COMMITMENT TO DIE

COMMITMENT TO DIE

A Kristin Ashe Mystery

Jennifer L. Jordan

BEAN
POLE
BOOKS

TUCSON, ARIZONA

COMMITMENT TO DIE

BeanPole Books and design are registered trademarks of Harren Communications, LLC.

Printed in the United States of America

Cover design by Mindthwack, Inc. Interior design by Libby Czopek.

ISBN: 0-9667359-0-0

9 8 7 6 5 4 3 2 1

www.beanpolebooks.com

For all of us who are different

MY HEART WAS BREAKING.

My brother David was dying, or maybe already dead.

It was midnight, and I was sitting in the intensive care unit at Denver Health Medical Center, reading a mystery aloud, hoping he could hear my voice through his coma.

Even there, between carefully pronounced, whispered words, I couldn't stop thinking about Lauren Fairchild and her "day to end all days."

It was probably the best day of her life.

Certainly, it was the most planned one.

After lunch with her sister and niece, she bought a book at the Tattered Cover, then stopped by her house to pick up a Walkman. She had already packed a picnic dinner of her favorite foods: wine biscuits with Brie, roasted chicken, au gratin potatoes, and raspberry cheesecake.

She drove west on I-70 for three hours to Exit 278, where she pulled off the highway, changed into boots, and hiked a mile, almost straight up. There, wedged between two mountains, she arrived at the edge of a blue-green lake fed by three stories of water.

She spread out a blanket and listened to music, perhaps leafed through the book, but never touched the food.

Instead, as the sun set over the adjacent peaks, she swallowed fifty painkillers.

In less than an hour, she felt no pain.

Thirteen hours later, in nearby Glenwood Springs, an early morning hiker hysterically informed authorities that she had found a body on the brink of Hanging Lake.

Shortly thereafter, everyone who loved Lauren Fairchild began to suffer.

I know this because ten days ago, Patrice Elliott, Lauren's sister, hired me to find out why she committed suicide.

1

The morning I met Patrice Elliott, everything that could go wrong did.

The discombobulation began when I woke up in Destiny Greaves' bed thirty minutes after the alarm had sounded. I dressed hurriedly in clothes pulled from a duffel bag, kissed a naked Destiny, told her I'd see her in three days, and ran frantically out the door.

Halfway down the Capitol Hill street, I realized I was wearing two shoes but only carrying one. I glanced at my watch and debated whether I should hunt for the missing Reebok or arrive on time for my appointment.

Unwilling to forsake an afternoon bike ride, I chose the shoe, turned around, and spent five minutes I didn't have searching for something I never found.

As I sprinted out the door the second time, Destiny's parting words left a distressing imprint on my brain: "Hey, Kris, maybe it's time to move all our stuff into one place!"

I glanced back and tendered a quick wave as an ineffectual reply.

I made the ten-minute drive from Destiny's mansion to my Washington Park office in eight. Harried, I opened up the thousand-square-foot studio that served as a base of operations for my part-time detective work and full-time marketing and graphic arts business.

None of the other six women who worked for me had shown up yet, so I did the early-arrival chores. I turned on the track lighting, adjusted the air conditioner, and fired up the coffee maker.

Spotting no sign of my new client, I headed for the bathroom to finish my daily grooming. I brushed my short, thick brown hair and washed my tiny wire-rimmed, oval glasses, thinking for the hundredth time I should get contacts.

I was thirty-five, yet looked like I had in high school. The freckles didn't help, and neither did a perpetual lack of make-up. My driver's license had always read five-seven, 118 pounds, a lie even at sixteen. I still hadn't grown the extra inch or lost the fifteen pounds it would have taken to restore truth. That day, like most others, my dress was casual. Pressed white shorts, black leather belt, purple blouse, loafers with no socks.

After one last peek in the mirror, I returned to my glass-enclosed office at the front of the building and waited for Patrice Elliott to arrive.

Thirty minutes passed before she walked through the front door, flustered.

"I'm sorry I'm late," she said in a young girl's voice. Dressed in a pink shirt, a navy blue jumper with matching mini-socks, and white sandals, the twenty-something woman looked as if she had recently completed a footrace. A bead of sweat dripped past her ear and into the unruly web of a home perm. She was inordinately thin, bordering on frail. The gray canvas bag on her left shoulder could have held a week's worth of groceries, and if it had, it would have toppled her.

I rose to greet her. "I'm Kristin Ashe."

Patrice removed taped-together sunglasses that were too wide for her narrow face and said, "I couldn't get my five-year-old daughter to cooperate this morning. I try to set a schedule, but she doesn't always follow it. Today was one of those days. It took so long to get her dressed, she missed the bus, and I had to drive her to preschool."

"Come in, sit down." I steered her into my office and gestured toward the couch across from my desk. "Where's she go to school?"

I had asked the question to help put the woman at ease, but it seemed to have the opposite effect. "Children First," she said, brow furrowed.

I had never heard of it. "Can I get you something to drink? Coffee, tea?"

"Water would be nice," she said, wringing slender hands that pressed into her lap.

I left to retrieve refreshments, and when I returned, Patrice had again donned her sunglasses.

I handed her a mug of water.

"Thanks," she said, grasping it tightly. "It's really hot out there, especially for June."

I sat behind a wooden desk and spun around in the swivel chair. Smiling, I said, "Would you mind taking off your glasses? Seeing my reflection is a little distracting."

"I'm sorry." She complied and, without the shield, looked even more lost and alone. An extra layer of cosmetics couldn't disguise red and swollen eyes. "I've gotten used to wearing them, and I forget they're there."

"How are you holding up?"

"Better," she began haltingly, speaking so softly I had to strain to hear her words. "At first, I couldn't eat or sleep, but now I can, a little. At least I go through the motions, but nothing tastes good, and I'm tired inside. Calling you last week and setting up this appointment helped."

The fingernails on her right hand dug into her other palm. "If my sister had to do this, why couldn't she have left a note? It wouldn't have taken long to write," she said anxiously.

"Maybe she didn't know what to say, or it was too hard to explain," I replied gently.

"Well, she could have tried!" For the first time, a hint of life sparked in eyes that registered events a moment too late. "If not for my sake, for Ashley's."

"Ashley?"

"My daughter."

"The one who didn't want to get dressed this morning?"

"The same." Patrice allowed herself a quick, slight smile. "I've told her Lauren's gone, but she doesn't understand. She has no concept of time. She thinks Lauren's on vacation, like when she and Nicole go away for a few weeks. Every morning, as soon as she wakes up, she wants to know if Lauren's coming over. Every day, I calmly say no, but sometimes, it's all I can do not to shake her and say 'She's never coming over! Never! She's gone for good! Don't ask me again!'"

"Be patient," I remarked mildly.

Patrice looked up from her feet and nodded. "I am. I would never hurt my daughter."

"I meant with yourself. Be patient about the loss. Grieving takes time and energy."

"It's not that I can't explain it to my daughter, it's that I don't have any answers myself. How could I not know my sister well enough to see the signs, to figure it out?" she asked, anger leaking into her tightly-controlled voice.

Before I could answer, she continued, "Everyone thinks I'm crazy, that I should accept Lauren's death and let it go, but I can't. I've finally accepted she died, and I'm making progress. I don't think about her every minute anymore, and I don't try to call her every time I want to talk. Still, I can't leave it like this."

"You have no idea why she committed suicide?"

"None, which makes it so frustrating! I had this picture of her, and now nothing fits. No one understands how important this is for me. They think I'm in denial, that this is my way of not dealing with it. My husband Stephen told me I need a therapist, not a detective."

"Sometimes I'm both," I said with a faint smile. "But I'm much better at investigating, which I'll start doing if you're ready to answer some questions.

"Go ahead," she said uncertainly.

"We'll tackle the easy ones first." I took a legal pad out of the bottom desk drawer. "What was your sister's full name?"

"Lauren Ashley Fairchild."

"Her age?"

"Thirty-five, she just turned thirty-five," Patrice said jerkily. "She killed herself on her birthday."

"Which was?"

"June third."

"What time of day?"

"The police think sometime before dark."

"Where did it happen?"

"At Hanging Lake."

I paused in my note-taking, peered at her, and raised one eyebrow. "Near Glenwood Springs?"

"Yes. You've heard of it?"

"My family vacationed near there every summer, and that was one of the day trips we took. I hated that hike—it was always hot and steep. Had Lauren been there before?"

"I'm not sure, but I know she's hiked a lot of trails in Colorado."

"You told me on the phone the cause of death was drug overdose, right? Tylenol with codeine?"

Patrice nodded, her hands clenching into fists.

"Where did she get the pills?"

"I don't know."

"She didn't leave any notes?"

"None."

"When did you last see her?"

Patrice bit her lip. "The day she died, she and my daughter and I went to lunch."

"How did Lauren seem at the time? Was she depressed?"

"No, actually, I thought she was happy."

"Happy, as in giddy?"

"No, more like peaceful or relaxed, which you never saw. Lauren always had a million things going on at the same time, and she never slowed down."

"At lunch, did she say anything to suggest that she was planning to kill herself?"

"No, just the opposite, which is what's so confusing. As she was saying good-bye to us after lunch, she gave my daughter a hug and a kiss, which she always did, and turned to me and said, 'I'll take good care of her.' Lauren's birthday was on a Thursday, and every Friday night, she came to babysit Ashley while Stephen and I went out. I assumed that's what she was talking about, but it's odd. Why would someone say something like that if she was about to kill herself?" Hope flickered across Patrice's drawn face. "Maybe Lauren was murdered. Do you think that's a possibility?"

"Had anyone threatened her?"

"Not that she told me."

"Do you think someone hated her that much?"

"No," she said glumly.

"Did anyone profit from her death?"

"Nicole, maybe, her lover. Lauren made out a will a few years ago, but I don't think she left much. Nicole called the other day to ask if Stephen and I could help with funeral expenses."

"Do you think it would be okay for me to contact Nicole?"

Patrice squirmed uneasily. "I'm not sure. Nicole's one of the people who thinks I'm crazy. She wants to get on with her life, as if nothing happened."

"Would you be willing to call and see if I could interview her?"

She didn't answer right away. "I guess."

"If you can introduce me, I'll take it from there. By the way, what kind of relationship did they have?"

"A good one," she said, not entirely convincingly. "Lauren and Nicole fought a lot when they first got together, but less recently."

"All right." I leaned back in the chair and put my feet on the desk. "Tell me about Lauren: What was she like?"

"You mean what did she look like?"

"Well, that, too, but tell me what mattered to her, how she lived her life."

"Let's see. She was about my height, a little over five feet. She had the same brown hair as I do, except lighter, and pale blue eyes. She was seven years older, and I always thought she was the perfect sister. She was pretty and smart and extremely thoughtful. She was kind of a protector, ever since we were kids, when she looked after me and my brother. She was very social, really good with people, and confident. Oh, and she was athletic. She loved soccer, softball, mountain climbing, almost everything outdoors."

"Anything else?"

Patrice became animated. "I think what I'll remember the most is how she lit up around children, especially Ashley. Lauren was so patient with her. They would play for hours on end, being silly until I made them stop."

"What did your sister do for a living?"

"She worked in the deli at Choices."

"The health food supermarket in Cherry Creek?"

Patrice nodded.

"Could she have been in any kind of financial trouble?"

"Lauren?" Patrice laughed for the first time, a tentative, forced sound. "She knew more about money than anyone. She made every dime seem like a dollar, and she was extremely generous with what she had."

"Could your sister have been sick, had an illness she didn't tell you about?"

"I don't think so. She looked healthy, and she never went to the doctor. Sometimes I tried to get her to go, but she believed more in holistic medicine."

I quit writing, and my eyes met Patrice's. "Do you have any idea why your sister would deliberately kill herself?"

"Maybe she didn't," she stammered, avoiding my gaze. "Maybe her death was accidental."

Quietly, I noted, "No one takes fifty pills accidentally."

"I'm sure it was a mistake. It had to be," she rattled on. "Otherwise, how could she leave like this, without a note or a good-bye or a reason why? She would never do this to me again, especially not on that day."

The hair on my arms stood up. "What do you mean again? Did your sister try to take her life before?"

"No." Patrice's head slumped forward until her chin touched her chest.

"What then, what day are you talking about?"

She fought to maintain control but lost as tears mixed with hysteria-edged words. "When Lauren was nine and I was two, our mother committed suicide."

I gasped.

Before I could offer condolences, she collapsed into sobs.

It took her a long time to add, "On her thirty-fifth birthday!"

2

Thirty minutes and a half-box of Kleenex later, Patrice had calmed down enough to drive herself home. I walked her to her car, and on the way out, she gave me a quick hug and thanked me again and again, as much for the chance to cry, perhaps, as for the work I had promised to do.

As I stepped back into the office, my older sister Ann grabbed me. "Destiny called to tell you she found your shoe."

"Good. I thought she had to be at the airport by nine."

"She called from there. Where's she going?"

"Durango. She's helping some women set up a center."

"Another one?"

"Yep," I said proudly. As director of Denver's Lesbian Community Center, Destiny had traveled all over Colorado in the past decade, lending support to small towns.

"Who was that woman in your office?"

"Patrice Elliott, a new client."

"For us?" Ann asked, referring to the half-million-dollar company she helped run, a company I had started eight years earlier. As art director, she oversaw production of the marketing materials we created for health care professionals.

People often commented on how surprising it was we could work together, and many days, the feat shocked me, too. Growing up, we had fought constantly. She was into sewing and boys, while I preferred sports and girls. The intersection of our lives mostly involved hair pulling and punch throwing, which we shared with Gail, the sister between us. My mother had given birth to all three of us in less than three years before regaining her senses and waiting a few years to add my younger brother David and sister Jill.

Ann would always hold the cherished spot of first, a ranking she seldom let me forget, and as adults, though we sounded the same on the phone (often confusing clients and vendors), in person we shared few similarities.

For starters, we didn't look alike. We were both about the same medium height and build, with large breasts and small behinds, but where Ann was soft, I was lean. Ann constantly poofed up her dark brown hair, while I wore my lighter brown, thick, wavy hair in a short cut that demanded nothing more than washing and combing.

We also didn't dress alike. Ann wore elaborate mix-and-match outfits in muted colors, dresses that clung to her and panty hose every color but tan. I hadn't worn a dress or panty hose since I quit my waitressing job in high school, and unless more than a foot of snow fell, I rarely bothered with socks. I favored what Ann called my "uniform" of starched button-downs or brightly colored polo shirts (depending on the season) and lean-cut faded blue jeans. In my mid-twenties, I'd improved my look when an ex-lover suggested I take my crumpled shirts and pants to the dry cleaners.

However, as I matured, my fashion skills remained stunted, and I still often chose outfits from a pile on the bedroom floor.

"No, this client hired me," I replied, indicating the investigations I did for women.

"What about the deadline we have coming up on that thirty-two-page newsletter for nurses?"

"We'll make it with time to spare," I said easily. "Let's go over our workload for the week, and I'll do this other job around it."

With that, we devised an arrangement that put Ann's mind at ease and freed me to begin the search for why a "happy" woman would commit suicide.

The day flew by, and not until late at night, shortly before I fell asleep, did I allow myself to think about Destiny.

I flushed at the memory of the way she had looked in the shower: tall, naked body; long blonde hair darkened with dampness; a steady stream of water dripping down the canal between her full breasts, veering across wide hips, onto sculptured legs.

Yet her last words brought on an instant frown: "Maybe it's time to move all our stuff into one place."

Was she serious?

Her suggestion did seem like the next natural step. After all, we spent practically every night together.

Eighteen months earlier, I'd met Destiny when she hired me to find her biological mother, but I'd fallen in love long before we shook hands.

From a distance, I'd followed Destiny Greaves' accomplishments for years. If she wasn't in the daily papers for her scathing assessment of the governor's insensitivity to the AIDS crisis, she was on the nightly news fighting for equal access for the disabled, or in the gay press chastising NOW for its discrimination against lesbians. She fought every important battle waged in Denver, and won most of them.

She never ceased to amaze me, and our time together had been wondrous.

With her, I knew we could explore every wrinkle and recess of each other and begin again. Over and over. I never tired of her, but that didn't mean I didn't find being in a relationship tiring. Stone-breaking exhausting at times.

Yet, I had to admit I was also weary from keeping two houses stocked. Not a week went by that I didn't need something at my permanent or temporary residence: a new toothbrush, a TV Guide, a fresh stick of deodorant. Also, the realization that we spent less time in each other's arms and more in transit had begun to irk me.

Still, the prospect of giving up my nineteenth-floor apartment made my temples throb.

I couldn't get the pounding in my head to stop until I realized I could postpone all thoughts of housing arrangements until Thursday, the day Destiny returned to Denver.

Meanwhile, I had a suicide to worry about.

The following morning, Patrice Elliott phoned to say that Lauren's lover had agreed grudgingly to meet with me. I called Nicole Carroll immediately and set an appointment for two o'clock that afternoon, wanting to strike before she changed her mind.

After lunch, I left for the Tech Center, an office park in southeast Denver, and found Nicole's place of employment in a nondescript one-story building off Belleview Avenue.

As I entered the office, I couldn't help wondering how many times Lauren Fairchild had walked through the same door.

A receptionist greeted me and reeled off elaborate directions to Nicole's office, all of which I needed. I walked through a maze of narrow hallways, constructed from cream and mauve partitions, and made three right turns and one left before I reached a dead end.

Here, Paige Werner, a somber, college-age administrative assistant, outfitted in plaid skirt and low heels, greeted me. At her desk, stationed directly in front of the door that led to Nicole's windowless office, she took her duties seriously. I introduced myself and commented on the uniqueness of her eyes, one blue, the other green. Showing no interest in casual banter, she directed me to a grouping of chairs, coffee tables, and reading material and ordered me to take a seat.

For the next ten minutes, I obediently read brochures about the company, a non-profit organization that brought exchange students to Colorado. Quickly tiring of this, I spent the remainder of the hour studying Nicole Carroll.

I had a clear shot of her through the open door, and while I'm certain she was aware of my presence, she pretended otherwise.

Physically, Lauren's lover was beautiful: high cheekbones, smooth complexion, and long black hair she flipped frequently to its best advantage. Her red business suit fit perfectly, complemented by a black silk blouse buttoned to the top and a strand of pearls. Probably nearing forty, she had the air of perpetual youth, frozen at twenty-five. The only noticeable flaw on a body otherwise destined for modeling came from eyebrows that remained permanently arched, giving her a disquieting air of continual skepticism.

Still in all, she was dazzling.

Yet, the more I watched, the more I disliked.

While I tapped my foot, she placed two phone calls, one in French. I tried to eavesdrop, but my high school lessons failed me. I could translate only inconsequential fragments of the conversation, and I never could determine what prompted frequent bursts of forced laughter.

When Paige, with great ceremony, finally ushered me into the inner sanctum, her boss couldn't stop shuffling papers long enough to meet my extended hand.

"You must rack up a ton of frequent-flier miles in this business," I said conversationally, unwilling to broach immediately the subject of her lover's death.

"If it really interests you, I never leave town on business. There's no need with phones and e-mail, but surely you didn't come to chat about airline freebies."

"Ah, no," I said, taken aback by her brusque manner. "As I said on the phone, I came to talk about Lauren."

Without looking up, Nicole said, "I don't have time for this, you know."

She had started to irritate me. First the wait, followed by no apology, now more rudeness.

I bent down to her level, cocked my head, and came within a foot of touching her. "Shall I leave?"

"Oh, could you?" She focused hazel eyes on me, and the phony smile that had surfaced all too frequently in the past hour reappeared. "That would be lovely. We have a group of sixty students from Montreal arriving tonight, and I'm up to here with it. You can reschedule with my assistant on the way out."

She proceeded to flip through three Rolodexes on her desk, as if I had already left.

I hadn't.

Fighting to maintain control, I said, "No, I don't think I'll do that. If it doesn't matter enough to you to find out why your lover killed herself, then it damn well doesn't matter to me. After all, I never even met the woman." Fuming, I turned to leave.

Her shrill cry caught me. "Christine, wait!"

In slow motion, I rotated until I faced her directly. "It's Kristin. Kristin Ashe," I said tersely.

"Fine." Nicole whipped back her sleeve, examined a Movado watch, and released a series of martyr sighs. "You've got five minutes."

I exhaled loudly. "Tell me this: Do you have any desire to know why she died."

"It would be lovely if I could give people a reason," she said flippantly, "but I don't believe there is one."

"Then why did you agree to this meeting?"

"As a last favor to Patrice. The woman desperately needs to regain control, and if this will help . . ." Nicole's voice trailed off, branding the notion ludicrous.

"Do you have any pictures of Lauren?" I asked, deliberately scanning the sparsely decorated office.

"Not here."

"At home?"

"Of course."

"Could I get a copy of one?"

"Didn't Patrice have any?"

I met her frosty gaze without blinking. "I didn't ask."

"I suppose I could arrange to get one to you."

"Good, that'll help." Still standing, I pulled a notebook from my shorts pocket and took delight in casually flipping through the pages while she tapped a Mont Blanc pen on the edge of the desk. "Okay, for starters, do you know where Lauren got the pills?"

"What's that have to do with why she killed herself?"

"Maybe nothing, but I'm looking into every angle."

"At this rate, we'll need twenty days, not five minutes," she muttered, causing my scant compassion to erode.

In full voice, Nicole added, "More than likely, they came from her rock climbing accident. Last year, she injured her knee going up a mountain north of Boulder. When the swelling didn't go down, she went to an orthopedic clinic. They X-rayed it, told her to have surgery, and prescribed painkillers. She had the prescription filled, which struck me as hypocritical."

"Why?"

"She usually wouldn't pollute her body with any kind of medicine."

"Did you see her take any of the pills?"

"No, which is why I deduced they're the ones she used. Wasn't that smart of me?"

In an even tone, I asked, "Did she have the surgery?"

"No, she claimed she couldn't afford it."

"Was she having financial problems then or right before her death?"

"No more than her usual cheapness," Nicole said matter-of-factly.

"Did you two share finances?"

"Not really. We split the house payment down the middle, but everything else was separate."

"Who benefits financially from her death?"

"No one. We have wills that name each other as beneficiaries, and we owned the house together, but we owe the bank as much as it's worth."

"Lauren didn't have any money saved?"

"Not that I can find. I have no idea where all her money went, but she managed to spend what she made and more. I'm borrowing to pay for the cremation, and I have no idea how I'll make next month's house payment by myself."

"You didn't have life insurance policies on each other?"

"Only the ones that come with our health insurance. Lauren's was for $5,000, which goes to me, but I'll need that to pay off her credit cards."

"Did you have any indication in the last few months that she was suicidal?"

"Au contraire."

"Excuse me?"

She tilted her head and spoke as if to a child. "Quite the opposite. In the last few months, she finally slept without screaming, which was a relief."

"What do you mean?"

"Lauren had nightmares. Dreams she could never remember when she woke up, or so she told me. They very nearly ended our relationship. For no reason at all, she'd wake up in the middle of the night, howling and screaming."

"How often?"

"Once a month, on average. Somehow, they always managed to occur the night before I had a stress-filled day at work and most needed sleep."

"You said they almost split you up. How did you manage to resolve it?"

"Very expensive earplugs and separate bedrooms."

"These went on the whole time you knew Lauren."

"No, not in the beginning."

"When did they start?"

"I didn't keep a record."

I smiled charmingly. "Approximately?"

"Four years ago, something like that. Check with her therapist. She'd know. Lauren started counseling shortly after the mess began."

I made a note in my book, more for effect than because I wouldn't remember. "Did Lauren suffer from depression?"

"Repression, more like," she said savagely.

"What do you mean?"

"She was extremely moody and withdrawn. She'd never talk about things that bothered her. Instead, she held them inside, until I thought she'd explode."

"Did she ever?" I asked casually.

"What?"

"Explode?"

Nicole flinched. "No."

"What about her mother's death, did Lauren seem upset about that recently?"

Condescendingly, Nicole replied, "Her mother died when Lauren was a child."

"I know, but there might be a connection. Did you know she, too, killed herself?"

"Of course I did. Lauren told me on our first date. She was obsessed with the suicide."

"Did you know her mother took her life on the same day as her daughter, on her thirty-fifth birthday?"

Nicole's eyes widened, then narrowed. "You believe this is relevant?"

"Maybe, but other things in Lauren's life might have caused her more distress. For example, were you and she having problems?"

I could barely conceal a triumphant grin when she drew back, startled, and nervously asked, "Why, what did Patrice tell you?"

"Actually, she said you were getting along."

"Well, she's right. We were. We weren't newlyweds, but we probably had sex as much as the average lesbian couple in their sixth year. In fact," she added with a hint of bravado, "we made love the night before Lauren died."

"Who initiated it?"

"She did."

"Was she usually the initiator?"

"I'd rather not answer that."

"Fair enough," I said comfortably. "Did she have any close friends I could talk to?"

"About our sex life?" she asked, bristling.

"No," I said meticulously. "About what might have been going through Lauren's mind when she swallowed all those painkillers."

"Just Cecelia." Her distorted smile resembled a grimace. "Her ex."

"Would you happen to have her phone number?"

"No, but go to Choices. You can't miss her."

"She shops a lot?"

Nicole scowled. "She works there."

"Okay. Anyone else you can think of?"

"Not hardly. That was the sum total of her friends, unless you count the mysterious Dr. W. Lauren certainly seemed to be seeing a lot of her lately."

"Who's Dr. W?"

"Now that's the question of the hour, but unfortunately my lover isn't here to answer it. She had thirteen appointments with her in the last three months, all of which she conveniently forgot to mention."

"How did you find out?"

"I read her appointment book."

"You have it?" I tried to contain my excitement. "Could I see it?"

Dismissively, she said, "I suppose, but it's a waste of time. I told you the best part."

"Dr. W's full name doesn't appear anywhere in the calendar?"

"Not that I could see, but you're welcome to pore over every last boring detail of Lauren's life." She paused before adding, "If you have nothing better to do."

I counted to ten and took a deep breath before I spoke again. "Could this Dr. W have been Lauren's therapist?"

She responded instantly. "No, that's a different entry. Gloria Schmidt. Every Thursday at three."

"You said 'with her.' If you have no idea who Dr. W is, how do you know she's a woman?"

"Simple," Nicole replied, more bored than contemptuous. "She and my lover were having an affair."

3

"So much for innocent until proven guilty, eh?" my friend and sometimes associate Fran Green commented six hours later while dabbing at a Bingo sheet.

"No kidding! The only evidence Nicole has are calendar entries and some vague theories about Lauren working late and acting secretive."

"That's it?"

"Seems like it." I glanced down but couldn't find B-6 on any of my grids. "Damn. Oh, and the suicide. She thinks that's the ultimate proof—that guilt drove Lauren to take her life."

"Sounds fishy coming from a dame who's more concerned about flipping through manila folders than helping figure out why her honey bit the dust."

"Exactly!" I said, brightening. Earlier in the day, I had phoned Fran, an ex-nun I'd met and befriended on a previous case, hoping she could offer feedback in this troubling one. In her work with the Catholic church, Fran had arranged adoptions, set up soup kitchens, visited the elderly, and developed prayer programs for prisoners.

She'd dealt with people at the highest and lowest points of their lives. A simple suicide wouldn't faze her.

At sixty-five, she possessed more energy than most people half her age. She had a runner's body, short and compact, and her gray hair was styled in what she termed a "wash and wear" cut. Chopped close to the scalp, it seemed to grow up, not down.

Having entered the convent at eighteen and left it at fifty-five, Fran matched her clothes to her no-nonsense personality. Sweat pants, loose-fitting Levis, or camouflage trousers always covered her legs. Tennis shoes—not fancy or flashy, just sensible sneakers—served as standard footwear and, in warm and cold weather alike, she wore T-shirts extolling her latest belief, cause, or vacation spot. This night's lavender garment was one of my favorites: "Just say no to men!"

My features grew flaccid when the announcer called four more numbers and my wrist never moved. Meanwhile, Fran, a blotter in each hand, whirred with activity.

"I can't believe you talked me into this. I hate Bingo!" I muttered, biting already short fingernails.

"But this is gay Bingo!" Fran said with a grin.

Meaning the same dull game, played in the same cloud of cigarette smoke, except every Tuesday night it was held in the basement of the Metropolitan Community Church in Capitol Hill and therefore attracted a predominantly lesbian and gay crowd.

I must have felt Destiny's absence. What else could have accounted for Fran convincing me to sit in for Ruth, her seventy-year-old lover and faithful companion at these weekly outings? Just my luck, Ruth had to skip so she could present the annual treasurer's report to her chess club.

I should have known the evening would be a long one when we walked in the door and Fran pulled out a customized set of blotters from a fanny pack and took her reserved seat at the front table.

In the next hour, I learned that scratch games were called pickles (pay a dollar and have a one in a thousand chance of winning fifty), that the two blue-haired ladies at the next table were really men, and that the announcer was a district court judge by day.

Through four rounds, neither of us had won a cent.

I'd consumed two Cokes and a handful of Tic-Tacs and was ready to go home and nurse my sugar headache.

"Aren't these seats uncomfortable?" I asked fidgeting on the folding chair.

"Didn't notice."

"Isn't the metal bar poking you in the back?"

No response.

I wiped beads of sweat from my brow. "It's hot in here. Don't they have air conditioning?" Once again, four numbers flew by, and I didn't touch my card.

Fran, arms in motion like an automaton, replied, "Need to buy more cards, Kris. Catch a ride on a bigger piece of the action."

"Good idea."

"So when can you get your mitts on Lauren's calendar?"

"Not until the weekend. Nicole can't spare a moment until then."

"What's up with—" Fran stopped abruptly.

"With what?"

"In a minute. Can't chat. One number from the big one," she said hurriedly.

Her delight vanished when a man in the rear yelled, "Bingo!"

We both leaned back, waiting for an usher to verify the winner's numbers.

After the early games, as they conducted this ritual, I'd gazed at the lucky person, listened intently to every number, and hoped one of them would be wrong, giving me another chance at the big pot. This time, I didn't bother to turn.

Frustrated, I wadded up the worthless sheet and threw it to the floor, letting it join hundreds of other failures.

"I'll be back." I rose to find an attendant who could sell game cards.

Three dollars poorer, I threaded my way through the dozens of conference tables and returned. Mere moments after the next round began, I was thoroughly agitated. Whereas three cards had been too few, six were clearly too many. Over the course of fifteen numbers, I placed countless dots and cast furtive glances at the numbers board above, all while trying to hold a coherent conversation.

"Sounds like this Dr. W might be the best lead you got," Fran said, showing no signs of fatigue from the stress of simultaneously monitoring eighteen game cards.

"Try the only one. Did they call B-4 yet?"

"Long time ago. Gotta pay attention, Kris." Fran took a leisurely swallow of tepid coffee. "Wonder what's up with the doc. No chance she's a love interest?"

"Slim," I said grudgingly.

"Shouldn't rule it out just yet. Cheating's as old as the hills. Girl steps out on her main squeeze, and guilt gnaws on her like a hungry bear until it eats her alive."

I shook my head as I thought out loud. "It doesn't add up. According to Nicole, the doctor's name didn't appear until a few months ago. The timing doesn't seem to match." I paused, searching for O-66. "Plus, something's not right with Nicole. It seemed like a stretch for her to come up with this half-baked theory. Personally, I think she's grasping at straws because she can't deal with her lover's death and her own feelings of guilt."

"Guilt over what? You holding out on me? Give me the juicy details." To emphasize her plea, Fran stretched out her hands.

I lightly pushed her arms away. "I don't have any, but there must be something. Think about it: If Ruth killed herself tonight, wouldn't you feel like you might have caused it?"

"Nope."

"Not even in a small way—a recent fight, or oversight, or insult? Wouldn't the slightest bit of guilt touch you?"

"No, siree," she said vehemently, meeting my stare. "What Ruth does with her life is her business, not mine."

Disbelieving, I studied my Bingo card. "I-17's been called, right?"

"Not yet."

"Shoot. I need white-out."

"Course if she did check out soon, I might feel bad enough to postpone that little affair I been thinking of having."

My head, which had been lowered, shot up fast enough to strain neck muscles.

"Gottcha!" Fran chuckled.

"Very funny," I grumbled. "Don't talk to me anymore. I'm one number away from Bingo."

"Whatcha need?"

"G-43."

"Been called."

"Are you serious?" I asked as the announcer belted out "B-1."

"You bet!"

I shot from my seat. "Bingo!"

Unfortunately, a slew of strident voices shouted the same word.

A middle-aged man in cowboy boots, starched white shirt, and tight blue jeans ambled over to confirm my victory. I couldn't take my eyes off his pot belly which protruded over a four-inch cubic-zirconium studded belt buckle, and my heart pounded faster as he checked each number.

Much to my relief, he congratulated me and forked over the winnings, which after splitting the pot with seven others, came to all of three dollars and seventy-five cents.

My mood didn't improve when Fran pointed out, "Should have called it when you had it. Would have won thirty bucks."

I glared at her.

"Oh well. No other way to learn. At least you got enough for a hamburger."

"Just what I need—a rubber patty on a stale bun."

"Don't knock it 'til you try it. They grill a mean burger here," she said, preparing her section of the table for the next onslaught of numbers.

"Fine. I'll go get one and sit out the next game. Can I bring you anything?"

"No can do. Ruins the concentration."

In minutes, I returned. Without cards in front of me, I relaxed and took a bite from the massive cheeseburger, piled high with tomatoes, onions, lettuce, and ketchup. "This is delicious," I said, wiping a trail of grease from my chin.

"Told you. Ruth thinks we oughta skip Bingo and come for take-out."

"She has a point. Do you ever win at this?"

"You bet. Little luck and some skill, Bingo can make a nice second income."

"How much have you won?"

"Lifetime earnings, $10,312."

"Ten thousand bucks at Bingo! Huh. Maybe I should pay more attention." I ate a potato chip. "That's how much you've won, but how much have you spent buying cards and pickles?"

"Hard to say. Probably eleven thousand." She laughed.

I pointed to a man two tables away who was surrounded by piles of discarded game cards and worthless pickles. "That guy probably needs a second income to play Bingo. Plus, he's creating a fire hazard."

She managed to glance at the man in question and dab N-33 a dozen times without missing a beat. "If Lauren wasn't warming up the sheets with Dr. W, what was she up to?"

"Good question. My best guess at this point is she was sick but didn't tell anyone. What do you think?"

"Possible. Might have had some newfangled disease. Didn't want to be a sidebar in a medical freakshow. Figured it was time to go."

"Exactly. On her own terms. In her own way."

"Could be. You need to snag this Dr. W, Kris."

"I know, but how?"

"Give me a few days—I'll sniff her out."

"Or him," I corrected.

"Whichever. Leave it to me."

"How?"

"Simple. I'll call all the doctors in the phone book whose last names start with W."

"That'll take forever."

"Nah, can't be that many. Piece of cake."

"Assuming you called every doctor in Denver, none of them will tell you if Lauren was a patient. Don't you think that'd be confidential?"

"Sure thing. They won't tell Fran Green diddly, but they'll be eager to spill the beans to Frances Blue, administrative director for Health Managers."

"What's that?"

"An insurance company I formed thirty seconds ago. Sounds good, don't it?" Fran cracked a smile at her own capacity for deception. When she spoke again, she used an immature, bored voice an octave above her usual pitch. "Perhaps you could help me, Miss. Lauren Fairchild recently filed a claim, and we're prepared to cut a sizable check for Dr. W this afternoon, except we're missing one teeny piece of information."

I watched with growing admiration. "Which is?"

"The date of her last visit." Her voice switched back to its normal baritone. "Guaranteed, this'll send 'em scrolling through the computer files or hunting in the cabinets. One of the suckers will confirm her appointments, and the rest will tell me she's not a patient."

"Beautiful! You really want to do this?"

"Consider it done. You sit tight, and I'll call you with the name." Fran punctuated her promise with a stroke of her blotter, and a split second later, she coolly shouted, "Bingo!"

This time, no one else chimed in.

The persuasive Fran Green kept me at church until the last number was called, a miracle that didn't transpire until after eleven.

Exhausted, I went home and fell straight into bed. Throughout the night, I tossed and turned and dreamed about Lauren Fairchild and Bingo.

By morning, I was as tired as if I'd been up all night.

I plodded into the office and, without much fervor, perused my to-do list. After prioritizing the day's tasks, I realized with a start that this was the last day to register for classes at the Adult Learning Institute, something I had put off for nearly a month.

I pulled the catalog from my top desk drawer, filled out the application on the last page, tore it free, and headed for the FAX machine in the back room.

As I walked toward Ann, who was busy lining up a chart of tooth eruption, she glanced up from her drawing board. "Is that the rough draft of Dr. Bennett's brochure?"

"No, it's a registration form for David."

"What's he taking?" she asked, her whine betraying the irritation that often surfaced in discussions about our brother.

"Beginning photography." I edged past her.

"I don't know why you bother, Kris. You know he probably won't go to half the classes. He'll get sick, or forget, or lose his camera again, like he did the last time you signed him up."

"I know," I said, bending down to punch in the FAX number of the school.

"How much are you spending on this little project?"

"Seventy-five dollars."

"When's he start?"

"Next Monday."

"Where will he get a camera?"

"I'm lending him mine."

"Your thirty-five millimeter?"

I nodded as the form crept through the rollers.

"I don't know why you do it," she said, dropping her resentful gaze.

Maybe because I was the only one foolish enough to try to relate to a brother who had no relational skills.

Long ago, my family had abandoned him to "the system," one ill-equipped to provide for him. The system consisted of social workers, psychiatrists, vocational rehab specialists, neurologists, counselors, physical therapists, and hundreds of other titled people. Yet none could determine what to do with David; not when he had his first epileptic seizure at age four, and not now when he was thirty-two chronologically, but thirteen mentally and emotionally.

Almost three decades had passed since doctors had first diagnosed epilepsy, and as the years mounted, the despair kept pace.

In the beginning, there had been hope.

Miracle drugs with names like Dilantin and phenobarbital were prescribed, in ever-changing dosages, to control his uncontrollable brain. Sometimes they worked at regulating the errant electrical currents. Often, however, they failed, leaving my brother to crash to the ground, his body the victim of a grand mal seizure.

The "experts" knew little about epilepsy. None of their testing, probing, or prodding could explain why David would go years without seizures and then have hundreds in one day. None would admit the long-term effects of taking massive doses of brain-deadening drugs.

Did the medicine contribute to learning disabilities? Would David have suffered from bouts of depression and explosive mood disorders without the pills?

Who could say?

All anyone knew for certain was that David had spent most of his adult life in mental hospitals and nursing homes. Most recently, he'd been living alone in a dank basement apartment near the University of Denver. Not because he was equipped to, but because Green Forest Rest Home had kicked him out after he'd thrown a full can of Pepsi at a nurse's aide.

No one else would take him.

No member of my family and no other facility. No one wanted him.

My divorced parents fought over him, but no longer loved him. My grandma "lost contact," though she lived five miles away. My two sisters in California had moved on with their lives. And Ann, despite my frequent pleas for involvement, lived as if we had no brother, as if he were dead.

I was the only one who stayed actively involved in his life, and not because I hadn't given up on him.

I had. A thousand times.

Initially, I had hoped he could have a job and friends and some degree of independent living.

I had hoped too much.

Still, something drew me back to him. I wouldn't have called it love or obligation. I didn't have a name for it, but I had been doing it since we were kids.

It would have ruined my life to let him live with me, but I did what

I could. I gave him money every month to supplement his disability checks. I bought him a bike, a television, clothes, and toiletries. I took him to the mountains and the movies.

I signed him up for evening courses, paid the tuition, talked to the instructors, drove him to and from each class, and tried not to expect too much.

There were a million reasons to give up and only one reason to fight: He was my brother.

Ann barely spoke to me over the next hour, but I pretended not to notice. I tried calling David, to tell him about the class, but never got an answer.

I spent the following sixty minutes lying on the couch in my office, contemplating Lauren Fairchild's fate.

What could have caused enough pain to make dying seem easier than living?

How far in advance had she planned her death? Was it one event, or a series, that had pushed her over the edge? How had she found the courage to follow through with such a terrifying plan?

Did death bring an end to suffering?

Who was the last person she saw when she closed her eyes, and what were her final thoughts?

As she lay dying, did she cry or cry out?

A phone call from my lover came as a pleasant interruption.

"Where have you been? I called you three times last night," Destiny greeted me, her tone more full of concern than accusation.

"If you can believe this, I was at MCC playing Bingo!"

"With Fran?"

"How did you know?"

"She seems the type, but I never knew you liked Bingo."

"I don't. I hate it. I won, and I still hated it."

"You won? That's great!"

"Three bucks," I said, curtailing her enthusiasm.

"That's all? Then I suppose I'll have to treat tomorrow night," she said coyly.

"What's tomorrow night?" I knew Destiny was scheduled to return from Durango, but I couldn't recall specific plans.

"Dinner at Ramano's, I hope."

"Won't you be too tired after your flight?"

"Not at all! If I come straight from the airport, I can be there by eight."

"Do you want me to call for reservations?"

"I already did," she said, a little self-consciously. "I'm planning something special."

"What?"

"I can't tell you."

"Will I like it?"

"You better!"

I laughed. "What am I going to do with you?"

"You'll think of something. I can't wait to see you this weekend."

"Me too," I said, before adding, "I almost forgot—do you think we could do something with David on Sunday?"

"Sure. What are you thinking?"

"Maybe take him to dinner and a movie, but I have to check with him first."

"Fine. Let me know what you decide."

"Thanks. I love you."

"Me, too. I'll see you tomorrow, and Kris—"

"Yes?"

Destiny's voice dropped to a seductive whisper. "Be prepared for the night of your life!"

I smiled all the way to Choices.

My arteries probably wished I'd been a regular customer at the health-food store, but in truth, I had never stepped foot in the place.

Despite the beautiful weather—eighty degrees, blue sky, slight breeze—I decided to drive the few blocks to the store, a decision I paid for in the congested parking lot. Drivers on both sides glared as I maneuvered back and forth to get my Honda into a parking space. Then, on foot, I had to dodge three vehicles before I made it to the entrance.

I passed through the atrium in the front of the store, took a right, and caught the attention of the first worker I could find. A woman in the floral department informed me Cecelia was not in the building. She had gone to the bank and would be back shortly.

At ten o'clock in the morning, I didn't feel particularly hungry, nor did I need all-natural groceries, but I had nothing more pressing to do, so I strolled through the store.

I had filled my carry-all basket by the time I reached the deli and, after standing a few minutes without anyone appearing to offer assistance, I strode across the room and hoisted myself up on a stool at the juice bar.

A young woman with her back to me stopped cleaning the espresso machine, turned, and cordially said, "Welcome to Choices Juice Bar, how may I help you?"

The standard customer service line fell flat coming from a worker who sported a tattoo of linked women's symbols on her right bicep and a helmet of green spiked hair that poked out of a clear shower cap. Wearing peace earrings, a tie-dye shirt, an oversized skirt, and Doc Marten boots, she should have been allowed to say whatever she wanted.

"What's good?"

"The carrot shake is royal!"

I grimaced. "No, it's too early in life for that."

She smiled. "Right on. How about the carob delight?"

"That fake chocolate stuff? No thanks."

"Water?" she said, grinning broadly.

I scanned the chalkboard menu behind her. "I'll take a strawberry smoothie."

"Bueno!"

As she expertly mixed frozen strawberries, kefir, guava juice, crushed ice, and banana, she explained the properties and nutritional value of each ingredient. Over the whir of the industrial blender, I asked if she had known Lauren Fairchild.

"Yeah, sure. She was my manager. Was she a friend of yours?"

"Not exactly. Her sister hired me to try to find out why she killed herself."

She nodded her head. "Cool."

"Did she manage the juice bar and the deli?"

"Nah, just the deli. I normally work over there, but the juice wizard is in a mountain bike race today. I told him I'd catch his shift."

She shut off the blender, removed the lid, and poured my drink into a fountain glass with an expansive flourish. She didn't spill a drop. "This is more people contact than I like. In the deli, I work in the back and don't account to anyone—except Lauren. And now that she's gone, I'm on my own."

"They made you manager?"

"Not even!" She laughed heartily. "They haven't found anyone to replace her yet, but if the chick they pick isn't as hip as Lauren, I'm out of here."

I took a sip of the smoothie. "This is pretty good. Maybe you should consider mixing drinks full-time."

"I couldn't. I hate waiting on the pretenders, but at least they tip." She inclined her head toward a crystal bowl with a handmade "Gratuities Accepted" sign. "This morning, I told Cecelia we should put in one of those cowbells, like they've got in bars, the ones they ring every time a drunk gives a buck. I told her we'd get better tips, because the debs and socialites would try to out-patronize each other, but she didn't like the idea. She should live a month on my take-home pay. Maybe then she'd like it," she added with a snicker.

I shifted in my seat to look around. "Actually, that's who I came to meet, Cecelia. Is she the one who manages the juice bar?"

"Bigger than that, she's the head witch around here." She leaned over and spoke conspiratorially, "But she likes it better when I call her the general manager."

"I checked earlier, and she was at the bank. When she comes back, do you think you could introduce me."

"Let's see if she's back. I'll call her over. I love to use the loud-speaker."

Before I could protest, the rebellious one picked up a microphone and transmitted her lilting voice across the entire store. "Cecelia Villareal to the juice bar. Cecelia Villareal, please come to the nearest juice bar."

She must have witnessed my distressed look, because smirking, she said, "I was just ribbing you. She didn't hear that. She never comes back from the bank in less than an hour, even though it's a block away."

Right then, an attractive woman with a deep furrow poked her head in the side entrance to the bar. "Colleen, stick to calling me and skip the theatrics."

"Okay, boss," Colleen agreed easily, no hint of remorse.

"What do you need?"

"This lady wants to meet you." She pointed at me with the ice cream scoop. "What did you say your name was?"

"I didn't, but it's Kristin Ashe."

Using the utensil as a wand, Colleen waved it back and forth. "Kristin Ashe, Cecelia Villareal. Cecelia, Kristin."

Cecelia stepped forward, and I stood, reached across the bar, and shook her hand firmly. "Patrice Elliott asked me to find out why Lauren died. Could I talk to you for a few minutes?"

Her body language immediately shifted, from open and friendly to guarded and pained. "Not here, not now," she said, moving to leave.

"Where? When?" I tried to catch her with my words.

She gave me a shrewd look, and paused. "Meet me at the park across the street in an hour."

"Okay."

"And you," she addressed Colleen with more affection than ire, "you quit paging me."

Colleen saluted her, and she left.

Exhilarated, yet strangely drained, I forced my attention back to Colleen. "Is she always like that?"

"She's one intense being. Yesterday, I told her if she focused all her energy, she could burn a hole in a brick wall." Colleen sauntered to the register, punched a few keys, and produced a receipt. "I meant it in a nice way, but she didn't like it. Here," she handed me the strip of paper, "give this to the dudes up front when they ring up your groceries."

"Thanks," I mumbled, bending down to tuck it in with my purchases. "It looks like I've got an hour to kill. Can I ask you a few questions about Lauren?"

"I'm not going anywhere." She propped her elbows on the counter opposite me.

"What did you think of Lauren? Was she a good manager?"

"Bust out! She was one rockin' lady. She was fair, and she cared— about all the kids who work in the deli and the earth—which most people here don't. She wouldn't kiss anyone's butt, especially not

Cecelia's, and she always asked us what we thought. She didn't act like she was better than us even though she was the queen bee. Plus, she always knew things."

"What do you mean?"

"Like she could take one look at people and know exactly what they were about, no bullshit, but she never judged people."

"When did you last see her?"

"On the day she did it. I freaked out later when I remembered she told me it was going to be a day to end all days, like maybe I should have felt the vibes. I just thought she meant she had some bitchin' birthday plans. I didn't have a clue she would do the deed."

"Did she work that day?"

"Nope, but she stopped to pick up a picnic dinner, and we all ragged on her about turning the big three-five."

"What did she take?"

"Her favorite stuff. These new wine biscuits we got in last week, some Brie, a piece of raspberry cheesecake, a really hefty slice, roast chicken, and my specialty, au gratin potatoes."

"How do you remember all that?"

"Easy, she made me pack it for her. She said she shouldn't have to work on her birthday. Blew me away when I found out it was her last meal."

"What time of day did she come by?"

"Maybe two or three o'clock."

"Do you know where she went after that?"

"She told me she wanted to cruise over to the Tattered Cover to buy a copy of something called *Our Town*. Weird, huh? I never heard of it."

"It's a play," I offered. "By Thornton Wilder. Didn't you read it in high school?"

"I must have been trippin' that semester. What's it about?"

"A girl who dies but gets to come back and relive one day of her life."

Colleen shook her arms. "Spooky!"

"Did Lauren seem different in any way in the weeks before she died, depressed or sad?"

She slowly shook her head. "She was truckin' along, like usual. Everybody around here's so freaked out about her offing herself, but I figure if that's her thing, what's the big deal? Death's just a change, a trip to another plane. It's not the end. I'm sure Lauren's out there now hanging out and meeting torqued beings. I thought I saw her myself the other day, near the frozen foods, laughing and jiving with this kid in a cart, having a righteous time."

I raised one eyebrow.

Colleen straightened up, turned her palms toward the ceiling, and shrugged. With an easy laugh, she said, "I know it sounds kinky, but it looked like her. Then again, I'd cranked out two shifts back-to-back and was pretty wiped, so who knows what I saw!"

I returned her infectious smile. "You didn't notice anything out of the ordinary about Lauren's behavior? Nothing at all?"

"Nope, sorry," she said, but something flashed across her face.

"What? What are you remembering?"

"She did have this schizo party one morning, the one she threw for herself with the breakfast square. That was out there, man!"

"What happened?"

"I came in early one morning, about a week before her birthday, and she was blowing out two candles she'd plopped on this granola bar. She acted queer, like I'd caught her at something, and told me she was having a celebration."

"Of what?"

"She wouldn't say. She said it was private, which yanked me, because we talked about everything, but hey, it was her life. The only thing she'd spill was that she was congratulating herself for reaching two years."

"Of working at Choices?"

"Nah, I've racked up almost three years, and she was the big cheese in the deli when I started. Plus, no one here cares about seniority or counts the days until retirement." Colleen snapped the dish towel she had been twirling. "Haven't you seen our employee manual? We're warriors, not fat cats waiting for pensions."

"Could she have marked two years of sobriety?"

"Maybe alcohol. She'd never touch it, not even a gulp of brew after a softball game."

"Was someone in her family alcoholic?"

"Big time! Her father died of liver disease."

"When?"

"I don't know, before she started working here."

"Hmm, maybe there's some connection. I'll have to ask her sister, or maybe her brother. Do you know if he lives in Denver?"

Colleen stared at me as if I were an idiot. "She didn't have a brother."

I scrunched my forehead. "I thought her sister mentioned a brother."

"No way! No male specimens in that family!"

"Are you sure?"

"Trust me, you spend the best years of your life hacking up vegetables with someone and stirring soups, you get to know them."

"Huh." I rose to leave and tossed a ten-dollar bill into her empty tip bowl. "Maybe I'm wrong."

"Darn right! There is no brother!"

I ambled back to the deli and, from across the room, Colleen yelled lunch suggestions.

I paid close to seventy dollars for my impulse buys and had two not-quite-full bags to show for it. With the exception of the food intended for lunch, I dropped everything in the car, picked up a *Westword* magazine from a corner stand, and crossed the street to the park.

I read for the next twenty minutes, one eye cast toward Choices, half-wondering if Lauren's ex-lover would show.

On schedule, Cecelia Villareal exited the store, and I watched her approach.

She walked purposefully, hands thrust deep in the pockets of purple and orange billowing pants. Her white sleeveless blouse did a remarkable job showcasing tanned, muscular arms. Her light brown hair, accented with natural blonde highlights, was parted on the side, shaved short in the back, and trimmed to a blunt cut.

Frequently she reached to brush back wisps that fell across her broad forehead, and each time she did, the sun glimmered off an inch-wide silver bracelet and matching ring.

When she came within five feet of me, I pushed off the ground. "Thanks for coming."

She drew up next to me and I realized that, while she seemed taller, we were the same height. "I almost didn't. This is unreal, having someone ask about Lauren. You're doing it for Patrice?"

I nodded. "As you can imagine, she needs some answers."

"And you think you can give them to her?"

"I hope so," I said, unnerved by the intensity of her brown eyes. My voice wavered as I added, "I bought lunch for us."

"At Choices?"

"Of course!"

"What did you get?"

"Protein burritos, wild rice, and fresh-squeezed limeade."

Cecelia looked at me thoughtfully. "That's what I eat every day."

I smiled. "Colleen told me."

"I wish you hadn't. I don't eat much."

"She told me that, too."

"I could have brought something," she said, chagrined.

"She said you'd never remember, that your mind's on other things, and you often space out eating."

She flashed the faintest grin. "Is there anything she didn't tell you?"

"Probably," I said easily, "but she crammed a lot into an hour, most of it about Lauren."

"Did she inform you that usually I eat over there, which at least gives me the illusion of being far from work?" Cecelia pointed to an area a few hundred yards away.

"She neglected to mention that."

"Good. Maybe she doesn't know. Don't tell her, or she'll follow me out here and talk about pesticides or supplements or dolphin-free tuna."

I laughed. "You have my word. Do you want to eat there?"

"Why not!"

Side by side, we crossed the lawn. There was something uncanny about the way we fit together, from the rhythm in our strides to the comfortable silence. Without a word, we both veered toward the same picnic table, a redwood near the adjacent schoolyard and away from the cluster.

As I unpacked lunch, Cecelia brushed away pine needles and twigs. I handed her a serving of everything, and we plopped down on the same side of the bench, our backs propped against the table, facing the playground.

She cast off black Birkenstocks and stretched her legs. "I love to come here," she said over the distant squeals of children playing on recess. "It reminds me of Lauren. She always wanted to eat at this table. She'd drag me out of the breakroom and tell me we should be with the children, even though they're always on that side of the fence, and we're over here."

I matched her pose, letting the sun warm my legs, while shade from a nearby tree cooled the rest of my body. "How long were you two lovers?"

"Four years."

"What made you break up?"

"There wasn't one reason. Mostly, I guess, because we were better friends than lovers," she said, fiddling with a turquoise earring.

"When did you last see Lauren?"

"On her birthday. She wasn't scheduled to work, but she came by to pick up a tape for her Walkman."

"What did you give her?"

"A Natalie Merchant tape. She called the night before and asked for it."

"Did she seem upset those last days?"

"Not at all! I think she was happier than ever."

"Colleen told me she had a two-year anniversary the week before she died. Does that ring a bell?

"Lauren? Of what?"

"I don't know. She told me she caught her having a private celebration, but Lauren wouldn't tell her why."

"This is the first I've heard of it."

"Hmm. How about a Dr. W? Did Lauren refer to anyone by that name?"

"No. Where did this come from?"

"Nicole picked through her appointment book and claims she found thirteen entries with this woman's initials, but she has no idea who she is."

"I don't either."

"She thinks Lauren was having an affair with her, that the guilt might be what caused her to kill herself."

"She's wrong," Cecelia said, her sharp features darkening. "Nicole never deserved Lauren's loyalty, but she got it anyway. Lauren wouldn't have cheated on her."

"Are you sure?"

"Positive! You can drop that line of questioning. It's an insult to her."

"I have to look into every angle," I said apologetically.

"I understand, but that's not the answer. Have you met Nicole?"

I nodded. "Yesterday."

"I'm surprised she had time in her busy schedule to see you."

"She didn't. She made me wait an hour and organized files the whole time I was there."

"That's Nicole." Cecelia shook her head in bewilderment. "I never could see what Lauren liked about her. What did you think of her?"

I chose my words carefully. "I think she's trying, but she doesn't understand what's happened, and she probably never understood Lauren."

"Exactly! Two days after it happened, she came into the store to talk to me about it, to see if I knew anything. It's like she wanted me to tell her, 'Lauren had a bad day at work, and she decided to kill herself.' She wanted a simple answer, but Lauren wasn't a simple person."

"You don't think there's one answer?"

"Not at all. Personally, I think she simply got tired of fighting every day."

"Fighting what?"

Cecelia stopped eating and changed positions. She pulled up her knees, rested her chin on them, and began plucking at her toes as if they were strings on a dulcimer. "Fighting to stay sane. I've never met anyone as strong-willed and disciplined, but Lauren never fit into this world. She was around people a lot, but she didn't really connect with them. All she wanted was a 'normal' life, something that was impossible after the crazy childhood she had."

"You mean her mother's suicide?"

"Hell, that was the least of it. When her mother was alive, she tortured Lauren."

"Physically?"

"Physically, emotionally, everything. She terrorized her. When Lauren was in the first grade, her mother shaved her head because she lost one of her barrettes. Lauren covered it up by telling the other kids in school she'd had a brain scan, which they thought was neat." Cecelia fell silent before wearily adding, "All her life, she invented ways to deal with things. Maybe she got tired of coping."

"What about her father?"

"He was never there. He was a sales rep for a pharmaceutical company, and he traveled a lot. When he was home, he drank. After Lauren's mother died, he withdrew completely. He sat in the bedroom in a rocking chair for five days straight. Lauren had to beg him to come out."

I shook my head in disbelief. "Why didn't Patrice tell me any of this?"

She shrugged. "She probably doesn't know. She was quite a bit younger than Lauren, plus I think Lauren shielded her from a lot of it."

"So, it didn't surprise you when she killed herself?"

"Not really. It wasn't like I expected it, but it also wasn't a complete shock. Her whole life, she was in pain, and now she's not."

"That's one way of looking at it, I guess."

She tensed, before saying in a measured tone, "It's the only way I can, or I'd wake up screaming every morning because I miss her so much." She stood abruptly. "I've got to get back to work."

We shook hands, and she walked away, shoulders bent with grief. She had almost reached the street before I remembered the brother. I chased after her. "Cecelia, wait up."

She halted, and I sprinted over, panting. "I almost forgot: I could swear Patrice said they had a brother, but Colleen thinks I'm crazy. Do you know anything about him?"

"She did have a brother—"

"See, I knew I was right. Where is he? I'll give him a call."

"You can't." She stared ahead, blank, and her voice became soft. "He died from sudden infant death syndrome. The same day their mother killed herself."

5

Thursday, I had no time to ponder suicides, dying babies, or two-year anniversaries. Instead, I had to deal with a crisis as soon as I arrived at work.

The big-screen computer had gone down, the one we used to produce all our artwork, the one that was supposed to be backed up daily, the one only a handful of companies in Denver could fix.

The hard drive hadn't been copied in a week, no repair firm could look at the equipment until Monday, and we had to recreate four days of work in two if we wanted to meet the deadline for our largest client, a nursing organization.

I immediately pulled two graphic artists from other projects and reassigned them the unfulfilling task of joining me in duplicating the lost thirty-two-page newsletter.

In the next twelve hours, I slowed down only long enough to order lunch for the staff, food I was too upset to eat. I had intended to swing by my brother's, either at noon or after work, to see where he had been for the last few days, and to invite him to dinner and a movie on Sunday. In the chaos, I barely remembered the dinner I had scheduled with Destiny, much less had time for an additional visit.

At the last possible moment, I dashed from the office and drove like a maniac to Ramano's, the Italian restaurant Destiny had chosen earlier in the week. I parked on South Broadway and sprinted the last half block to the eatery, located between a gay bar and a lesbian health spa.

I slid through the door and had to push through a crowd (the byproduct of a recent sterling review in *Westword*), to reach Destiny. In black jeans, starched white shirt, navy blazer, and loafers, she looked as if she had stepped out of a dressing room, not off an airplane.

Before I met Destiny, the friend who introduced us had described her as having a "hot body" but never mentioned the character in her face, the depth of her green eyes, or the tall forehead that readily registered any sign of laughter, concern, confusion, or frustration. Every range of emotion played across the plane of her forehead as it wrinkled in expression.

This night, as she walked toward me extending a dozen white roses, joy came across as if the word had been scrawled in all caps across a movie-theater screen.

"What's the occasion?" I smiled and hugged her tightly.

She kissed my cheek. "You'll see. C'mon. Our table's ready."

She flagged down the host, who led us to a tall, mahogany booth in the back of the candle-lit room.

We scanned the menu and chose our usual: chicken alfredo for me, vegetable lasagna for her. After ordering for both of us, Destiny reached across the table to squeeze my hand. "God, I've missed you!"

"It's only been three days."

"I know, but it seemed like four." She grinned mischievously. "I should have come straight from the airport, gone to my bedroom, and had you meet me there with take-out."

I raised one eyebrow. "It's not too late."

She laughed, a light merry sound. "We'll get there soon enough. By the way, do you know what tonight is?"

Worried, I said, "Should I?"

Stroking my hand, she leaned forward and whispered, "It's our eighteen-month anniversary."

"You keep track?"

"Of course I do, which brings me to my next subject: Have you thought about my proposal?"

"Which one?"

"To live together?"

"You weren't serious the other morning, were you? You didn't—" I caught myself when she pushed back from the table. "I'm sorry, Destiny. I didn't mean to—"

"Forget it," she said quietly, the twinkle in her eyes gone.

"I haven't really considered it, have you?"

"Yes. It's all I've thought about this week."

"Couldn't we keep dating?"

"Why?"

"I don't know. Practice, maybe."

Openly crestfallen, she said, "Kris, I've never met anyone I loved as much, or liked as much, or laughed with as much. I want to spend my life with you."

"Your whole life?" My voice fractured.

"Maybe not my entire life, but at least this portion of it right now."

"We'd grow old together?"

"Maybe we could set a more reasonable goal, like growing older. Although, I'll never be as old as you," she said kidding about the ten-month difference in our ages.

I overlooked the humor. "But we spend time together, tons of it."

"It's not the same."

"Aren't you afraid we'll jinx what we have?"

"I think we'll make a statement, to ourselves and everyone else, that this relationship is a priority in our lives."

"But you've never lived with anyone before."

"So?"

"How do you know you'll like it?"

"I just do."

I studied her. "You're really ready to do this?"

"Yes."

"Because you want to save money?"

"No!" she exclaimed, hurt.

Trying a different tactic, I said kiddingly, "Because you're tired of losing stuff between your house and mine?"

She cracked a thin smile but refused to make eye contact.

"I know: You're afraid some woman will come along, think I'm single, and put the moves on me?"

She glared. "No, Kris. What I'm afraid of is that we'll live like this, half in a committed relationship and half not, for years, and I don't want that."

"It won't take years."

"How long then?"

"I don't know. A few more months, maybe," I said, and as soon as I did, my stomach began to hurt. The pain sharpened when I saw Destiny glow.

She switched to my side of the booth and scooted close. "Really?"

I nodded feebly, unable to explain why every muscle in my body had tightened.

What was causing the tension? Destiny and I, we fit together. She was the best friend I'd never had, the lover I'd always desired.

An insomniac since childhood, I'd had the deepest sleeps of my life next to Destiny. The light weight of her body next to mine comforted me in a way nothing else in the darkness could. I could listen to her breathing and relax in the space between her breaths.

So what was the problem?

I had no idea. I only knew that I had just lied.

I carried most of my entree out of the restaurant, diplomatically protesting to the waiter and Destiny that I had eaten a big lunch.

After dinner, we went back to Destiny's house, put the roses in a vase, and made love, she with abandon and I with another's body. I had thoroughly disconnected from her, and me, yet was still there going through the motions.

I slept fitfully and left at first light, careful not to wake her.

At the office, I fell back into the groove of pressing to meet the printer's deadline, thoughts of Destiny far away. I was absorbed in my ninth pediatric endocrinology article of the morning when I heard a knock on the door.

I raised my head and smiled at the sight of Fran Green.

"Hey, there! You look terrible!" she said, never one to withhold an opinion. She strutted around the desk and patted my back.

"I've had a stressful few days. Our computer crashed yesterday."

"Enough said. Hard knocks from the hard drive."

"Something like that." I ran a hand through disheveled hair. "We lost four days worth of work, all of which has to be redone by the end of today."

"Need a hand?"

"Do you know how to spell endocrinology?"

"Bet I could sound it out," she said, reclining on the couch.

"No thanks. What brings you down here anyway? Don't tell me you need a newsletter today, or I'll scream."

"Nope. Came to talk to you about Dr. W. Got a minute?"

"One." I leaned back in my chair. "What took you so long? I figured I'd hear from you by noon Wednesday."

"No such luck," she growled. "What a stinker! Made so many phone calls, felt like a Ma Bell operator on Christmas."

"Well, spit it out: Who is Dr. W?"

"No idea."

I tried to disguise my disappointment. "None?"

"Not a one. Spent all day Wednesday calling every MD in the book whose last name starts with W. Fifty-three in all. Couldn't find hide nor hair."

"Damn," I muttered.

Frowning, I moved a client's file to the side of my desk and pulled out a legal pad, ready to brainstorm a new angle. Reflexively, I glanced back at the manila folder. Rebecca Kowalik, D.C. Doctor of Chiropractic.

Excitedly, I said, "Maybe we should have thought of this before, but what if Dr. W is a chiropractor or some other kind of doctor?"

"One step ahead of you, Kris. Took yesterday and called every chiropractor, homeopath, osteopath, dentist, psychiatrist, acupuncturist, and heaven knows what else. You name it, they have a shingle hanging, I called 'em."

"Veterinarian? I could call Nicole and ask if she and Lauren had pets."

"Don't bother. Called them, too."

"What now?"

"Gotta give it up."

"We can't," I said desperately. "I have a feeling this ties in somehow. Lauren visited her thirteen times in the three months before she died. Can't you think of anything else?"

"Sure can, and it knocks the wind out of me. On one of the last phone calls, hit me like a lightening bolt: The W might be shorthand for her first name, like Dr. Wilma. I ain't about to go back through the phone book again."

"Thanks anyway," I said, despondent. "It was a good idea."

"Not good enough," she said gruffly. "Don't you worry, though, won't leave you stranded. Tracking down a couple other leads."

I sat up straight. "Like what?"

"Can't say. Don't want to get you in another dither. Give you a buzz when I have something. Fair enough?"

"At least give me a clue."

"Rather not." Fran stood. "I'll let you get back to the grindstone."

"What if I'm chasing down the same path? It could happen!"

"Doubt it. You got plans to go to the library today?"

"No. Why? Should I? What's there?" A hint of panic crept into my words.

"Gotta go, Kris. Catch you later." Barely able to conceal a parting grin, she shuffled out the door.

"What does the library have to do with Lauren's suicide?" I called after her, but she never answered.

I was still cursing Fran Green and shaking a fist when Ann popped in to tell me Destiny was holding on line three. I took a deep breath before picking up the phone.

"Destiny!"

"Hi, honey! I know you're busy, but I wanted to touch base—do we have plans for this weekend?"

"Not yet."

"You never got ahold of David about Sunday?"

"I haven't had time."

"Do you want me to call him?"

"I'll do it as soon as I get a minute," I said, a shade irritably.

"Okay. What about tonight? I could pick up a video and Chinese food and come to your apartment."

"I don't think so."

"Okay. Dinner out, and back to my house?"

"Not tonight."

Her upbeat tone faded. "Do you have to work late to finish the nurse's newsletter?"

I swallowed hard. "No. We should be done soon, but I thought I might want a night to myself."

"On a Friday? You just had three nights alone, when I was in Durango. Wasn't that enough?"

"Umm, yes and no." Why did it suddenly feel like my life belonged to Destiny, and I had to borrow back parts of it?

"Kris, what's going on? Are you mad at me? Have I done something wrong?"

"Of course not!"

"Is it that suicide case you're working on?"

"No," I said slowly. "It's intense, but I'm handling it."

"What then? Is this about our moving in together?"

"I just want one night alone," I said, a hollow ring to my protest. "I'll come over in the morning and take you to breakfast at Stan's Kitchen."

This represented an extremely generous offer. Destiny loved the diner on East Colfax but could rarely convince me to eat there. I objected to the smoke, grease, and ever-present slab of gyros meat, and I had no tolerance for waitresses who slung food too hard and turned their backs too soon.

"Okay," she said breezily. "Maybe I'll have dinner with Suzanne tonight."

My heart skipped a beat.

Suzanne? The lesbian who lived on the third floor of Destiny's house? The one who was always available?

"You sure have been seeing a lot of her lately," I said, deliberately casual.

"I'm helping her write a grant for a literacy program she wants to start."

"Hmm."

"Nothing's going on, Kris."

"I didn't think it was."

"Good. I'll miss you tonight. Promise you won't have too much fun without me."

"Don't worry, I'll be miserable," I guaranteed with a laugh.

True to my word, I spent the evening moping and contemplating my newfound "freedom." What I was free of wasn't exactly clear, and as the hours ticked by, the exercise became increasingly pointless.

A late night call broke the monotony.

"Destiny?"

"You wish, girl."

"Jesus, Fran, you scared me to death."

"What gives? It ain't even midnight. You're a night owl. Didn't interrupt a snooze, did I?"

"No," I sighed. "I was almost bored enough to go to bed, but not quite."

"Why aren't you with your main squeeze on a Friday night? Nothing's wrong between you two lovebirds, I hope."

"Everything's fine. I'm seeing her tomorrow morning, if that makes you feel better. I hope you called to tell me you found Dr. W at the library."

"Nah. Forget about that. We got bigger fish to fry. You ain't gonna believe what I sniffed out at the big book house downtown."

"What?"

"Quite the place, the bibliotheque! They got more information in one building than you and me could fit in our heads, even if we started stuffing now and didn't stop for a hundred years. You ever thought about that, Kris?"

I yawned. "No, and I'm not about to start. Does this relate to Lauren?"

"The trick is to plow through all the useless stuff until you come to one tasty morsel, and that's not as easy as it sounds. Not even with all the high-powered computers and cross-referencing mumbo jumbo they got. Not by a longshot. I'm telling you, not just anyone can do it."

"Do what?"

"Matter of fact, almost couldn't myself. Strained my eyes so bad peering at the screen, started to cry. Ruth's been telling me I need new glasses, but what's she know? Next thing, she'll be buying me a shawl to go with my granny glasses. That'll be the day! She's half-deaf, but you don't see her pricing hearing aids."

"Surely," I said between clenched teeth, "you didn't call to discuss your eyesight."

"No, siree. Last time I checked, you weren't an optometrist," she said with a deep chuckle. "Speaking of, I plumb forgot to call them, the eye docs, when I was looking for Dr. W. Maybe on Monday, I'll—"

"Fran," I exclaimed, "the next word out of your mouth better be about what you found at the library, or I'm hanging up."

"Easy, testy!"

"I mean it!"

"All right already! Called to tell you Lauren had a brother. Poor shaver died the morning her mother bit the dust."

"I know. I talked to Lauren's ex-lover, Cecelia, and she told me he died from SIDS."

She snorted. "It was SIDS all right, but not in the way you think."

"What do you mean?"

"The name Fairchild's been bugging me, but I couldn't place it for the life of me. Spent all day digging through microfiche of old newspapers. Finally hit paydirt a few hours ago. Would've called you sooner, but Ruth dragged me to a chess club shindig."

I almost dropped the phone. "You read about this kid's death in the paper."

"Front page headline."

My stomach felt like it had a fist inside it, pounding. "Since when does a case of SIDS make the news?"

"Since Lauren's mother, one Nell Fairchild, killed her ten-month-old son, one Brian Fairchild."

"How?" I croaked.

"Seems he'd been fussy the night before, probably with colic, and early in the morning, the mother cracked. Hit the kid with an iron."

I covered my eyes and lowered my head. "Let me guess: She did this on her thirty-fifth birthday."

"You got it! After, locked herself in the garage and started the family stationwagon."

My next words were barely audible. "Where were Lauren and her sister Patrice when all this happened?"

"Good question. Newspaper accounts don't say precisely. Seems it was January, snow on the ground, and, here, let me read something."

In the pause that followed, I tried to catch my breath and slow my pounding heart.

Fran's calm, collected voice mixed with the sound of rustling papers. "Found this in the *Denver Post* the day after their deaths: 'Gilbert Fairchild arrived home at eight o'clock last night and found daughters Lauren, 9, and Patrice, 2, clad only in nightgowns and huddled in a backyard doghouse with Beau, the family's golden retriever, at their feet.'"

6

By the time Fran and I hung up, I felt sick.

The mystery wasn't why Lauren Fairchild had killed herself at age thirty-five, but rather how she had survived the twenty-six years following her brother's murder and mother's suicide.

How much of this did her sister know?

Possibly all of it, but why hadn't she said anything at our initial appointment? Possibly none of it, and how would I break it to her?

Bracing for my client's ignorance, I had asked Fran to drop off a copy of the article at my office, a request she agreed to fulfill the next day.

An hour later, curled in bed with a cold, wet cloth on my forehead, the phone rang again.

Didn't Fran Green ever sleep? I reached for the receiver. "Hi, Fran."

"Kris, it's me."

"Ann? You sound funny, what's wrong?"

"David's in the emergency room at Denver Health."

I threw off the covers. "Who called you?"

"Dad. He's down there now."

"What'd he say?"

Her voice shook. "Paramedics found him an hour ago at his apartment. He's unconscious, and they think he's had a bunch of seizures."

"Oh my God!" I gulped. "Is Mom there?"

"I don't know. I hope not."

"I'll get dressed and be right over."

"No, wait. I'm not sure I want to go."

"Why not?" I rose from the bed, dragged the phone over to the bathroom, and began rummaging through a pile of clothes on the floor.

"I can't face it."

"Seeing David?"

"That, plus seeing Mom and Dad."

"All right," I said, planning rapidly as I retrieved a crumpled polo shirt, bike shorts, and a fairly clean pair of underwear. "I'll call Destiny and ask her to come get me. We'll stop by your house on the way to the hospital, and you can decide then, okay?"

"Yeah."

"He might be dying."

"I know," she said, no life in her words.

"See you soon."

"Bye."

I disconnected from Ann, dialed Destiny's number, and waited through ten long rings.

Her cheery voice interrupted the eleventh one. "Hi, Kris. I knew you'd miss me too much. Should I come over to your place, or do you want to come here?"

"Destiny, David's in the hospital. Can you come get me?"

"I'll be right there."

I hung up, grateful for her immediate, unwavering support. I dressed hurriedly, then sat in the darkened living room for a few minutes, my legs shaking, trying to slow my breathing. Right before I left the apartment, I dashed back into the bathroom and brushed my teeth.

I took the elevator down and stepped outside the building just as Destiny pulled into the circular driveway. I hopped in and told her what little I knew. In a light rain, we drove the mile to my sister's house.

We never discussed whether Ann would come with us, she simply joined us, and on the short ride to Denver Health, no one spoke.

We parked on the street south of the hospital and walked briskly toward the entrance, a nervous pace that almost propelled us past my mother, who stood between two parked ambulances, smoking a cigarette.

It had been almost six years since I had seen her, yet she looked the same, her rail-thin figure almost lost next to the bulk of her long-time friend Sharon. A few strands of gray poked through her brown, curly hair, and the trademark dark circles under her green eyes were visible beneath the cover of round, brown eyeglasses. She wore blue jeans with cuffs several fashion-styles too wide and a sweatshirt two sizes too large.

She didn't recognize me until, in a faltering voice, I called out, "Mom."

Startled, she turned, and Ann and I approached.

I pulled Destiny from the background, introduced her as my lover, then broke the silence that followed. "How is he?"

My mother shrugged, one hand shielding her glasses from the drizzle.

"Who found him?"

"The apartment manager."

"You called her?"

"Yes." She puffed on the cigarette, hand jerking. "I finally got ahold of her a few hours ago. He missed a doctor's appointment this morning, and the nurse called me. I tried to reach him all day. Finally, about nine o'clock, I called the police and asked them to do a welfare check, but they said there wasn't cause to believe he needed one."

"The manager found him and called the paramedics?"

"Yes."

"How long has he been having seizures?"

She folded her arms tight around her chest. "Probably off and on all day, maybe longer."

"Oh my God," I shivered.

Why hadn't I made the time to go to his apartment, to prevent his head from flopping side to side, to quiet his flailing arms?

As suddenly as these guilt-ridden thoughts raced through my mind, I blocked them. "How can they tell?"

"By the abrasions on his body." She glanced toward Destiny. "David's been having trouble with seizures for the last three months. They haven't been able to get them under control."

"We know," I said coldly, stealing her attention. "We see him every week. I'm going in." I turned around abruptly and walked away, Ann and Destiny close behind.

Before we could reach the door, Sharon caught up and pulled me aside. "Kris, I can't stay," she breathed into my ear. "I only came because someone needs to be here for your mother. I know you and she don't get along, but she needs your support right now. Can you take care of her?"

My chin dropped. "How?"

"She's very upset."

"Of course she is. My brother's dying."

Sharon strengthened her grip on my arm. "Not about David, about Martha. She doesn't think your dad's wife should be here. She and your brother aren't exactly friends, and it might upset him."

"But he's not conscious, right?"

"Not yet. Still, do you think you could talk to your father?"

"Now?"

"Yes. Could you ask him to have Martha leave?"

I had been here less than two minutes, and it had already begun, the same twisted family drama, relived against the backdrop of my brother's death bed.

I shook my head and took a deep breath, ready with the exhale to explain to Sharon that I couldn't fight my mother's battles.

Before I could bother, she hit me with a hateful sneer. "This family is so screwed up! I don't know why I bother. I've got problems of my own!"

Shaking, I watched her storm off. Destiny and Ann rejoined me, and we went inside, where an aide steered us to the "Ashe" waiting room, a ten by ten holding area temporarily assigned to the family and friends of David Ashe.

There, we found my father and his wife of seven years, Martha, sitting on a couch in the corner of the room, next to each other, but not really together. They rose to greet us.

My dad, in dress shorts, golf shirt, tennis shoes, and Beaver Creek baseball cap, looked as if he had come straight from the eighteenth hole, while Martha played the part of an architect's spouse, a role she cherished. Every hair in her styled coif was in place; half-glasses dangled from a gold necklace; and the hue of her pink shoes perfectly matched that of her mauve jumpsuit and belt.

My father embraced me. "Hi, pal. I was afraid you wouldn't come."

"I'm here for David," I said curtly, pulling away to hug Martha.

Ann intentionally held back, mumbled greetings, but didn't touch either of them. In a voice wrought with tension, she said, "Have you seen him?"

Martha answered. "Not yet. They're working on him now, so no one can go in."

"How is he?" I asked.

"Who knows?" my dad said quietly, in sync with Martha's, "They won't say."

Destiny and I sat down in a love seat across the room, but Ann ignored the row of chairs, choosing to stand near the doorway.

"When did you last see him, Kris?" Martha asked.

"On Saturday."

"How was he?"

"He had a few tiny seizures, but he was pretty coherent. I had no idea . . ." my voice trailed off.

"We took him out to dinner last Christmas," she said, half-apologizing. "He seemed healthy then."

On this hot June night, I didn't have a reply to that statement. Destiny wasn't involved enough to comment, and Ann acted as if she had laryngitis. My father wouldn't meet my eyes.

We sat silently until Destiny volunteered to get coffee and soda for everyone. In her absence, Martha commented that she seemed nice. I agreed, and my dad and I started discussing the Colorado

Rockies. Inane conversation, to be sure, but it kept us from talking about anything that mattered.

At least thirty minutes passed before Destiny returned with the drinks, my mother at her side. My mom stayed in the room only briefly before returning to her post in the hall.

Over the next hours, I used two cans of Dr Pepper more as massage tools for my throbbing head than refreshment. Twice, I left the room to go to the bathroom, and each time I returned, I tried to slip by my mother as quickly as possible, afraid to talk to her.

A hundred feet from our cell, they struggled for seven hours to save my brother's life. They put him on a respirator. They pumped in massive amounts of intravenous drugs. They performed a CAT scan, an EEG, and a spinal tap.

In the end, he was alive, in critical condition, in a coma, and that was when the doctors finally allowed us to see him. One by one, we went, allotted five minutes apiece. First my mother, then my father, Ann skipped, and I went in her place.

Destiny remained in the waiting room, forcing me to stumble down the long hallway alone. Nobody had bothered to prepare me for how my brother looked and, entering his room, I almost fainted.

I had seen him six days earlier, but clothed, not naked in a hospital bed, surrounded by and attached to a dozen machines.

He looked as if he had lived under a viaduct for a year, with a head too big for his torso and dark brown hair that was stringy and greasy. His face was unshaven, and his fingernails were long and dirty. In answer to my question, a nurse in the room guessed he had less than a hundred pounds on his six-foot frame.

His body was bruised and abraded from hours of thrashing on the orange shag carpet in his bedroom. Open sores on his pelvic bone, arm, chin, and left cheek told the story of how he had spent the day.

Alone and writhing.

I sat on the chair next to the hospital bed and bowed my head until it almost touched his emaciated elbow, but I didn't cry, and I didn't say a word.

I couldn't.

When my five minutes were up, the nurse touched me gently on the shoulder, and I rose, a bit unsteadily. I asked if she could return to the family room and retrieve Ann and Destiny. She complied, and in a few minutes, the three of us met outside.

Destiny put an arm around my shoulder, and I buried my head in her neck. She held me until I opened my eyes and choked, "What am I going to do if he dies?"

7

As the sun poked faintly through the clouds, we crossed the wet hospital parking lot, Destiny and I arm in arm, Ann a stride ahead.

I didn't try to talk to my sister until we were in the car, driving toward her house, and then, I had to fight to control anger. "Why did you even come to the hospital if you didn't want to see David?"

"Some sick desire, I suppose, to see it all played out again. He's really outdone himself this time, hasn't he? I felt sorry for him at first, but the longer I sat in that little room listening to everyone chat, the more I figured out, and it made me furious."

The depth of her rancor stunned me. "What are you talking about?"

"His whole life, everyone's cared more about David than he's cared himself. How convenient that he brought us all together tonight. One big, happy family," she said bitterly. "He certainly went to great lengths to do it. He's holding us hostage again, just like he's done every day of his life. Except this time, I'm not falling for it. I won't be pulled back into this family's perverted games."

"You think he did this on purpose, that he chose to lie around convulsing for the fun of it? Christ, Ann, he's sick, and he's—"

She cut me short. "What's new? He's been sick his whole life."

"You think that's his fault? You think he wants to have epilepsy?"

"Yes, I do. I think people choose their own reality, and for whatever reason, this is the one he wants. It must serve him in some way."

"How? How does he benefit from his brain fucking up? What does he get out of falling to the ground uncontrollably, talking funny, and having kids make fun of him and adults stare at him? His hands shake all the time, and his gums are rotting from the medicine he takes. He's never had any friends, never! You wouldn't know this, because you never visit him, but he's lived in places that smell like urine, places designed to warehouse people until they die, stations for the elderly. That's his reality, Ann, life in a nursing home, except it came fifty years too soon. How the hell could you think someone would choose this?"

"Lots of people have epilepsy, and they don't live like he does. He's always been an underachiever. No matter how meager the expectations, he always managed to fall below them. He could do better than he's done. At the very least, he could find some kind of job."

"How? It's more than the epilepsy: his IQ is ten points above the retarded level, he has the emotional maturity of a thirteen-year-old, and he's mentally ill." My voice surged to a fever pitch. "Can't you understand any of that? My God, if he were paralyzed, would you shout at him until he got up and walked? Would you hate him for being in a wheelchair?"

"If I believed his legs could function, yes!"

"This is crazy!" I threw up my hands and turned to face her. "Our brother is probably dying. Can't you have any compassion for him?"

"What about me? Or you? Who ever cared if we were in pain? Just because we don't have epilepsy doesn't mean we haven't suffered." She opened the car door and stepped onto the curb. "I used up all my compassion for David a long time ago."

"Obviously!" I shouted, long after the car door had slammed.

Destiny drove to the end of the block, parked around the corner, and shut off the engine. She reached across to touch my cheek. "Are you okay?"

"I guess."

"Was it weird seeing your parents?"

"Very."

"I can't believe how much Ann looks like your mother."

"Don't tell her. That's her greatest fear."

"I can understand why you've had problems with your mother. It's hard to like her, especially because she doesn't seem to like you."

"Is it that obvious?"

Destiny nodded.

"Did she ask about me?"

"No. Your name came up only once, when she said ever since you were kids, you were David's favorite sister, and she could never understand why."

I grimaced.

"Mostly what she talked about is how much she's done for David. She's under the impression she's the only one who has contact with him. I pointed out that you and I visit him at least once a week. She seemed surprised."

"I'll bet."

"She doesn't really listen either."

"No kidding!"

"Three times, she called me Desiree, and each time I corrected her, but it was like she was too self-absorbed to comprehend my name's Destiny."

"That's Barbara Ashe for you!"

"And she blames everyone else. The first thing she said was that your father's always been embarrassed that David's his son, that he was too easy on him when he was growing up, and that he raised him to be handicapped."

"She's not far off the mark."

"You think he was responsible?"

"Absolutely, but so was she. That's the part she conveniently forgets."

"At one point, your mother said the strangest thing: 'David didn't ask to be brought into this world, and neither did I.'"

"Yuck!" I fidgeted. "What did you think of my father?"

"He's harder to pin down. It's as if he's there, yet not. On the surface, he's pleasant enough, but underneath, there's this other side, a distant and controlling one."

"Some family I have, huh?"

Destiny rubbed my arm. "My relatives wouldn't win any citizenship awards either."

I smiled weakly. "Are you sure you're ready to marry into this mess?"

"I intend to live with you, Kris, not them."

"It's impossible not to—they all live inside me."

"I know, but you have to remember you're separate."

"It didn't feel like it tonight," I said wearily. "I haven't seen my mom and dad together in seventeen years, and it made my skin crawl to be around them again. I could feel their hatred for each other, even though they never spoke. Could you?"

"A little."

"Scary, isn't it, that I spent eighteen years under their influence. They had separate bedrooms and barely spoke except to fight. It's no wonder I'm afraid of commitment."

"You are, aren't you?" she said gently, though her gaze was intense. "We don't have to move in together if you're not ready. I didn't mean to rush."

"You didn't."

"I don't want you to feel pressured. If you need to back out—"

"I don't," I said unconvincingly.

"Living together is a big step, and this probably isn't the best time to make a decision."

"I'll think about it," I said softly.

Because I couldn't bear to honor my promise of breakfast at Stan's Kitchen, Destiny and I went to Village Inn for a meal I moved around more than ate. By the time she dropped me off at my apartment, I was so tired, I had a headache. I didn't dare lie down, or I knew I'd never rise in time for my appointment with Nicole. I debated canceling, but suspected if I did, she'd never again offer me access to her dead lover's appointment book.

I took a long hot shower and bath, neither of which compensated for the night's lost sleep, but they both helped. I spent the next hour flipping through the *Denver Post*, unable to retain much of what I read. I settled for skimming the ads and headlines, but even that proved to be too much. It seemed odd to live a piece of my weekend routine—digesting the Saturday paper—when nothing about the past twelve hours had been routine. My thoughts never strayed far from David.

My headache worsened, causing me to put down the comics and practice yoga poses until I had to leave for my eleven o'clock meeting.

I stretched the ten-minute drive to Nicole's Congress Park townhome into fifteen and still arrived a few minutes early. I easily found the two-story gray duplex, marked by a distinctive black awning over the small porch. I climbed up flagstone steps, past a coifed row of hedges and two large planters of pink geraniums, and rang the bell.

When the door didn't open, I pounded on it, irritated I had forsaken sleep for what could prove to be a fruitless errand. Only the sight of a sprinkler watering the lush, trimmed parkway kept me from leaving. Someone must be home, I thought hopefully.

I hiked around to the back of the house to see if Nicole was in the yard, but I couldn't peer through the solid six-foot gray fence, and I couldn't locate a gate.

I was about to give up when I saw a kitchen chair protruding from a dumpster in the alley. I retrieved it, lugged it over to the fence, and climbed up. From the elevated angle, I saw a grapevine-covered arbor, a swing and hammock, a fountain, a two-tiered deck, and Nicole, oblivious to my gyrations, sprawled on a lawn chair facing the house.

"Nicole!" I yelled, trying to overpower the blare of her headset. "Nicole!"

"Screw this," I muttered, clambering over the wooden wall. Up was easy, down a different matter. Dropping to the ground, I felt the weight of my body compress into my ankles, which led to a string of profanities that captured Nicole's attention and almost caused her to jump out of the loosely-tied top of a neon green bathing suit.

"What do you think you're doing?" she said, peevish.

"We had an eleven o'clock appointment."

"Did you ever think to use the doorbell?"

"I did," I said flatly. "No one answered."

She sat up, plucked a towel from the chair next to her, delicately wound it around her shoulders, and took a sip of lemonade. Beads of moisture on the tall glass matched those on her body, and I looked at them longingly as she said, "I'm afraid this really isn't a good time."

"All I need is Lauren's appointment book."

"Oh, right." She slid into thongs and veered toward the door.

"One other thing."

She stopped but wouldn't turn.

"How much did Lauren tell you about her family?"

"Very little. She hated to talk about anything personal."

"Did you know she had a younger brother?"

"Brian. He died from SIDS," Nicole replied, bored.

"No, it wasn't SIDS. Lauren's mother killed him with an iron."

She spun around and laughed, abrasive and mirthless. "Where do you get this stuff?"

I didn't smile. "From a twenty-six-year-old newspaper clipping. The Fairchild case made the front pages. Nell Fairchild killed her son, then herself."

"You can't be serious."

"I am."

"Why? Why would she hurt him?" For the first time, Nicole's tone held no flippancy.

"He had been crying a lot the night before, and she snapped. She probably hit him to try to quiet him, and unfortunately, succeeded in doing it permanently."

"Where was Lauren?"

"I don't know."

"You don't think she—"

"I don't know, " I interrupted, nerves frayed. "All I have to go on is what was in the *Denver Post*, which isn't much."

"Does Patrice know?"

"I'm not sure. I was hoping you could help me find out."

"Me? How?"

"By talking to her."

"Why me? We're not as close as you might think."

"But you've known her for six years."

"I'm sorry, but you'll have to do it yourself. I'm finished with the Fairchilds."

"Please!"

"Listen, I have no intention of getting in the middle of this. If Lauren didn't have the guts to tell me, I'm certainly not going to tell her sister."

"Maybe you shouldn't be so hard on Lauren. Maybe she forgot."

Nicole snorted. "She was nine years old! How could she?"

"Very easily," I said softly. "It happens all the time. It's the most merciful human instinct: amnesia."

"I'm sure it happens to some people, but I rather doubt that's the case here. What's more likely is that this is one more tidbit Lauren kept to herself. The story of our relationship. End of discussion." She climbed onto the deck. "Wait here, and I'll get the calendar."

Nicole entered the house and firmly shut the door. I lowered myself onto the vacated lawn chair and watched a squirrel perform tricks in a spruce tree. I was about to take a swig of lemonade when, from an upstairs window, I heard two women engaged in heated arguing. I could identify Nicole, but not the adversary, and as hard as I strained, I couldn't discern words.

Five minutes passed before a red-faced Nicole, having donned an oversized T-shirt, returned. She handed me the appointment book.

"Thanks!" I patted the leather binder. "I hope this will help."

"Don't count on it. I told you before, find Dr. W, and you'll have your answer."

"Hmm."

"You don't believe me, do you? Don't you suppose I'd know if my own lover was having an affair?"

I shrugged. "Maybe, maybe not."

"I certainly would," she retorted haughtily. She inspected her watch and added, "I'd love to keep chatting, but if you don't mind . . ."

"Okay," I said and stood awkwardly, waiting for direction. Surely she didn't expect me to exit the way I had entered.

After an uncomfortable interval, she said, "I'll show you out."

She led the way, through an all-white, modern kitchen and a cluttered dining and living room, to a black-tiled entryway, where she grabbed my arm. "I almost forgot—you asked for a picture of Lauren." She reached onto a nearby shelf and retrieved a photo, which she wouldn't immediately relinquish. "You probably expected a picture of the two of us, but I couldn't find any recent, flattering ones. This was taken three months ago, on Ashley's fifth birthday. Don't bother returning it. I had double prints made of the roll."

She thrust the photo and almost struck me with it. "Don't they look happy together? Lauren was a different person when she was around Ashley."

I stared at the print, blinking rapidly. "But Ashley's—" I couldn't finish my sentence.

Nicole gave me a curious look. "Patrice didn't tell you?"

"No."

"I should have known. She never tells anyone. She wants them to believe she has a perfectly healthy child."

A lump formed in my throat. "But she's wearing hearing aids. Is she deaf?"

"Partially. That's why she goes to Children First. It's a school for children with disabilities. She had spinal meningitis when she was a baby, and it damaged her brain. She's never spoken a word."

It took several seconds for me to close my gaping mouth.

8

Returning home from Nicole's, I counted the blocks, anxious to finish the commute and begin a nap. Once inside my apartment, I ignored the message light on the answering machine and went straight to bed, if not to sleep.

I closed my eyes, relaxed my body, and tossed and turned, but sleep wouldn't come. Not in the first hour, or the second, or the third. By the fourth, I gave up.

Exhausted beyond reason, I stumbled into the living room, found Lauren's photo and calendar, and collapsed to the floor, ready to plow forward with my investigation.

Just as I opened the appointment book, a buzz interrupted my stupor. Only partially coherent, I rose and spoke into the intercom. "Hello?"

"Fran Green here. Let me up."

"I'm kind of busy now."

"Never mind, I'm on my way."

So much for the tight security I paid a fortune to enjoy in my luxury apartment. Although I never pressed the button to unlock the front door, Fran nonetheless gained entrance by attaching herself to a resident entering with a passcard.

I barely had time to shove the photo and calendar underneath the couch before I heard a knock. Reluctantly, I cracked open the door. "Hi."

"Hey, kiddo, how ya doing?"

"I've had better days."

She pushed across the threshold and patted my arm. "Destiny called and told me about your brother. Terrible thing."

"She didn't have to do that."

"Said you wouldn't. You ought to let her in more."

"She has a key," I said, deliberately missing the point.

"You caught my drift."

"Yeah, yeah," I said dismissively. "Come in if you want. There's pop in the refrigerator, or water, or something. I don't know." I gestured lamely toward the kitchen.

"This ain't no time to worry about hostessing. You slept yet?"

"Not really."

"Better do that. How about the suicide case? You haven't told the sister about the kid's murder, have you?"

"No, Fran. I've been a little busy since our last call."

"Good," she said, overlooking the sarcasm. "Better postpone it, or leave it to me."

"You?" I slumped against the wall.

"You forgetting comforting folks used to be my job, in my former life as a nun?"

"No," I said slowly. "But I can't believe you'd do something like this."

"Believe it. I'll work the case awhile, if you like, just 'til your motor's humming again. It's your call."

I sighed. "I appreciate the offer, but I can handle it."

Her eyes narrowed. "You sure?"

"I felt fine this morning when I stopped by Nicole's and picked up Lauren's appointment book."

"Hot diggity!" Fran danced. "What's in it?"

"I haven't opened it yet," I lied.

Her face fell. "No rush, I guess, but you sure you want to do this?"

"Yes!" I said emphatically. "All I've thought about all day is David convulsing, and all I've heard is his grunting and moaning, these awful sounds he makes when he's seizing. The only time any of that left my head—even for a second—was when I was at Nicole's."

"You ain't trying to be a hero?"

"Not at all."

"Okay, but the offer stands. You call on me for anything, you hear?"

I rolled my eyes. "I will."

"Good. Meanwhile, how would you like to speed things up, find out why Lauren did it?"

"I'd love to, but how?"

"Easy. Stroll in to the shrink's office and dip into Lauren's file."

I gasped. "Gloria Schmidt, the therapist she visited every Thursday? We can't!"

"Why not, the patient's dead. What's the harm?"

"I don't know . . ."

"Look, if we can ease the pain of some folks in Lauren's life, don't you reckon it's worth it?"

"Maybe. But what if we get caught?"

"Won't happen. I'll case the joint beforehand, get a feel for it. Took a spin by there earlier. Schmidt works out of a triplex, shares it with two other head docs and a rolfer. I'll schedule an appointment with the rolfer, get the lay of the land."

"Have you ever been to a rolfer?"

"Heck no, but seems easier than therapy."

"It's too risky."

"Not on Thursday night, it ain't, not between nine and eleven."

"Why then? What if Dr. Schmidt has group therapy or comes by to meet a client?"

"She won't."

I looked at her sharply. "How can you be sure?"

"I happen to know our friend Gloria's in a bowling league on Thursday nights. It's the only time she don't take her pager with her."

"What marker did you call in to find this out?"

"Freebie," Fran said, smug. "Ruth has a friend in her league. The lady hasn't missed a match in years. I'm telling you, it's foolproof. You in?"

"No way! I'm not desperate enough to break the law."

"Forget the law. What's the ethical harm? Tell me one thing morally cuckoo about providing comfort to Lauren's loved ones. I betcha G. Schmidt, PhD, would cough up the files herself if she could, but she can't. Think of it as helping her along."

"You're amazing," I said, viewing her with awe. "I'd never do this, but if I did, I wouldn't read any other files, just Lauren's."

"Same here. You and me, we're this close to a collision." Fran squeezed her thumb and index finger to within an inch of each other. "We're on the same track, running out of rail."

"You really think someone could do it without getting caught?"

"You bet! Never seen such a cakewalk!"

Excitement crept into my voice. "What would you wear?"

"The darkest clothes I could find."

"Your habit?" I said, cracking a wan smile.

Fran laughed heartily. "If I'd kept it, I would."

"What about gloves?"

"You watch too much TV. Who cares about prints? They only count against a con who pulls more heists."

"Which you'd never do, right?" I asked nervously.

"Nope. One-shot deal, not a career."

"Is there anything you haven't thought of?"

"Hope not. Even planned the getaway. Ruth'll give us a lift."

"Your seventy-year-old lover?"

"No, Dr. Ruth Westheimer. Heck yeah, my honey. How many Ruths you think I know?"

"The one who can't see at night? The one you told me hit a yield sign the last time she drove after dark?"

"Not to worry. She's got new lenses. You give me the green light, and the caper's good as done! We strike this Thursday, you could be calling Patrice Friday morning with the answer. Case closed, give you more time to spend with your brother."

For longer than I'd care to admit, I considered the tempting short-cut but eventually shook my head and let out a deep breath. "I can't, Fran. I wish I could, but I can't."

Deflated, she said, "Suit yourself."

After Fran left, I listened to messages on the answering machine and elected to return only Destiny's call.

She asked how I was and if I wanted to visit David. I told her tired and no, not yet. She asked if she could come over and spend the night, and I told her I'd rather she didn't. She asked what I was going to do and when she could see me again. I told her rest and I'd call in the morning.

I hung up drained, from the emotions of the past twenty-four hours and from the demands of being in a relationship.

I sat on the gray carpet, leaned against a chair, and tentatively reached under the couch to reclaim the treasures I'd hidden from Fran.

I brought the photo of Lauren and Ashley close, rubbed my eyes, and studied it carefully, mesmerized by the image that sprang from the flat surface.

The picture was of Ashley swinging, with Lauren pushing, and the photographer had managed to freeze the exact moment of Lauren letting go and Ashley flying away. Ashley, eyes wide, huge smile, hands clutching the swing, dominated the foreground, while Lauren, in motion, grinning and straining, filled in behind her.

I touched each of them, irresistibly drawn to the moment the camera had stolen. I wanted to climb in the photo and join them.

What they shared seemed sacred, and as the room went dark, I began to feel uncomfortable spying on them.

I turned on a light, and my conscience pricked: Was this invasion so different from digging into therapy records?

Probably not, but then again, neither was scanning private calendar entries, and soon I set the picture aside and began to do that, too.

I skimmed through the binder once, careful to stop before I arrived at late May, the week before Lauren's death. Somehow, I wasn't quite ready to peek into her final days, and it struck me as even more unnatural to look beyond, into a dead woman's future.

After I grew accustomed to the large, artsy loops of Lauren's hand-writing and managed to decipher bits of her shorthand, I was able to piece together parts of her life from January through May.

I pulled out a blank sheet of paper and began to take copious notes, dividing her activities into weekly and monthly categories.

Weekly contained: Babysit Ashley every Friday night, GS Thursday afternoons (which had to be Gloria Schmidt, the therapist), and CF on Wednesday mornings (possibly Children First, Ashley's school).

Monthly included: Draw up work schedule; a Choices duty on the first of every month; payday, an event Lauren marked on the fifteenth with a smiley face; and period starts at about every thirty days.

A chill washed over me as I realized the dates of Lauren's menstrual flow coincided exactly with mine, and I shuddered when I realized I would be the only one alive to face the next round of tampons and Advil.

I continued to organize the other happenings, eager to spot a pattern: Dr. W, thirteen meetings from March to April, most on Wednesday afternoons, some on Tuesdays and Fridays. I reviewed these until they blurred, but none provided a useful clue.

The "2 years" duly noted on May 28, the Friday before her death, confirmed what Colleen had said about Lauren's private celebration but offered no new insight.

Hiking and soccer, flag football and racquetball, lunch with Patrice and dinner with Cecelia, meet plumber, and get oil changed—all randomly scattered through the winter and spring.

And then came words that made my heart beat faster: Nicole out of town on business. Aroused, I flipped back to examine them again. Three in all, each with an accompanying line drawn through a four or five-day weekend, they surfaced in mid-January, early March, and late May. Suspect entries in light of Nicole scoffing at my frequent-flier suggestion and insisting she never traveled on business. Either she had lied to me or she had lied to Lauren, and I was willing to bet on the latter.

Adrenaline pumping, I stood and paced, half-planning how to confront Nicole, half-postponing delving into the last week of Lauren's life. My nervous energy quickly evaporated, and I plopped down again and re-opened the calendar to the section I had avoided.

Monday, May 31: Haircut.

Tuesday, June 1: Meet with Dr. W.

Wednesday, June 2: CF at nine, movie with Cecelia at five.

As I came closer to the last hours of Lauren's life, my hands began to shake, and I could barely move the pages.

Thursday, June 3: the big day, so noted in underlined, capital letters. Kill self. It didn't say that, but it may as well have. Her "To do" list was comprised of the following tasks: Lunch with Patrice and Ashley; pick up dinner and tape, Tattered Cover, get gas.

Below it lay a "To pack" list: boots, backpack, blanket, Walkman/tape, book, windbreaker, water bottle. So organized was Lauren that she had included the most important ingredient as the final item on her list: pills.

Nothing had been left to chance.

This was confirmed on the pages, which didn't contain a single scribble, following Lauren's birthday, "the big day." If there had been a shred of doubt as to whether her suicide had been planned, none lingered after I thumbed blank page after blank page. Lauren must have known she would kill herself on June 3, because no life existed after that fatal day. No dental appointments, haircuts, oil changes, periods, or paydays. Nothing!

Clearly, she'd made a commitment to die, but why?

The more I discovered, the more I wanted to know answers to questions that could never be asked.

How far in advance had she plotted the suicide? Could anything have changed her mind? Why did she celebrate a two-year anniversary—of what? Who was Dr. W? Were they having an affair, as Nicole suspected?

And I had even tougher questions.

What did Lauren see when she woke up mid-scream in the middle of the night? Was it something from her childhood? How had she managed to survive those years? Why did she take Patrice to the doghouse the day her mother killed her ten-month-old brother, and what did she think about while they huddled together? Did she believe she had saved her sister's life, and did she miss the brother who never grew? Did she forgive her mother or ever again feel safe?

Then suddenly, my mind took a dangerous turn, and I wanted to know things about Lauren that had nothing to do with the case.

Who was her first love, and when did she know she was a lesbian? What was her favorite part of her body and of other women's bodies? Why had she chosen Nicole, or Cecelia, and what type of woman was she usually attracted to?

I felt desperate to know more.

I wanted to get inside a woman who was no longer alive, to touch her.

Nothing else mattered but knowing!

That's when I decided to break into the therapist's office and read Lauren's records.

9

The next morning, Fran Green wisely didn't ask, and I didn't volunteer, a reason for my change of heart. We simply agreed to pay an illicit visit to Gloria Schmidt's office on Thursday night. Fran promised she'd take care of everything; my only obligation was to wait in front of my apartment building at nine, sharp. She and Ruth would find me, she said.

That business concluded, I called Destiny to see if she wanted to go to the hospital. Having slept a solid ten hours, my coping mechanisms felt somewhat back intact.

Unfortunately, Destiny was either out or ignoring the phone, so I dialed Ann instead and asked her to accompany me.

She immediately declined, prompting me to ask, "Are you ever going to visit him?"

"Probably not."

"Why?"

"Because I have no desire. I'd probably scream if I went to see him now. All I want is for him to let go, to let us go. He's had enough pain for one lifetime, and he's caused enough. He's like an open, throbbing sore, this ugly, oozing reminder of the past."

"What a horrible thing to say!" I exclaimed, responding to the coldness in her tone, as much as to the statements.

"It's true. Everything we were subjected to as kids, you can see in David: the violence, dysfunction, depression. What little our parents had to give, Kris, they gave him. They still do. They took care of him, and instead of taking care of us, they expected us to take care of him, too."

"You can't blame him for that."

"Didn't you ever wish you had epilepsy?"

"Of course not!"

"When I was in fifth grade, I told my friend Heidi I wanted to have it. Maybe then, someone would have noticed I was alive. Without it, I was invisible and worthless. A bomb could have exploded in my bedroom, and no one would have noticed."

"I know we didn't get enough love and attention, Ann, but what did you expect Mom and Dad to do? David didn't fake those seizures."

"Even so, what did epilepsy have to do with the special meals Mom fixed him every time we had to eat something with gravy on it?"

"What do you mean?"

"He hated gravy, so Mom made him a grilled cheese or hamburger, right?"

"Yeah, so?"

"And what did she do for you when we ate shrimp?"

"Nothing. I made my own peanut butter sandwich."

"Later you did, but before that, how many times did you throw up because she forced you to eat shrimp?"

"I have no idea," I said tersely.

"A lot. She said she wasn't a short-order cook, and she kept forcing you to eat what the rest of us ate. She only gave in after you threw up on the table, and she never did admit you were allergic to shellfish. And what about the garage?"

"What about it?" I said, fury causing a pain behind my eyes.

"Dad never made David eat out there, but Gail and Jill and I had to, and you were out there practically every night."

I closed my eyes to block out the memory of my father's twisted punishment for expressing an opinion at the dinner table that didn't match his. I couldn't count how many times I'd choked down oil fumes with my dinner or heard chunks of snow breaking from the wheel wells in the foreground as my family carried on merrily in the background. But I could track how many times David had been subjected to the isolation: zero.

I stopped twisting the phone cord. "You really hate David, don't you?"

"Yes, I do." Ann paused. "And it's taken me about fifty therapy sessions to stop hating myself for it, too."

"Don't you feel any connection with him?"

"Not usually. I did dream about him last night, though," she said, artificially cheerful. "I dreamed I killed him. I put him, and me, out of misery."

"I can't believe you're saying this."

"Haven't you wished it was over, that we could grieve for him all at once, instead of every day of our lives?"

My voice sank to an ominous low. "All I wish is that he'll get better soon and be able to come home."

"To what, Kris? To the life he had living alone in that gross basement apartment, waiting for the next trip to the hospital?"

"God, Ann, are you that far gone? Don't you have any hope left?"

"Yes," she said quietly. "I hope he'll die."

Fuming, I clamped down the receiver and kicked the air until my leg was sore and I was out of breath.

I struggled to compose myself and called Destiny ten times in the next hour. Unable to reach her and tired of trying, I left a detailed message and set off for the hospital alone.

I parked in the south lot and came in through the main entrance of Denver Health, having to first pass by a mini McDonald's and through a horde of smokers. The fast food and cigarettes seemed out of place in a hospital, but then, very little about hospitals made sense.

At the front desk, I learned David had been moved to an intensive care unit on the eighth floor. On the crammed elevator ride, blocking out the smells and sorrow, I tried to concentrate on getting ready to see David, whatever his condition.

I checked in at the ICU nurses' station, and a male aide offered to lead me to David. I followed him through an open area where a dozen patients, mostly unconscious, lay. One man, about fifty years old and awake, if not coherent, unnerved me with his incessant shrieks of "Mommy." I hadn't realized I was holding my breath until we came to a glass-enclosed area at the perimeter of the room, and I saw David in it. I exhaled loudly, relieved to be able to physically separate myself from what was going on around me and stunned at the sight of my brother.

Still in a coma, he looked angry and surreal, a human hub with wires and tubes and machines sprouting from his body, some miracle of modern medicine.

I entered, shut the door, and decided against closing the mini-blinds. I sat on the edge of a chair next to the bed and lightly touched his left forearm. "Hi, David. It's Kris." I looked closely but couldn't detect any movement.

"You sure are quiet. I haven't seen you this still since we hid from Mom and Dad in the fort," I said, referring to the childhood dwelling, five feet north of my parents' brick home, where David and I had spent days and nights, frequently ignoring my parents' calls.

My older sisters and I had built the two-story structure when we were in junior high, assembling it from scraps of plywood and discarded nails scavenged from the sites of new homes in the neighborhood. Soon after we furnished the fort with remnants of carpet, discarded pillows, and crudely sewn curtains, Ann and Gail lost interest in it, and David and I claimed it as ours.

Every summer day, he and I spent hours in the fort. Through blazing heat and ferocious rainstorms, we talked and read and played games and napped. We snacked on Zotz, Vanilla Wafers, and Ruffles we secretly bought and smuggled in.

In the winter, we used the crude edifice as a shelter. We shoveled a path to it and cleared the snow that blocked the door and windows. We lit candles for light and warmth and passed the time in our parkas, boots, and mittens. Many times, we huddled and shivered, but we seldom abandoned the fort for the house next door, a place that seemed colder still.

"You've got a nice room here," I said, glancing around. "At least it's private."

No response. Not even a tic.

"I tried to call you last week. I wanted to tell you I signed you up for a photo class. It's supposed to start in a couple of weeks, but we can reschedule. I was going to come by, but things got hectic." My voice trailed off helplessly, and I lowered my head.

When I spoke again, it was with great difficulty. "I'm glad you're still alive. When I saw you on Friday, I didn't think—" Suddenly, I couldn't finish my sentence. I couldn't utter another syllable.

Tears began to form, and I paused and looked up, trying to regain control.

What I saw outside David's room made me freeze inside, and my heart started pounding uncontrollably. On the other side of the window stood my mother, and I caught a glimpse of her just as she turned to leave.

Realizing I had spotted her, she must have concluded a retreat would have been too obvious, because without warning, she altered her course and in seconds sat across from me.

What a nightmarish scene: four feet away, a mother I hadn't talked to in six years; between us, a brother's inert body.

My mother reached to hold David's right hand and addressed me, as if we were alone in the room. "Someone needs to clean out his apartment."

My eyes flickered toward David's. "Isn't it a little early for that?"

"He can't go back there. A nurse told me he'll need months of rehabilitation after he comes out of the coma."

"Do they know when that'll be?"

"They won't say, but he can't go back to where he was. Something needs to be done."

I didn't respond. I knew what she wanted, but I refused to volunteer. I couldn't bear the thought of returning to the dark, dingy apartment where my brother had been writhing and convulsing.

"Have you ever stepped foot in his place?" my mother asked accusingly.

"Ah, not recently, not inside." I coughed. "I always tell him to meet me outside."

"I just came from there, and it's filthy. There were pornographic magazines everywhere and dirty clothes and rotting food."

"Did it smell—" I asked, unable to add, of semen? A peculiar odor, strong enough to cause gagging, often clung to David.

"Yes, it smells," she snapped. "What would you expect? He should never live alone. He doesn't have the skills, but your father can't be bothered with him. He and his new wife—"

"Dad and Martha have been married seven years," I couldn't resist correcting.

"—don't have a place for him."

And neither do you, I thought. Not in your house and not in your heart.

"He can't find time for David. He never could deal with his son's problems. Or anything else, for that matter. This entire family has problems, and no one will confront them. I'm tired of doing it alone, and I'm not going to any more. It's someone else's turn. You live the closest, Kris. It would be easier for you to clear out his apartment."

My throat felt dry. "I can't."

"It won't take that long."

"No," I said quietly, but firmly.

"That's typical," she said nastily. "You've only been in David's life when it was convenient for you."

"I've been in his life," I said between clenched teeth, "when I could emotionally handle it, and a lot of times when I couldn't. I can't take care of the apartment."

After she said, "What do you know about emotion? You never cry, and you never care about anyone but yourself," it all came back to me.

All the times in my childhood I had tried, but failed, to win the verbal wars she waged. All the times I had held back tears, then stomped off to my basement bedroom and screamed into a pillow all the vicious, clever comebacks I hadn't thought to say.

This time, the cruel retorts raced through my head while I was still in her presence: You were incapable of loving four overachieving, socially acceptable girls. What about a mentally ill, physically embarrassing boy? You were ashamed of him.

You gave birth to him; I didn't. You raised him, and what a poor job you did. All my life, you've tried to foist him off on me, but this time it won't work. I'm not his mother!

My rage came to a full, silent boil when my mother added, "And I didn't appreciate you introducing Destiny as your lover the other night. She had no right being at the hospital, and you didn't need to taunt me with your homosexuality. If your intention was to humiliate me in front of my friend Sharon, you succeeded."

Those comments, as incensing as they were, brought a strange tranquillity to me. I calmly stared at my mother, unwilling to believe I had ever been inside her body, unable to fathom how I had lived through the toxins.

In a measured tone, I replied, "I brought Destiny the other night because she's my friend and David's. When he wakes up, he can tell you himself that they're buddies. And I introduced her as my lover because that's what she is. It shouldn't have come as a shock to you. When I was eighteen, I told you I was a lesbian. I still am." I stood. "Not everything is about you, Mom."

I patted David on the shoulder and walked past my mother, careful to avoid eye contact, eager to leave.

But her next words stopped me. "You think you know your brother, fine! If you're so close to him, tell me why he was seizing uncontrollably."

"Because he has epilepsy," I spat, shaking with disgust. I reached for the doorknob, a step away from fleeing her mocking attempt to draw me back into the sick family circle.

"I found thirty unopened bottles of medicine under his bed. He filled the prescriptions but hadn't taken any medicine in months. That's why he had the seizures."

I turned around, expecting to see a shred of sadness on her face, some acknowledgment of my brother's pain, but only spiteful triumph registered.

I left without speaking.

On the way out, I had to refrain from strangling the man whose haunting "Mommy" cries had reached a hysterical pitch.

10

From the hospital, I headed straight to my office.
A broken computer, important two days earlier, now seemed meaning-
less. It was the least of my worries as I ripped open the envelope Fran
Green had dropped through the mail slot. I swallowed hard when I
saw the headline of the article: Mother Kills Infant Son and Self.

I turned on a light in the front room and dialed the phone, half
hoping no one would answer.

"Hello."

"Patrice, this is Kristin Ashe. We need to talk. Can I come over?"

"Now? Is it about Lauren?"

"Yes."

"Is it bad?"

"I have to show you something. I can be there in about fifteen
minutes."

She hesitated. "Okay. I'll see you soon."

I photocopied the article and in ten minutes had parallel parked
in front of the Elliott home in Park Hill, while Patrice, in a yellow
sundress, frantically paced on the sidewalk.

"What is it? What's happened? Why did Lauren do it?" she shouted before I could slam the car door.

"I don't have all the answers yet," I said calmly, "but I discovered something I thought you should know."

I crossed the lawn and sat on the concrete steps of the 1930s brick bungalow, motioning for her to join me. She came over, pushed one of the dozen toys out of her way, and slowly kneeled, teetering on the top stair. "It's not good, is it?"

"Did anyone ever tell you why your mother committed suicide?"

"Of course."

I exhaled loudly. "Thank God!"

"She was sad because my brother had passed away. He died from SIDS several months before Mother killed herself."

I winced. "Ah, that's not exactly what happened. Friday, I found out your mom and Brian died on the same day."

"Did Lauren know this?"

I nodded.

"Why would she lie to me?"

"Maybe because she didn't know how to tell you the truth," I said squirming. "Your mother killed your brother."

Patrice gasped and began to wring her hands. "Accidentally?"

"I think you'd better look at this."

I unfolded the copy of the newspaper clipping and passed it to her. Watching her eyes widen as she read, I felt heavy with the realization that I was destroying memories of her family. She would never again view the people she loved in the same light. She would see her brother dying a violent death, her mother beating him senseless, her father deceiving her, and her sister hiding behind the silence.

After she finished, Patrice laid the paper on the porch and ironed it smooth with the back of her hand. "There must be some mistake," she said dully. "You have the wrong family."

"The names fit," I said gently.

I reached across to pat her, and without sound, she began to cry, chest heaving with muffled sobs. I put my arm around her shoulder, and she leaned in and collapsed against my chest. "I hate being cold."

"You hate being held?"

"No, I hate being cold." she said between labored breaths. "I always have, but I never knew why. It's that doghouse. This is why Lauren killed herself. That's what you came to tell me, isn't it?"

"Not exactly."

"It can't be coincidence she chose the same day, her thirty-fifth birthday."

"Probably not."

"She did it to send a message, didn't she?" Her moist eyes hardened. "To me, the lone survivor of the Fairchild family. You've found the answer, right?"

"I'm not sure I have," I said delicately. "I never met your sister, but from what I know, I don't think she'd choose a date and kill herself to intentionally hurt you. I'd like to continue investigating."

"What could you find that would top this?"

"Nothing, I hope. But maybe I'll discover a more simple explanation."

"Like what?"

"Lauren might have been ill. Her calendar is filled with appointments with a Dr. W, and I'm working on that lead. Also, Nicole swears she was having an affair, so maybe that's it."

"She's one to talk. Nicole was probably cheating on her."

"Exactly. See what I mean? There could be a thousand reasons."

"I still think she might have been murdered," she said, hope creeping into her voice.

"Patrice, don't start that again. You know Lauren committed suicide."

"But not necessarily because my mother killed my brother?"

"Not necessarily." I rose and stretched, then leaned against the side of the porch. "If I'm going to continue with the case, I need to ask a few questions about Ashley."

"What does my daughter have to do with this?" she asked, hands tightening into fists.

"From everything I've gathered, Lauren loved Ashley more than anything or anyone."

She relaxed. "That's true, and the feeling was mutual. I think Ashley misses my sister more than she would miss me or Stephen if we died."

"I doubt that," I said softly.

"No, honestly, there was a bond there, a spirit they both had when they were together. Lauren had an infinite amount of patience with Ashley. A few years back, I saw her sit for three hours, waiting for Ashley to come out of a tantrum."

"What happened?"

"Ashley had misbehaved somehow, I can't remember what she did, but Lauren reprimanded her. This made Ashley mad, so she scrunched down on her hands and knees in the middle of the kitchen floor. Lauren sat down next to her and stayed until she was ready to get up. She stroked her back and kept repeating she loved her until Ashley finally came out of it."

Patrice started to cry again. "I miss my sister so much. I don't know what I'm going to do without her. Lauren practically raised Ashley."

"Nicole told me Ashley had spinal meningitis when she was an infant, and that the infection caused brain damage. Is that true?

Patrice nodded. "But I'd rather not talk about it. No one understands about disabilities."

"I do." I studied my fingernails. "My brother's had epilepsy since he was four. Right now, he's in a coma because he had so many seizures in a row."

She blinked rapidly, lips quivering. "I had no idea. I'm sorry."

"I know what it's like to wonder when he'll fall or what else will go wrong with his body," I said in a monotone.

"Does it ever end?"

"What?"

"The fear."

"I don't know," I said, fighting tears.

"Last month, the doctors told us to watch for puberty in Ashley. That's the latest thing."

"How? She's only five years old."

"They're worried this thing in her brain, the master gland, might be damaged. I guess it's happened with other babies who had meningitis. Every day I have to check her for signs of pubic hair or breasts."

I felt sick. "And if you find any?"

"What else," she said, straining, "more medicine. Even with it, though, she'd probably have a spurt of growth, then stop growing altogether. She'd start out too big for her age, then she'd end up too small. I can't think about it. All I can do is pray it won't happen. If it does, we'll face it like we do everything else, one problem at a time. Is that what you do with your brother?"

"Something like that," I said, unable to make eye contact.

"I can't remember what it's like to live without worry. We've been doing this since she was eight months old, and there's no end in sight."

"That's when she contracted the meningitis?"

Patrice nodded. "On a Wednesday. I've gone over it in my head a million times, trying to think what else I could have done. She had a fever and was vomiting, and I took her into the clinic, but a careless doctor looked at her for less than two minutes and said she had an ear infection. He sent me away with a prescription.

"I gave her the medicine, but it didn't seem to help. Friday night, Stephen and I were supposed to go out, and Lauren was going to babysit. I tried to cancel, but Lauren wouldn't hear of it. She said she could handle her, even though Ashley was crying almost nonstop. What an awful weekend. Saturday, Ashley seemed to be worse. In the afternoon, I paged the doctor, and while I was on hold, Ashley had her first seizure."

My stomach tightened. "What did you do?"

"I called an ambulance, and they rushed her to Children's Hospital. They put her on IV medications and a cardiac monitor, and she was there for two days before anyone told me she had bacterial meningitis. She stayed two weeks, getting a little better each day. The fever went down, and she wasn't as fussy, so I thought she was cured."

"You didn't know about the brain damage?"

"Not then. There was no way to tell. By the time they discharged her, she seemed normal, but the nurse who gave homecare instructions told us the meningitis might have caused slight brain damage. Actually, her exact words were 'neurological deficit,' which I didn't understand, and she had to explain. She said Ashley might develop at a slower rate than other kids, and that even if she seemed to be okay, just as a precaution, we should have her checked at eighteen months. She gave us the name of a developmental specialist. Over and over, the nurse kept insisting what she told us was standard procedure, and it didn't mean anything was wrong."

"But you were worried?"

"A little. I tried to put it out of my mind, but I never really could. I waited until she was eighteen months before I took her for the evaluation, but by then, I knew something was wrong. Ashley could barely crawl, much less walk, and sure enough, the specialist said there were significant delays and referred us to a neurologist, Dr. Pamela Brock. That's when my whole world fell apart."

"What did the neurologist find?"

"Lots of things, but the thing that stuck with me most was mild mental retardation. Stephen went ballistic when he heard those words. He didn't even care about the hearing loss. As soon as we left the doctor's office, he told me not to tell anyone we had a 'deformed' child."

"Oh, no."

"He's better now, but he was really upset. Fortunately, I didn't listen to him. I called Lauren and asked her to come over. I told her everything."

"How did she react?"

"She didn't. Not in front of me, anyway. I remember she stared out the window and wouldn't say a word."

"Did she ever talk about it?"

"The next time we got together, she did. She wanted to devise an action plan, and that's how she was until she died, always thinking of solutions. She's the one who taught me to trust myself, instead of depending on other people, like experts who don't know my daughter."

"You must really miss Lauren."

"I do! I can barely cope without her. She always calmed me down when I'd think about Ashley's future and panic. Ashley has support now, at her school, but what about in ten years, or twenty, or fifty, when Stephen and I are gone? I wish we could afford to do more.

We're saving for a special computer, but the raise Stephen expected hasn't come through yet."

I glanced toward the house. "Is Ashley around? I'd love to meet her."

Patrice shook her head. "Stephen took her to the zoo."

"Some other time." I reached into a front pocket and pulled out car keys. "I'd better get going."

She grabbed my arm. "What are you doing Wednesday morning?"

"Just work, but I can do that anytime. What did you have in mind?"

"You could come with me to Ashley's school." She smiled shyly. "I go there every week. Lauren and I used to do it together."

"Sure, what time?"

"Eight o'clock. We can meet outside and go in together. Wait here, and I'll get the address."

Patrice ran inside and returned with a slip of paper. "I drew you a map."

"Thanks." I folded the directions. "By the way, I thought of something else, but it might be too late."

Patrice's brow furrowed with concern. "What?"

"Did you ever consider suing the doctor who thought the meningitis was an ear infection, to get money for Ashley's care?"

She groaned. "It's all I used to think about."

"But you never did?"

"No. It would have been impossible to prove, and it was more important for me to accept Ashley for who she was and move on. At least that's what she told me after she researched it."

"Who, Dr. Brock, the neurologist?"

"No, Lauren."

11

The rectangular brick building, playground, and parking lot of Children First occupied half a city block in north Denver. On Wednesday, as I waited near the driveway in front of the special education preschool, a full-size, yellow school bus eased to a halt.

The sixty-six seater was empty except for two occupants: a child who sat halfway back and a driver who activated the flashing lights and opened the door.

He lowered the child to the ground, a pigtailed girl in a red dress, pink socks, and green plastic sunglasses. She made a beeline for the entrance, her gallop unbalanced and awkward.

A lump formed in my throat as I watched the driver jump back into his seat, put the bus into gear, wave good-bye, and pull out into traffic, having safely deposited his lone passenger.

A tap on the shoulder broke through my thoughts, and I turned to see Patrice proudly smiling. "That's my daughter."

"Ashley?" I said, whirling to catch another glimpse. "Why didn't she come with you?"

"She has a routine, and I try not to throw her off. Plus, she loves to ride the bus. She and Harry, the driver, are inseparable."

"Does she always sit in the middle?"

"Always. Harry's tried her in just about every other seat, but that's her favorite. Unless it snows, then she likes to sit up front, right behind him. I think bad weather scares her."

"Where did she get the cool shades?"

Patrice looked perplexed until I pointed to my own glasses.

"Oh, those!" She let out a laugh. "I forgot she was wearing them. They were a surprise in her Happy Meal. Come on in, and you can meet her."

Side by side, we headed toward the building.

"I have to tell you: Ashley's a little shy, and it takes her awhile to trust people, so I don't want you to feel bad if you don't get a response."

"That's okay," I said, holding open the door. "I don't have any expectations."

"Please, don't take it personally."

"I won't."

We proceeded through the reception area and down two halls before we arrived at Ashley's classroom. Mobiles of the sun, moon, earth, and stars hung from the pale yellow ceiling and walls, and giant cut-outs of a flower, bird, and tree separated the large, sunny space into smaller areas.

In the middle of the red-carpeted room rested a handful of miniature tables and chairs and one tiny house with an extra-wide doorway and no roof. At the far end of the room, a wall of windows opened onto a courtyard full of grass, trees, and playground equipment.

Patrice introduced me to Jean McNaulty, the early childhood specialist, and to Ashley, who had moved to stand in the protective shadow of her mother. I shook hands with both of them, firmly matching Jean's grip and lowering myself to meet Ashley's solemn brown-eyed gaze. After I stood again, she continued to gape over thick, long lashes, her mouth partially open.

I flashed her a broad smile. "Where are your sunglasses?"

She scanned the room as Jean patted her pocket. "We can only wear glasses when we're outside, right, Ashley?"

Ashley wrinkled her nose and pointedly stared at the eyeglasses on my face.

Jean countered, "Not those kind of glasses. Kris needs those all the time so she can see. I was talking about sunglasses, the kind with dark lenses that you wear for fun."

The explanation seemed to satisfy Ashley, and she transferred her attention to a little girl who rapidly approached.

Imitating a power walk, the youngster wore a dirty white T-shirt, blue jeans she had outgrown, and red cowboy boots. "Who are you?"

Before I could answer, Jean intervened. "Erin, it's not polite to approach people you don't know."

Unrepentant, the young charge squinted. "What's she doing here?"

"Her name is Kris, and she's a friend of Ashley's mom's. She's going to spend the morning with us."

"I got a star for not hitting."

She held up her right hand, and I admired it. "That's great! Do you get one of those every day?"

"Nope. I hit a lot. Wanna play cars?" She grabbed my fingers and pulled me to the center of the room.

For direction, I turned to Jean, who said, "That's a good idea. We'll meet up with you at snack time."

In the next hour, Erin and I drove miniature versions of tanks, plows, motorcycles, sports cars, and cranes. The three-foot semi truck, big enough to support Erin's weight, was her favorite. She kept insisting I push her around on it, which I did until I was exhausted. Between rounds on the big-wheeler, I rested by telling stories involving one of the other vehicles. My break always ended with Erin's shrieking command, "I go zoom."

Several times, I propelled her by the computer station where Ashley and Patrice were working on shapes and colors. Whenever we came close to her, Ashley stared at me.

Jean's "Snacktime!" shout came as a relief to my aching back muscles.

At the large plastic table, I met Tyler, a three-year-old autistic boy who had spent the morning working with Jean. Out of the corner of my eye, I had caught sight of his most common response to her lessons: frustration, which he usually displayed by going limp.

During the meal, Tyler indicated which foods he wanted by pointing and making guttural noises. Ashley reached for her favorites but never made a sound. Erin ate a little of everything—Fruit Loops, barbecue potato chips, raisins, and orange slices—chatting between, and often during, bites.

She told me bits and pieces about the homes she had lived in. She also informed me her grandmother had given her the red cowboy boots, and I had better not touch them. After I told her how pretty they were, she took my hand and placed it on one of the soles.

At this, Ashley rose from her place across the table, came around, and tried to sit on my chair.

Patrice followed, attempting to lead her back to her original seat, but Ashley wouldn't budge.

"Maybe you could move her chair over here," I suggested. "Would you like that Ashley? You can sit by me, and I'll touch those nice white tennis shoes you're wearing."

This must have suited her, because although she wouldn't soften her deep frown, she did become less agitated.

Patrice brought the stool, placed it six inches from me, and in no time, Ashley had a hand on my knee, and Erin sat in my lap.

Shortly after, Patrice took Ashley and Erin out to the courtyard while Jean and I cleared the dishes. Tyler, in an almost catatonic state, lay on a red beanbag near the windows.

"You're so patient," I said, picking raisins from the floor.

Jean wiped the table. "That's because I go home at four. Also, I get weekends off and thirty days of vacation. My job is easy. The people I admire are the family members. Did you know Lauren?"

"We never met."

"She was a wonderful person. Her death was hard on all of us, especially the children."

I poured leftover cereal back into the box. "Do you think Ashley understands Lauren's gone for good?"

"Oh, yes. She's a perceptive child. We've all spent extra time trying to counsel her through the loss, but it's been hard to reach her. She's fallen back several levels in terms of developmental progress."

"Do you think Ashley will ever speak?"

"We're hoping so. At this point, we're not sure if she can't talk or won't. Her hearing is almost perfect with the hearing aids, and her vocal cords aren't damaged. We know she understands language, but she hasn't used it. Once a day, Beth, our speech therapist, works with her, and she's heard her make all kinds of sounds—she'll laugh, cry, growl, and groan—but she's never formed a word. And it's not just her lack of speech that baffles us. Sometimes, it seems as if she comprehends complex ideas, and other times, she struggles with the simplest task. "

I watched through the window as Patrice guided Erin and Ashley down the slide. "How come Tyler didn't go outside?"

"He has a slight cold, and his mom asked us to keep him in."

"But it's supposed to hit ninety today."

"I know." She shrugged. "You should see him in the winter. She stuffs him into a thousand dollars worth of ski clothes, and he can barely move. It takes us five minutes to set him free," she said, smiling wryly.

"Is it hard dealing with the parents?"

"Sometimes, but other aspects of the job are worse."

"Which ones?"

It took her a moment to answer. "I think the hardest part is knowing most of these kids are here as a result of abuse. We see lots of children because of fetal alcohol exposure, which is a leading cause of developmental problems. And Erin is here because her mother used crack when she was pregnant. The mother got high, and now her daughter, whom she immediately gave up, is extremely high-strung and prone to violence. Erin's only four, and she's been in and out of eleven foster homes because no one can cope with her temper. It's sad really."

"Is the abuse that widespread?"

"Absolutely. The general public has no idea what the long-term effects of drug, alcohol, and child abuse are, what a price these children pay for the rest of their lives. I see it all the time at our reunions.

Once a year, we invite back kids who have been through our program, and it's heartbreaking."

"Why?"

She sighed. "When they're this age, there's still hope, and for the most part, despite their disabilities, they're accepted. The older they get, though, even with our best attempts at integration, the less they're welcomed. They fall farther behind, and they have a tough time of it." Jean folded the wash cloth and moved to a green beanbag near Tyler, who seemed oblivious. I sat on the floor next to them.

"I shouldn't complain. I'm lucky to work here. We have a staff ratio of two to one, which is terrific, and we do good work."

Jean's last words were lost in a burst of banging. Startled, I flipped around and saw Ashley pounding on the glass, eyes riveted on me. Patrice crept up behind her, waved at us, and captured her in a bear hug. She carried a flailing Ashley back to the far edge of the playground and put her in a large red wagon. By the time the wheels were in motion, Ashley was smiling again.

I turned to Jean. "She's incredible."

"For some reason, Ashley's taken with you. She's not usually this involved with other people, but you have a way with children. Do you have any of your own?"

I shook my head.

"You should consider getting involved here. We'd love to have you. If you're interested, we can always use more ESPs."

"What's that?"

"An educational surrogate parent. You can be an ESP for a child whose parents or guardians are unknown or unavailable. After receiving training, you oversee the child's educational programs. We have a specialist on staff who conducts the trainings, Wendy Henderson. I'd introduce you, but she's on vacation this week."

"Hmm."

"Or, if that's too much commitment, you could volunteer here. We can always use a hand, especially with field trips, which we're trying to do more frequently."

"Where do you go?"

"Simple places, like the grocery store or park or zoo. A lot of times a mother will ask us to work with her child in a different setting, to reinforce appropriate behavior."

"I could do that, go to the zoo, I mean."

"Next week's the grocery store," she said pointedly.

"Really? Okay, I'll have to check my schedule," I said vaguely.

"Great! It's a fun trip," Jean said, rising to greet Patrice, Erin, and Ashley as they came through the door.

In short order, Jean decided she and Erin would learn to count with blocks, while Tyler visited the physical therapist, and Ashley, Patrice, and I played house.

Without prompting, Ashley shuffled into the plastic hut and opened canvas curtains. That accomplished, she leaned out an opening and pointed to me.

Patrice translated. "She wants you to sit in the house with her, but you don't have to. It's pretty cramped in there."

"I don't mind."

"Here, take the stool," she said, handing me a round disk attached to three ten-inch legs. "It's much more comfortable."

I crawled inside the house and sat on the single piece of furniture I had carted in. My left elbow dangled out a window, and my head poked out the roof. "There!" I said to Ashley. "Are you happy now? I am. Thanks for inviting me. It's pretty neat. A little bit cold, since our roof seems to have fallen off, but we'll get by."

She smiled.

"Let's see, what should we do next?"

She didn't respond, but I had her full attention.

"I know. We'll call someone," I said, taking the pretend phone off the hook. "But who should we call?"

I snapped my fingers. "I've got it! We'll call Santa and ask for Christmas presents."

I made a big production of dialing the telephone. "Hello, Santa, this is Kris and Ashley. We're calling to tell you what we want for—"

I stopped mid-sentence and, in mock embarrassment, plastered a hand over my mouth. "What?! Oh, you're right, it is a little early. Sorry to bother you on vacation. Tell Mrs. Claus hi for us."

I replaced the receiver, raised both hands to my head, and slowly moved back and forth. Ashley eyes bulged as I feigned shock. "Can you believe that?" I said, grinning, "Santa told me to tell Ashley we have to call back in five months. It's too early. He's not taking orders yet."

I laughed and laughed, and after a few seconds, I felt like bursting when I heard her join in. I'm not sure if she even understood the humor, but peals of happiness bounced off the walls.

At her command, a slight tilt of the head toward the phone, I called everyone else I could think of—the Easter bunny, Donald Duck, Little Mermaid, Big Bird—and told them what had happened to me and Ashley when we tried to call Santa in June.

Every time I re-explained the situation, I punctuated my points with loud guffaws, and every time, she giggled with me.

I debated who to call next, when Patrice poked her head in the far window. "It looks like you two are having a good time." To her daughter, she said, "Ashley, it's time for you to take a nap, and Kris has to go home now."

"We're on our way," I replied, crawling out.

I turned to help Ashley, and my chest hurt when I saw her dejection. She grabbed my right index finger and wouldn't release it. Gently, I led her through the doorway, and outside the roofless house, Patrice pleaded with her, but she stubbornly refused to let go of my hand.

I knelt beside Ashley and whispered, "I have to go home now, but I'll come back and see you again."

She wouldn't relent.

I put my other hand over hers and clasped it tightly. "You know I will, don't you? Who else is going to help you call Santa? I'll come back next week, and we'll do it together, okay? But right now, you have to take a nap."

After I hugged her and added, "I promise I'll be back," she finally let go.

I spun around before she could see the tears pooling in my eyes.

12

Outside the building, Patrice dug in her purse and handed me a Kleenex. "I'm sorry Ashley wouldn't let you leave. She's really attached. I've never seen her laugh like that with anyone except Lauren."

"You don't have to apologize. I could have stayed the whole afternoon."

"You meant it, didn't you, when you said you'd see her again?"

"Of course. I'll come next week and help out with the field trip to the grocery store, if you're agreeable."

"I'd love that." She hesitated. "But isn't it difficult, with your brother and all?"

"No, actually, it helped. This may sound weird, but I wish I could go back and do it again, have us both be young, but I'd act grown up and be more understanding." My throat tightened. "I think I could have been nicer to David than I was."

"You shouldn't feel guilty, Kris."

"I don't—" I couldn't finish the lie.

"Before Ashley came to Children First, I used to feel guilty."

"Really?"

She nodded. "No matter how much I did, I thought I should do more. After she started coming here, I finally relaxed a little, but I still felt guilty about the two hundred dollars a day the state pays for her care."

"You shouldn't. This is the best use of tax dollars I've seen."

"I don't as much, but it took a long time for the feelings to change. As part of the evaluation for her to get into this program, they asked about things like my health, family history, drugs, drinking. There were all these questions, and I couldn't stop thinking about the one glass of wine I had when I was pregnant. I thought the woman who interviewed me could tell I was a bad mother."

"You're not."

"I know, but we all look for reasons. Maybe we'd feel more secure if we knew what caused the illness, more in control. I bumped into Tyler's mom one day, and she told me she and her husband had wished for a girl, and she thought maybe that's why Tyler's autistic, that they caused it."

I shook my head in amazement.

"You never really get over not knowing," she said quietly. "Even when you learn to deal with it, there's always someone around to remind you how tragic it is to have a disabled child. They stare at Ashley in malls, but they never see her accomplishments. Six months ago, maybe even six days ago, she would have ignored you. Today, she talked to you. Not in the way other kids her age would, but I saw progress. That's what I live for, the little steps. They're all I have." She glanced back at the building in which we'd spent the morning, and a shadow crossed her face. "I don't know what I'd do without them, but I guess I'll find out next year."

"What happens then?"

"Ashley leaves the program to attend a neighborhood school. I have no idea how we'll cope. I wish Lauren were here to help me."

I had no reply for that.

From Children First, I drove to Choices. I had an eerie compulsion to buy fresh fruit and vegetables, and they, reportedly, had the best in the city.

I entered the sparkling store and headed straight for the juice bar. No sign of Colleen, my erstwhile informant, there or in the deli. However, her equally wild, nonconforming male counterpart was busying whipping up drinks for three society ladies who balanced on stools in front of him.

One of the women, in a green leather jacket, flashed $10,000 worth of cosmetic dental work as false gratitude for the vegetable mixture he placed in front of her.

Nonplussed, he threw his ponytail over his bare, tattooed shoulder and gave her the peace sign.

She giggled—a vacuous sound—and leaned closer to her fifty-something friends who probably thought the proper make-up, jewels, and designer clothes subtracted, not added, a decade.

I had hoped to run into Cecelia but couldn't summon the courage to ask for her. I felt a pang of disappointment when I overheard the juice clerk tell another employee that Cecelia had the day off and wouldn't return until morning.

I left without buying anything.

The image of privileged, beautiful people haunted me all the way back to my office. I wanted to cry, for the children I'd left behind, the ones whose lives were already determined. Three or five years behind them, seventy or ninety to go, and yet, so much already had been sadly, irrevocably set.

Back at work, I made a feeble attempt to concentrate, but my thoughts kept drifting. After rationalizing that the computer was back from the shop, work was caught up, and no deadlines loomed, I gave myself the rest of the afternoon off.

I spent my free time biking around Cherry Creek reservoir, trying to forget David lying in a bed, trying to remember Ashley laughing in a playhouse. After three hours, guilt and tired muscles surfaced, prompting me to journey to Denver Health in a crazy attire of padded bike shorts, tank top, and leather gloves. Much to my relief, I didn't run into any family members in David's room, and I spent a satisfying hour telling him about my visit to Children First.

From the hospital, I drove to Destiny's mansion in Capitol Hill. Built in 1896 for a wealthy family, the building now housed Destiny and two other women in separate residences. With her parents' help, Destiny had bought the house years earlier when Denver's real estate prices had crashed. One of the tenants, a carpenter, renovated in exchange for rent. One room at a time, she was restoring the building to its original splendor, an ambitious plan that had stretched over more than a decade.

Rolling up to the house thirty minutes before our scheduled date, I planned to sneak in, clean up, and change clothes before Destiny arrived.

I parked my car in a space off the alley and was opening the back gate when I heard Destiny's voice. I looked up in time to catch the silhouette of her and Suzanne hugging at the top of the stairs, outside Suzanne's third-floor apartment.

Unaware of my presence, Destiny bounded down the stairs, two at a time.

"Hi, there," I said, loudly.

Shocked, Destiny almost missed a step and fell headfirst. It took her half a flight to regain her balance.

"You're early," she said, a touch accusingly.

"I thought you were at work," I countered.

"I left an hour ago," she said, flustered. "I thought I'd check the pipes in Suzanne's apartment. I've been hearing a vibrating noise for a few days."

My girlfriend moved to hug me. Arms limp, I returned her embrace. When I smelled a new scent in her hair, my body stiffened, and I almost collapsed. Apples—the fragrance of green apples—clung to her.

"How was it?" I asked, coldly.

"What?" she replied, stung by my frost.

"The plumbing."

"Oh, that," she said frivolously. "I couldn't find anything. I'll get

Claudia to look at it when she gets home."

"Maybe you should leave all the handyman tasks to Claudia."

Destiny gazed at me intently, concern rippling across her forehead. "Are you okay, Kris?"

"Yeah," I said dully. "I just need to take a bath and a nap."

"Come on in," she said. She grabbed my hand and gaily led me around the side of the house to the front entrance. "We'll get you all clean and rested."

Once inside, as she leafed through her mail and turned on the stereo, I undressed in the bedroom. Naked, I shuffled down the long hallway to the bathroom, devastated. What was going on with Destiny and Suzanne?

I spotted a bottle of New England Orchard bubble bath and let out a breath. I picked up the bottle to confirm it matched the smell in Destiny's hair and almost jumped out of my skin when I heard a knock.

Destiny peeked in. "Do you want me to order dinner—maybe Chinese?"

"Sure," I said. "Whatever you want."

I returned the bottle to the counter and crouched to turn on the water.

Destiny crept up and put her arms around me. "Do you like the smell? I bought it at a shop in Durango. You should use it in your bath."

"No thanks." I wiggled out of her grasp. I lowered myself a half-inch into the of water in the tub and instantly scalded my legs and buttocks. I vaulted out and adjusted the mix of hot and cold.

Destiny handed me a towel to quell my shivering. "Speaking of Durango, they asked me to come back tomorrow. The women at the Southern Colorado Lesbian Community Center are meeting with town leaders, and they'd like my input."

"Great," I said under my breath.

"I told them I couldn't go."

I held the towel tightly, afraid to let go. "You should."

"I explained the situation with you and your brother. They're trying to reschedule. I want to be here for you, Kris."

"I don't need you to stay." I sloshed water around the tub with my left foot. "Nothing's happening. David just lies there. There's nothing we can do," I said bitterly.

"I know he's in stable condition now, but things could change. I'll stay if you want."

"Don't," I said, venturing into the tub cautiously. Perfect temperature. "Really, I'm fine."

"If I leave early tomorrow morning, I could be back Friday night."

"You shouldn't cut it that close," I said feebly. "It's a five-hour drive one way. If you do it all in two days, you'll be exhausted. Why don't you spend the weekend down there?"

"Six hours," she corrected. "And I'm coming home to spend time with you this weekend, Kris, whether you like it or not." She bent to kiss the top of my head. "Are you sure you don't want to try the new apple bubble bath?"

Suddenly self-conscious of my drooping breasts, I could have used the foam for protection, but I declined.

"You'll be okay while I'm gone, right? You'll have Ann to talk to, and Fran. And you can call me on my cell phone if anything changes, right?"

"Sure," I lied on all counts. What was the point of honesty? After a long pause, I willed lightness into my tone. "By the way, are you and Suzanne still working on that literacy grant?"

"No, thank God. She finally submitted it last week. I was going to ask her earlier if she'd heard back from the foundation, but she wasn't upstairs when I checked on the pipes."

"No kidding. Then exactly who were you hugging when I came in the back gate?" I thought but couldn't articulate.

My throat was too raw with emotions of the past weeks to confront her.

After Destiny left to call in our dinner order, I slid as low as I could into the recesses of the giant tub, mouth submerged, nose and eyes a drop above drowning level.

The water turned cold and my skin shriveled up, but I dawdled until long after the Chinese food arrived.

The next day, preparing monthly financial reports occupied so much of my attention that I would have forgotten the upcoming evening's illicit activity were it not for Fran Green's hourly reminder calls. Any eavesdropper would have guessed we planned to break into the Denver Mint, not into Dr. Gloria Schmidt's office.

At four o'clock, the temperature hit ninety-eight, a record for that day in June. Five hours later, I felt hot and conspicuous in the darkest clothes I owned: heavy blue sweats, a purple turtleneck, and burgundy knee socks. Exaggerating the potential danger that lay ahead, I had even taken a black magic marker and darkened my beige Topsiders.

I was ready for anything.

At precisely one minute before nine, a large car pulled alongside the curb. In it sat Fran, wearing a purple workout suit and Colorado Rockies baseball cap. Next to her, at the wheel, was the owner of the Oldsmobile Eighty-Eight, her lover Ruth, clad in a flower-print house-coat and orange-juice-can hair rollers.

I tried to hop in behind Fran, but the passenger door wouldn't open. The two ladies gestured for me to get in from the other side, and as I passed the back of the car, I couldn't help noticing the enormity of the trunk, large enough to comfortably store four bodies. Attached to the bumper was a yellow sticker: "I smoke and I vote."

It was bound to be a long night.

Shaking my head, I slid in behind Ruth and scooted to the middle of the seat. I reached between the headrests and patted my comrades.

"Good to see you, Ruth. Hey, Fran."

"Pardon my outfit, Kris, but it's what I wear this time of night. If an officer sees me, Fran said to tell him I went out for a quart of milk and became confused."

"The helpless old lady scam," Fran interjected. "Fools 'em every time."

"Good cover," I laughed. "By the way, Fran, I'm glad we're on our way to a burglary in this inconspicuous orange car with SISTER vanity plates."

"Persimmon," Ruth corrected. "And I'm glad you like the plates. I sent for them last month. Isn't it rich: ex-nun and dyke."

"My honey looks good in the car, like she belongs," Fran explained. "That's what counts. And it's an older car, shouldn't turn any heads. Plus, you gotta see the engine—it'll chew up street faster than a police cruiser."

"God forbid," I said vehemently.

The two older ladies exchanged glances and chuckled.

Ruth took one last drag from her cigarette, threw the butt out the window, and applied a fresh coat of pink lipstick before shifting the car into drive. "Off we go!"

She peeled out of the driveway, taking the first corner at such a sharp angle she ran over the curb. Between silent curses, I wished I had worn a neck brace, or at least a bra.

I reclined in the plush seats, using my knees as a brace. "So, how was the rolfing?"

Fran shuddered. "Don't ask."

"That bad?"

"Oh, it was a great experience, if you like having your body chopped in half. Good thing I arrived early and did the gumshoeing beforehand, because I'm here to tell you: I was in no shape after."

Ruth turned to me. "She felt so puny, we had to miss Bingo."

"Wow," I said as Ruth, her focus back on the road, swerved to miss a parked bus. "You must have been sick!"

"You said it."

At the next stoplight, Ruth hit the brakes three times before we came to a complete stop five car lengths behind the truck in front. The way things were going, chances were decent the cops would pull us over long before we reached Lauren's therapist's office, much less got in.

"I'm no stranger to crime myself, you know," Ruth said conversationally, hands tightly gripping the steering wheel.

"Oh, really?" I said, praying she wouldn't try to make eye contact again on the two-mile drive.

"Two years ago, some hooligans stole this very car you're riding in."

"You're kidding!"

"I'm not. They took it from in front of our house—in broad daylight, if you can imagine—and went on a joyride."

"Lucky to get it back in one piece," Fran chimed in. "Nothing damaged."

"Now that's not exactly correct, dear. There were Cheeto stains on the back seat and Pepsi dribbles in the front."

"True enough," Fran agreed as we inched past a Ford Escort on the narrow street.

"What a hog!" Ruth exclaimed. "These drivers act like they own the road." She punctuated her point with a long lean on the horn.

"And how!"

"Good thing we're almost there!" I commented nervously.

When we pulled up to the triplex that housed Dr. Schmidt's office, fortunately, there were no other cars on the dark street, or Ruth would have hit them. As it was, she parked with two wheels on the grass. I scurried out of the car, grateful to touch the ground.

Fran clambered out and gestured for me to follow her around to the back of the house, where she pointed to a window six feet off the ground. "That's the one. Leads into the kitchen. I unlatched it the other day. Let's hope they left it that way. Time's a wasting. Hoist me up."

"Can't we go in a basement window?"

"No can do. Basement has a separate entrance. Might not be connected to the shrink's office. No problem, though. Give me a boost, and I'll be there in a jiffy."

"What about me?"

"No sweat. I'll bop around front and let you in. Deadbolt operates without a key."

"No, I meant why don't I go in the window first."

"No dice. Even with my butt and gut, I only weigh an even hundred." She surveyed my body as if I were a steer at auction. "If you don't mind my saying, you look a tad beefier than that."

"Only by thirty pounds," I protested. "Plus, I'm six inches taller."

"I'm thirty years older. C'mon, Kris, quit bellyaching and give me a lift."

"All right," I muttered, lacing my fingers into a cup. "But you better not forget to let me in."

"Would I do that?" She flashed an evil grin and placed her right foot into my hands. "When I say 'Go,' heave me up."

"Fine." I hunched over.

"Go!"

I lifted the lithe ex-nun high enough, but something was wrong. "Damn! Window's stuck."

"Locked?"

"No, stuck. Push me higher. I got a bad angle."

I took a deep breath and obliged, straining my back, stretching my arms, and burning my legs.

When I couldn't stand the pain one more second, I squealed, "I'm about to drop you!"

She let out a triumphant cry. "I've got it!"

Fighting spasmodic muscles, I held on long enough for her to get her head and shoulders inside the house. Unfortunately, that left a lot of Fran Green still facing out.

"Push, Kris!"

"Push what?"

"This ain't no time to be shy. Push my rear end and pray Ruth don't come looking for us. She'll be madder than a hatter if she sees this. You don't want to tangle with her jealous side."

"This is hardly pleasurable," I growled, letting go of her foot. Gritting my teeth, I put a hand on each cheek and shoved, causing Fran to fall into the office with an ominous thump.

"You okay?" I whispered, trying to suppress uncontrollable laughter.

Looking a little wobbly, she rose, dusted off, and straightened her cap. "No thanks to you. You threw me like a shotput."

"Yeah, but you're in."

"That I am." She returned my smile. "Meet me in front."

She closed the window, and I darted around the corner, past Ruth dozing in the car. I sprinted up the porch steps, and my partner in crime opened the door.

Suddenly frozen with fear, I couldn't move forward. "I don't think I can do this."

"What gives?"

I swallowed hard. "I'm too scared."

"Well, I ain't. I'll do it myself. You hunker down and wait here on the porch."

"What if you get caught?"

"They wouldn't send a sixty-five-year-old lady who spent most of her life in the convent to the slammer, would they?"

I shot her a doubtful glance. "Maybe."

"Heck no! What a great human interest story that'd be. I'd play to the media and be out by morning. You worry too much. I'll be fine."

With that, she turned and slinked down the narrow hallway, a thin beam from her flashlight leading the way.

I sat on the cold concrete and tried to stop shaking. Clearly, I wasn't cut out for this line of work. I slumped down and tried to ignore the sounds of the night—crickets chirping, a siren in the distance, dogs howling—but the crescendo built to a deafening pitch.

I scurried into the office for shelter and almost bumped into Fran.

"There you are. Knew you couldn't miss out on the action."

"What have you found so far?"

"Pringles. Want some?" She held out the can, and a chip fell to the floor.

"Jesus, Fran, I can't believe you're snacking at a time like this." I dropped to my hands and knees and frantically searched for the missing potato piece. "If you keep this up, we'll have to vacuum."

"Soothes my nerves. There's herbal tea in the kitchen and cans of juice and crackers."

I found the lone Pringle and pocketed it. Disgusted, I said, "I didn't come here to eat."

"Plate of homemade chocolate chip cookies, too."

"I'll be right back. Give me the flashlight."

Toward the back of the house, in the kitchen, there was a full-size refrigerator, a microwave, an oak table and chairs, and a small television. Not bad. The set-up made the furnishings at Marketing Consultants look shabby, and I was embarrassed to discover the contents of the fridge and cupboards outshined the combined stock of my office and apartment.

Maybe I need to spend more time in grocery stores, I thought as I peeled back foil from a dish on the table and helped myself to a giant cookie.

I carried the purloined treat back to where Fran waited. "Which one's Dr. Schmidt's office?"

"This baby." She stepped through a doorway into a large windowless room. "Get in, and we'll close the door so we can turn on the light."

After I obeyed, she flipped a switch, and a marble floor lamp softly lit the room. Fran let out a low whistle at the sight of plush hunter green carpet, an executive-size mahogany desk, and an eight-foot-long cream-colored leather couch positioned between matching loveseats. "The doc's doing pretty well for herself. Must be beaucoup bucks in examining heads."

"Hmm," I said, distracted. I was too busy sorting out my feelings to frame a more complete reply.

Oddly enough, for the first time in days, I felt untroubled. No remorse. No guilt. No fear.

I felt like I belonged.

I lay on the couch and felt strangely at ease in the setting a dead woman had visited every Thursday afternoon from four o'clock to five. I was in a safe place. The world could rage by outside, but in here, everything was still. I could have lain there for days, without ever reaching the edge of my sorrow.

For a moment, as I rested, chewing the stolen dessert, I almost felt as if I were Lauren.

I imagined I had come in for an hour of therapy, to sort out my life, to make some sense of it, to find a peace in the world.

Then I remembered the unhappy ending: the painkillers, the isolation, the last breath, and I shivered for this woman who had tried but failed.

The sound of Fran rattling a file drawer broke into my thoughts. "Got to find her records. Lucky for us, Doc Gloria is organized. Check out all these categories: active patients, inactive, group therapy, personal growth, journals, professional associations. Whaddya think?"

"Try inactive," I suggested, wrapping myself in a blanket I found on one of the loveseats.

"Will do." She rifled through the rows of files. "Wrongo! Think it's in active, and she hasn't gotten around to moving it yet?"

"Sure."

Fran ransacked another pile. "Nope. Have to hold a seance and talk to Lauren directly if we can't find this confounded file."

"That's not a bad idea. Do you know any psychics?"

"Kidding, Kris. Put on your thinking cap and help me."

"How about the desk?" I suggested, half-heartedly. "Maybe she's been looking through it recently."

"That's the ticket." Fran took a seat behind the desk and began exploring the contents of the bottom drawer. "Pack of gum. Half-written letter to her mother. Last year's Denver Brass schedule. Birthday card."

"I don't need an inventory."

"And one file folder with Lauren Fairchild's name on top."

"You're kidding!" I sat bolt upright and cinched up the blanket.

Fran shuffled through the papers. "You ready for this?"

"No, but go ahead. Don't tell me all of it. Just read the important stuff."

"You got it." She took out a sheet, held it at arm's length, and squinted to decipher the letters. "Let's see . . . looks like Lauren came in for her first visit four years ago. The doc describes her as intelligent, empathetic, intuitive, high functioning."

"Sounds good."

"Also a loner, hypervigilant, mildly depressed, subject to extreme mood swings. Distance between her and permanent partner, N-something. Can't read the handwriting."

"Nicole."

"Right-oh." Fran scanned the private notes. "Night terrors about physical abuse. She's being attacked; she's attacking someone. No deep connection with anyone, except disabled niece. More and more references to guilt. Unusual attachment to Ashley, probably sees self as disabled."

"No kidding, given her childhood."

"Perhaps reliving trauma of not being able to 'save' sibling. Get this, Kris—" Fran's voice rose with excitement before breaking off completely.

"What?"

"Here's a whole page detailing how her brother died."

Suddenly the walls seemed too close. My heart started pounding faster and louder, and panic filled me. "Someone told her about it?" I croaked.

"Worse."

I felt sickeningly hot and threw off the blanket. "Don't tell me—"

Fran's head moved in slow motion, up and down, then became still. "Lauren saw it all, Kris. Every last bit of it."

13

"I think I'm going to be sick," I cried, darting from the office. I fumbled in the dark until I found the bathroom and, oblivious to the exposed window, turned on an overhead light.

For five minutes, I hunched on the toilet, chilled, head between my knees, until the last wave of nausea passed.

I staggered back to Dr. Schmidt's office and propped myself against the doorframe, afraid to enter, scared of what more we might find.

Weakly, I said, "Did Lauren see her mom kill herself, too?"

Fran gathered the materials and began to pace. "No. According to this, she went upstairs, found Patrice, and hightailed it to the dog-house."

"Read me all of it," I said, reclaiming my spot on the couch. I put a pillow over my eyes to block the glare of the light.

"You sure you're up to it?"

"Yes," I said feebly.

"Okay. Looks like she told Dr. Schmidt this six months ago."

"It took her that long?"

"Apparently. Now, don't interrupt. Here goes verbatim: 'Brother Brian cried all night. Probably sick. Early in morning, after father left for work, mother brought infant down to kitchen. Ironing Lauren's dress. Two-year-old Patrice upstairs asleep. Lauren sitting at kitchen table eating cereal. Waiting to give mother birthday present she made in school. Brian in playpen in kitchen screaming. Mother calls for quiet several times, each time becoming more agitated. Approaches child and hits iron against playpen walls, yelling for quiet. It works. Baby stunned silent by violence. Mother returns to ironing board five feet away. Crying starts again. Without warning, mother hurls iron at 10-month-old child. Hits him in stomach.'" Fran gulped and stopped to catch her breath.

When she resumed, her voice was soft. "'He wails even louder. Lauren runs to playpen to stop mother. Mother crosses room, picks up iron and beats child on head and chest until there is no sound. Lauren clutches mother, afraid to make any noise. Mother brushes off daughter and returns to ironing. Lauren runs upstairs, wakes up Patrice, stuffs pillow over her head to quiet her crying, and goes outside. Confused as to what to do. Knows she'll get in trouble for missing school, but too frightened to go back inside house for clothes, and doesn't know what to do with sister. Hides both of them in the doghouse. Shivering cold. Tries to cover Patrice with her body. Calls dog, Beau, in to keep them company. Hears sirens late in the afternoon, but won't come out. Night falls. Father comes home and drags her out. Policeman says her mother and brother are dead.'"

A few moments after Fran stopped reciting, I removed the pillow from my head and blinked rapidly. Fran, stunned, had returned to her seat behind the desk.

"How did she ever survive?" I asked, a hitch in my voice.

"She didn't, kiddo. That's why we're here, because she killed herself."

Our tear-filled eyes met. "You think this is it, this is the answer?"

"Could be."

"But why a month ago? Why not ten years ago or twenty years ago? And what about her recent contentment? Where did that come from? Why did she celebrate a two-year anniversary the week before she died? What was that about? Clearly, her childhood affected her, but it can't be what pushed her over the edge, not after all these years. Is there anything in those notes, anything at all that refers to suicidal thoughts?" I asked desperately.

"Not a word."

"Something doesn't make sense." I flopped onto my side. "It all seems related, but there—"

I never did finish the sentence. The blare of a car horn startled Fran and me into new positions.

"Jiggers, that's Ruth!" Fran tore out of the room, down the hall, and into the kitchen, and I followed, struggling to match her breakneck pace. When we reached the side window, we crouched below it and listened carefully. Hearing nothing, we slowly lifted our heads to peer out. Fran raised the glass.

"What's up, Ruth? Uniforms?" Fran hissed.

Her lover rolled down the window. "I'm bored, and you said we'd be home in time to watch the news."

Fran turned to me and shrugged. "Give us a few more minutes, and no more honking, or I'll be getting a pacemaker installed tomorrow."

"Whatever you say, dear."

Fran lowered the window. "Better speed it up, or she'll drive off without us. Done this to me before. One time at the video store, told me I took too long to pick a flick and left me there high and dry."

"You go. Get her calmed down before we're both arrested. I'll straighten up the office and go out the front."

"Can't lock it, you know."

"So what! I'm not about to jump out the window. We'll hope whoever opens up in the morning thinks someone forgot. Now, go! And you better damn well wait for me!"

"I'll stay, even if that darn Ruth takes a powder." She handed me the flashlight and jogged down the dark hall.

The last sound I heard was the door creaking shut.

I crept back to the office and put everything in order. Before I returned Lauren's file to its resting place in the bottom drawer, though, I held it to my chest.

I could almost feel her heart beating next to mine, and it made me ache. From the therapist's meticulous notes sprang the story of a lifetime of pain, more than anyone should have endured.

Maybe Cecelia, the ex-lover who seemed to know her better than anyone else, was right. Maybe Lauren's death was a blessing, a chance to be free.

That's what I contemplated as Ruth and Fran drove me home and right before I went to bed that night.

For the first time in weeks, I enjoyed a deep, sound sleep. The slumber of the innocent. Or maybe of the guilty who no longer care.

Unfortunately, it only lasted about two hours. The rest of the night, I flopped around, unable to escape the cold, stark images of Lauren and Patrice, crouched in the doghouse on the worst day of their lives.

14

The next day, I couldn't stop fantasizing about napping. Through meetings, proofreading, and bike riding, my thoughts drifted toward sleeping.

I ate dinner with Destiny and dreamed of dozing.

Finally, at nine, Destiny and I went to bed. Within minutes, she fell asleep, and I tried but couldn't. I tossed and turned and watched the hours cascade by on the digital clock on the night stand.

I was beyond exhaustion, eyes burning from lack of sleep, but I couldn't rest. I couldn't slow my mind enough to stop thinking about David or imagining Lauren. In between, I worried about Destiny's proposal, Patrice's grief, and Ashley's future.

Every time I closed my eyes, I watched events of the recent past flash across my lids, but I had lost all ability to concentrate. Before one thought could be completed, another replaced it, causing me to try frantically to retrieve the lost images. If only I could have organized them, perhaps I could have brought a semblance of sanity back to my life.

At midnight, I felt on the verge of imploding.

Careful not to wake Destiny, I rose, picked up clothes from the floor, and went into the living room to dress in an outfit that wouldn't have won any awards, but at least contained one of everything: underwear, T-shirt, shorts. I rounded out the wardrobe with an old pair of tennis shoes I retrieved from the hall closet.

I grabbed a wad of money, keys, and my driver's license and left, not sure where I would go or when I would return.

Outside, the chill in the night air made me wish I had taken an extra second to grab a jacket, but within minutes, I had the car moving and the heater blasting.

I drove for miles, in a circuitous route that took me all over the uncommonly quiet city, but eventually drew me inexorably to Denver Health Medical Center, to my brother.

I parked on Bannock Street and cut through the mostly empty lot, ever conscious of the dark surroundings.

On the eighth floor, a compact woman with smooth brown skin and hair cut short, almost square, blocked my passage to David's room. The nurse's professional demeanor was marred only by the red high-top sneakers that poked below her lab coat. The depth and seductiveness of her voice surprised me. "Hold it there, honey, where you going?"

"To visit David Ashe."

Her bright eyes scanned me from head to toe. "You're coming by mighty late."

"I didn't realize there were set hours," I said, contrite. "I couldn't sleep."

"Are you his sister?"

I nodded. "Is it that obvious?"

"You're a dead ringer. The eyes and the freckles."

I grimaced. "I don't have quite as many as him. When he was little, we used to kid him about the ones on his ears."

"They're still there." She chuckled and extended her hand. "I'm Rose."

"Kris."

"I hear he's got a pack of sisters."

"Four."

"Have the others been by?"

"Not yet. Two of them live in California. They're on standby right now, but one's in school, and the other's expecting a baby."

"That makes three of you," she said, one eyebrow raised.

"The other one's in Denver," I said, shuffling my feet and glancing downward. "She doesn't want to see him."

Rose nodded knowingly. "Some folks can't, and maybe shouldn't."

"Is it okay if I go in?"

"Sure thing, but I don't want to hear any loud partying in there." She punctuated her admonition with a wink.

"Don't worry, I'm too tired for that," I sighed. "I thought I'd read to him."

"What's on the menu?"

I pulled an *Alfred Hitchcock Mystery Magazine* from under my arm.

"Whoo-ee. That might be a tad frightful for the boy."

I laughed. "The scarier the better. He loves these things, but I'll be careful," I promised.

"You better. I don't want his first sound to be a scream. It's bad for business," she said, chuckling. "You go on in now. Holler if you need anything."

She walked toward the nurse's station, rocking from her own humor, and I entered David's room. I closed the blinds on the window that faced the other patients and opened the ones that looked out on Denver's twinkling skyline.

I set the tin of nuts I had brought next to a package of diapers on the dormant heat register below the glass. I pulled a chair closer to his bed and sank into it.

"Hey, Dave," I said quietly, squeezing his hand.

In recent years, I had been afraid to look directly at my brother— unable to face his greasy brown hair and acne- and whisker-covered cheeks. That night, though, he seemed cleaner. I studied him, trying to picture the resemblance Rose had seen, hoping it wasn't there.

My brother and I shared intense blue eyes, thick eyebrows, and freckles, as if we came from the same cutter, but every feature of his was exaggerated. His eyes were more sunken, his eyebrows bushier, and his freckles more dense. He also had lush eyelashes, gaunt, angular features, and a perpetual cowlick I didn't possess.

I had spent years trying not to get too close to him, repulsed by the smell of his breath and the state of his teeth and gums. Medications had caused halitosis and deformed his gums to the point that his teeth barely protruded.

By a curious twist, he looked healthier in a coma than out of it. The nails on his long, thin fingers were clean and trimmed, and his hands weren't shaking. Absent were his thick, black-framed glasses, the helmet he wore during periods of frequent seizures, and the heavy, tattered coat he favored even in warm weather.

"I know it's late, but I couldn't sleep, so I thought I'd come read to you."

I curled up, knees propped on the bed, and in carefully pronounced, whispered words, read a six-page mystery about a man who murdered his only friend.

My mind wandered constantly: to Lauren and her last day, to Ashley and the rest of her life, and to the happy moments I had shared with my brother when we were young.

As children, David and I had been great friends and companions, but as we grew, so did the manifestations of his illness, and with it, my fear and discomfort.

There was a day, when I was fourteen and he was eleven, that marked the beginning of the end of our closeness.

It was fall, and we had ridden our bikes to the library and checked out books, mysteries and adventures for me, *Willy Wonka and the Chocolate Factory* for him, a story he had read a hundred times. After, we went to a nearby Burger King to eat.

There, at the counter, in the middle of a lunch-hour throng, David had started to seize. He crashed to the floor, and customers scattered. I knelt next to him, made sure he wasn't choking on anything, and settled in to wait it out.

A woman behind the counter yelled for the manager to call 911.

I tried to explain to her, and the sea of adults surrounding David, that there was no need to panic, that my brother had epilepsy, that he'd be fine. After a few minutes, the convulsing subsided, but not the strangers' anxiety. An ambulance came, and over my protestations, the paramedics insisted on placing David, who had recovered completely, on a stretcher and transporting him to the hospital. For legal reasons, they said.

I called my mom, who, after bawling me out for the medical bills that were sure to follow, left to retrieve David.

Alone, I wheeled our two bikes home, crying all the way.

What if he had seized five minutes earlier, as he and I had zipped across the busy four-lane street? What then? I couldn't have prevented it. He would have died.

I had never before felt so helpless or hopeless.

I had always protected him from the taunts of other kids, but this was worse. I couldn't block the image of a crowd of horrified grownup faces looming over me, judging my brother, judging me.

Suddenly, the world was too big and ugly, and I was too small and frail.

I think I gave up on him that day.

Remembering it all, almost two decades later, drained me. A pain shot through my neck, and the muscles in my shoulders tensed to the point of cramping.

I leaned on the bed, my head cradled in folded arms, and lay next to my brother's lifeless hand, lost in the stillness.

I almost shrieked when I sensed a movement and heard someone say softly, "Kris."

I sat up and blinked at the sight of my lover standing in the shadow of the doorway, the faint light shimmering off her blonde hair.

Destiny gave me a slight wave. "Hi, honey."

"How did you know I was here?"

"I took a guess after I woke up and you were gone." She scooted a chair next to mine, perched on the edge of it, and put her arm around my shoulders. She pointed to the container below the window. "What are those?"

"Cashews. He loves them. Maybe he'll smell them and wake up. If not, I'll give them to the nurses," I said, numb.

She shot me a look of concern. "Are you all right?"

"I guess."

"You couldn't sleep?"

I shook my head.

"You should have woke me."

"I couldn't," I said simply. "I thought I'd come by and read David some mysteries, but I only managed to get through one."

"Do you want me to read?"

"No, thanks. I think I want to sit here and rest awhile."

"Okay if I stay with you?"

"Sure," I said half-heartedly.

After a few minutes, Destiny broke the aching silence. "What are you thinking about?"

"Nothing."

"Okay," she said, hurt.

"High school," I said after a short pause. "David's hormones kicked in, and the doctors couldn't control his seizures. They medicated him so much, he became a zombie. He fell asleep all the time, even in class, and when he was awake, he was seizing. David had so many seizures while he ran to catch the bus that my mom asked me to start picking him up from school."

"Why didn't she do it?"

"Who knows? I can't remember her excuse, but I said I would. I was about twenty years old, living in my own apartment, but I had a job near the school. I agreed to take a late lunch every day and drive him home. I'll never forget the first day I went to get him."

I paused and rubbed my head. "He wasn't where I told him to meet me, and it took me an hour to find him—in the nurse's office. He'd had a seizure in one of the crowded hallways, in front of a bunch of kids."

My lower lip started quivering. Destiny pulled me closer but didn't say anything.

"All the way home, I wanted to cry, but I couldn't. David was still out of it, unfocused. When we got to my mom's, I helped him change out of his pants—he'd peed in them during the seizure—then I went back to work."

I let out a deep breath. "Years later, I wondered why my mom wasn't there, why she didn't help David when he needed it, but you know what I thought about that day?"

Destiny shook her head, her eyes a pool of sadness, and reached to stroke my hair.

That gentle motion, the tenderness that came naturally to her, made me explode with grief.

I started sobbing and could barely talk. "I felt like a hero and a fake," I said between gut-wrenching cries. "For doing so much . . . and so little."

Destiny drew me into her body and kissed my cheek. "You've done enough, Kris," she whispered. "More than most people would have or could have."

I looked up but couldn't speak.

She brushed hair back from my eyes. "Now let's go home so I can hold you while you sleep."

On wobbly legs, I stood up and walked out of David's room, my hand in Destiny's.

I spent most of the next day, Saturday, in bed.

I tried to convince myself I was catching a cold and needed to rest, but truthfully, I felt depressed.

Sunday morning, a phone call from Patrice roused me.

She began enigmatically. "I found out something yesterday I think you need to know. I'm not sure it has anything to do with Lauren's death, and I probably shouldn't be telling you this . . ."

"Yes?" I prompted, stifling a massive yawn.

"Maybe it's nothing, but it feels important. No, never mind. I shouldn't have bothered you on the weekend."

"At this point, anything would help," I said dully. "I'm not really getting anywhere."

"But this may not relate."

"Patrice, what?" I practically barked.

Stunned by my change in tone, she answered immediately. "I think Nicole's having an affair."

I frowned. "Lauren's gone. I agree it might be a little soon, but there's nothing wrong with Nicole dating."

"There is if she started last year," she said righteously.

I riveted my attention. "What are you talking about?"

"I don't have much to go on, but last spring, while Lauren was babysitting Ashley, Stephen and I ran into Nicole and another woman at the movies. At first, I didn't think much of it. Nicole seemed awkward, as if she wished she hadn't run into us, but she introduced us to the other woman. She called her a friend from work."

Patrice's pace quickened. "When we got back to the house, Lauren mentioned in passing that Nicole had been working a lot of overtime, including that night. This was before we had a chance to tell her we'd bumped into Nicole, so of course, I didn't say a word. I felt terrible about it, but I didn't know what else to do.

"After Lauren left, I started remembering little things. Like how Nicole's cheeks were red, how she seemed happier than when I saw her with Lauren, and how the other woman looked at Nicole when she talked. Stuff like that."

"But you never said anything to Lauren about any of this?" I probed.

"No. I considered telling her, but Stephen said I shouldn't interfere. Plus, I didn't have much to go on, and I didn't want to cause trouble. I guess that's why I never brought it up."

"Why didn't you tell me about this when I asked you if Lauren and Nicole were getting along?"

"I honestly forgot," she said guardedly. "Right after it happened, I thought about it a lot, but it sort of faded, until yesterday anyway."

My interest piqued. "What happened?"

"I saw the two of them at Cherry Creek Mall, but they didn't see me. I was in the dressing room at Foley's, trying on shorts when I heard Nicole in the next stall. I started to go over and say hi, but then I heard another woman's voice. The two of them were trying on bathing suits, and from what I could tell, they'd done this before."

"Done what?"

"It was pretty clear they were more than friends," she said, her words caked in indignation.

"And you recognized this woman from her voice."

"No, her eyes. Nicole left to go to another department, and this woman came out to look at herself in the full-length mirror outside my door. The door was the kind with slats you can see out of, but people can't see in. I got a good look at her."

"And you remembered her eyes, even though you only met once?" I asked, skeptical.

"You would have, too," she said adamantly. "One's blue and the other's green."

Barely able to see through my anger, I dressed and drove straight to Nicole's house.

I'd had plenty of time to study the blue and green eyes of Paige Werner, Nicole's assistant, thanks to my hour-long wait for Nicole.

I rang the doorbell but didn't bother to wait for an answer. I stomped around to the backyard, lifted myself up on the fence, and yelled at a stunned Nicole to meet me out front.

Having covered her skimpy pink two-piece bathing suit with a sleeveless denim shirt, Nicole had regained full composure by the time we met at the front door. I couldn't decide whether I hated her more for her abrasive personality or for her wiry, tanned legs.

I bellowed through the bars of the security door. "We need to talk."

She pinched her lips. "I doubt that."

"Are you going to let me in?"

"I'd rather not," she said, drawing the sides of the unbuttoned shirt tighter.

"Fine, we'll do it here."

"Why don't you give it up?" she said, irked.

"You'd like that, wouldn't you?" I sneered.

"Yes, but what's that supposed to mean?"

"You already have your answer, don't you? You know why Lauren committed suicide, but you couldn't bother to share it with the rest of us."

"I have no idea what you're talking about," she said, genuinely perplexed.

"C'mon, Nicole, give it up. From the beginning, you were against Patrice hiring me. You thought it was a dumb idea. The only reason you agreed to talk was to salve your guilty conscience. You never really cared why Lauren killed herself. The only thing that interested you was knowing whether she had caught you."

"Excuse me?"

"You were—or are—having an affair with Paige Werner. Funny how Lauren wrote all the dates of your business trips in her appointment book when you told me you never travel on business."

Nicole blanched, but I didn't relent. "All those mysterious four- and five-day trips you took to another woman's bedroom. Maybe you keep tolerating me because you want to know if Lauren suspected or knew, and if that might have led to her death."

"I take great offense at what you're saying," she said coldly.

"I take equal offense at your lack of morals."

She feigned boredom. "I assumed you'd get around to finding out about Paige. Who told you?"

I shrugged my shoulders.

"Perfect Cecelia, the ex-love of Lauren's life, right?"

I forced my facial muscles to remain passive.

She glared at me, her eyes burning into my smooth forehead. "Whatever. My relationship with Paige, or with Lauren, or with any other woman, is none of your goddamn business. I've tried to be pa-tient while you ran around making a big show of trying to know some-thing about my lover. But what right do you have to know why she killed herself?"

"None, but Patrice does."

"The hell she does," she spit.

"She's her sister."

"And I was her lover, her life partner, her best friend," she said between clenched teeth. "But what did that matter? You can't possibly know what it's like to deal with a suicide. Now get the hell off my porch."

I caught my breath and checked my temper. When I spoke, it was in a lifeless monotone. "You think I have no idea what it's like? You don't know a thing about my life. My brother is in a coma at Denver Health. He's there because he tried to kill himself. Don't you dare tell me what I know and don't know. You should thank God every day Lauren escaped this world. At least if she didn't want to live, she was able to die. She's not trapped in some unreal, inhumane place in between."

I trembled so hard, I didn't have the energy to protest when Nicole opened the door and guided me inside the house, to a bench in the foyer. She stood uncertainly five feet away.

I sat for a few minutes, silent, eyes dry and cast downward, shaking my hands, trying to regain control.

Nicole spoke first, almost gingerly. "Do you have any idea how hard it is to live with someone who has checked out, who doesn't care anymore?"

I couldn't look up. "You mean right before she died."

"No, years ago. There's always been a part of Lauren that was dead. I knew it the first time we made love, but after Ashley was diagnosed with spinal meningitis, Lauren withdrew from the world. She took it harder than Patrice and Stephen. I tried to reach her, to console her, but she shut me out. After that, all she cared about was making money and being with her niece."

She joined me on the far end of the bench, and I started when she touched my elbow.

"I hated her eyes, Kris, because there was no life in them except when she was around Ashley. There was no life for me, none at all. That first time you came to see me, in my office, I pretended not to care about Lauren, because I was tired of loving someone who stopped caring about me."

"Maybe she couldn't care," I said faintly.

"Couldn't. Wouldn't. What's the difference?" Nicole said restlessly. "I put up with it for years, then Paige came to work for me. After a few months, we started doing activities outside of work. At first, I invited Lauren to join us, but she never had an interest. If she had come, maybe none of this would have happened."

She looked at me for a hint of agreement. I displayed none, but she continued.

"One night, after an office seminar, the whole staff went to a bar. For some reason, Paige and I waited for everyone else to leave. The second we were alone, she leaned across the table and asked if I was attracted to her."

Suddenly uncomfortable, I shifted on the bench.

"She stunned me, and I couldn't talk, but I nodded my head. Then she asked if I wanted to make love with her. I told her I was in a relationship, but I paused. That's where I should have stopped—right at that point. But I didn't. I couldn't. Not after I looked into those eyes that were incredibly full of life, something I missed in Lauren's eyes. They were alive and dancing and free."

I cleared my throat, to no avail.

"She has the most intense eyes. One's a gorgeous shade of green. The other's a deep, rich blue. I couldn't help it—those eyes, they made me say 'Yes, I want to touch you and I want you to touch me.' The instant the words came out of my mouth, I knew I was going somewhere I'd never come back from."

I no longer tried to conceal my revulsion. "You really don't have to justify—"

"I'm not justifying anything. I'm telling you how it happened," she retorted before softening her tone. "After my answer, Paige smiled. She didn't say a word, simply smiled, this quirky half-smile, and then stood up and walked past me to the bathroom. A few minutes later, she came up behind me and leaned over to grab her purse from across the table. She was so close to me, her body was like a blanket around me."

"Really, you don't have to tell me all this," I said meekly.

Nicole continued her reverie without embarrassment. "Her breasts brushed against my shoulders, and her hair fell and touched my ear. I could smell her deodorant and lotion and soap and sweat, and they all blended together into this magical potion. The whole thing lasted five seconds, but I felt such a rush. She was like a drug, and I was addicted. Even then, some part of me knew I'd ruin Lauren's life, and my own, but I couldn't stop."

For the first time, Nicole gave me her full attention. "Have you ever had an affair?"

I locked my eyes into hers and shook my head.

"The deceit eats away at you a little bit each day, until suddenly, it stops. That's when you should be worried, because by then, something has died inside of you. Maybe it's the ability to know right from wrong, maybe it's self-respect, I don't know. I just know it's gone, and it never returns, not even when you don't have to sneak around anymore."

"Lauren found out about Paige, didn't she?"

"She did," Nicole admitted offhandedly. "Three months before she died, she knew."

"How can you be sure?"

"I told her myself."

My eyebrows shot up. "What did she say?"

"At first, she didn't believe me. I started to use details to convince her, but she cut me off. She said it was my business, and she didn't want to hear about it, but Paige had better never step foot in our house."

"That was it?" I said, flabbergasted.

"We never talked about it again."

"She didn't scream and holler and call you names?"

"That wasn't Lauren's way." Nicole flashed me a fake smile. "She was too controlled to make a scene."

"And she didn't talk about breaking up?"

"Never."

"Didn't you think it was odd?" I pressed.

"Possibly, but at the time, her reaction suited me, so I let it go. If I analyze it now, I think she was passive because she'd already planned to kill herself, leaving her no right to protest."

"Why didn't you end the affair?" I asked, curious.

"I was prepared to," Nicole replied eventually, "but when she didn't put up a fight, I couldn't do it."

"What did Paige think?"

"She was impatient. She still is. She can't understand why I haven't forgotten Lauren. She wants me to sell this house and move away from the memories. Paige and I fight all the time, and I find myself comparing her to Lauren. Paige is jealous and paranoid that I'm cheating on her. She tracks my movements, almost to the point of stalking. She calls dozens of times every night, and if I go to lunch with someone else and come back fifteen minutes late, she goes ballistic."

Nicole clasped her hands together. "Meanwhile, I haven't washed the sheets on Lauren's bed, and I can still smell her. You don't think Lauren killed herself because of my relationship with Paige . . ." Nicole's voice trailed off, and for the first time, I felt a scrap of empathy.

"No," I said quickly. "Her suicide was too calculated. Nothing about it was done in a fit of distress."

"I'm certain Lauren was having an affair, too," she said, a shade viciously.

I framed my dissent carefully. "I haven't found any evidence of one."

"What about Dr. W?" she interjected.

"That's a deadend. I can't figure out who he, or she, is."

"Meaning there's still a possibility Lauren was involved with someone?"

"I doubt it," I said gently.

Her voice rose an octave. "Why?"

"Did you notice any of her patterns change in the last year?"

"No."

"Did you see her light up when she talked about another woman?"

A terrified look came into her eyes. "Not particularly."

"Did she make any changes in your sex life? Did you make love more or less often at her request?"

"None of this is proof," she said acidly. "How can you be sure?"

Weary with the knowledge that after a few weeks, I understood her dead lover better than she had, I rose to leave. "It wasn't in her nature, Nicole."

15

From Nicole's, I headed straight for the drive-thru at Arby's. Back at my apartment, out on the balcony overlooking the highrises of downtown Denver, I used a ham sandwich, potato cakes, and cherry turnover to restore equilibrium.

As I chewed the last fatty bite, I realized I had run out of ideas for new angles to pursue. Seemingly, I had moved no closer to solving the mystery of Lauren Fairchild's suicide and had little to report to her sister.

I gulped, grabbed the cordless phone, and grasped at the only straw left. I called Fran Green.

"Hey, Fran," I said cheerfully.

"Kris, what's shaking?"

"Not much." I briskly updated her on the case. "Listen, I need to try something new. Do you think you could come with me to visit a psychic?"

She guffawed. "You pulling my leg?"

"No, I'm desperate, and I figure it can't hurt. No one in this realm's helping much. Don't forget—I agreed with your idea of breaking into the psychiatrist's office."

"Worked out well, too," she said smugly.

"Speaking of which, when you were glancing at Lauren's file, did you see any mention of this Nicole-Paige affair?"

"Heck, no," she said, a tad nettled. "Would have mentioned it right off."

"Of course," I replied slowly, distracted. "I guess Nicole was right— Lauren didn't care about it. At least not enough to bring it up in therapy. Or," I added, thinking aloud, "she knew she'd be killing herself on her thirty-fifth birthday. I think she chose that date deliberately. I'm also certain she accomplished something, marked it with a celebration, and then was ready. I just wish I knew what it was, what prepared her to die."

"Strange when you put it that way."

"This whole thing's bizarre, which is why we need outside help," I hinted.

"Not that again, Kris. Could be the Catholic doctrine, but I ain't hankering to mess with spirits. Better to leave well enough alone," she said nervously.

A side of Fran Green I'd never seen. "You're scared," I gibed.

"You bet I am, and you should be, too."

"Well, I'm going to do it, with or without you. I have the name of a woman who teaches at the Learning Institute. I saw her course description when I was looking for a class for David. You can pass if you want," I said belligerently.

"How is your brother?"

"The same. He just lies there."

"How you holding up with those hospital visits?"

"I'm managing," I said curtly.

After a long delay and a succession of exasperated sighs, Fran said, "I'll go with you, kiddo. Probably not safe for you to be alone with crackpots at a time like this. But don't expect me to believe every half-baked, pea-brained, ill-cranked theory that comes out of this psychotic's mouth."

"Thanks," I said smiling widely. Rarely did I win a round with Fran. I gloated for a few seconds before adding, "Back to the therapist for a minute. You're sure there wasn't anything else in her notes?"

"You saying I missed something?"

"No, not at all," I replied quickly. "But we got sidetracked reading about the day her brother died. I just wonder if we missed anything. Did she mention Ashley at all?"

Fran snorted. "She did, but didn't make any sense. I skimmed it."

"Can you remember the gist of it?" I pushed, excited.

"Maybe I need hypnosis to recover my memory or someone with psychic abilities to pull it from my noggin."

"Funny, Fran," I fumed. "What did Lauren tell Gloria Schmidt about Ashley."

"No biggie," she said offhandedly. "Something about getting agitated every time she talked about the kid, maybe not feeling safe around her. Can't recall exactly. Wasn't scribbling notes, and you weren't pitching in from your nest on the couch."

"She didn't feel safe around a child?"

"Something like that, but you got to go easy there, girl. You'll give yourself an aneurysm."

"Yeah, right," I said sarcastically, "my brain will bleed."

I hurriedly made closing remarks with Fran and immediately dialed up Noni Inlight, psychic. I secured an appointment for Thursday morning and replaced the receiver, contented.

I hadn't mentioned it on the phone, but in the back of my mind I thought if we could contact Lauren's spirit, we could also spend a few minutes finding out where the hell my brother's had gone.

Maybe, just maybe, Noni Inlight could help me out of the darkness.

Later that afternoon, at Destiny's, I slogged through the Sunday paper while Destiny watched television.

In the middle of her flipping through channels, I peered over the top of the comics. "I've been giving a lot of thought to our living together," I began hesitantly.

"And?" she said, thrilled, hitting the mute button.

"You've dated a lot of women."

Her enthusiasm vanished instantly. "What's your point?"

"Are you sure you're ready to give up all that?"

Miffed, Destiny jabbed at the remote and darkened the television. "I already have. You know I don't want to see anyone else."

"No one?"

"No one!"

"But living together is more final," I said timidly.

"Kris, you make it sound like death."

"You know what I mean."

She sat up on the couch and stared at me. "Actually, I don't."

I squirmed on the loveseat. "What if you feel trapped and have an affair the week after we move in together."

"That particular week, I'll be too busy unpacking," she said lightly. When she spotted the concerned look on my face, she added, "I'm kidding. Honestly, I can't guarantee I won't feel trapped, but I can promise I won't cheat on you."

"But where would we live?"

"Here, wouldn't we? I mean it would be a lot more comfortable. You just rent, and your apartment isn't big enough for both of us. I own, and it wouldn't be easy to sell a house this size."

"The real estate market's pretty hot right now," I countered.

"I thought you liked it here," she said, pained.

"I do, but what about all the women you've been with . . . in there?" I pointed to the bedroom behind us.

"First of all," she said tightly, "I rarely invited any of them over. I went to their places so I could leave in the middle of the night. Secondly, that's never seemed to bother you before."

I folded the newspaper carefully and set it on the floor. "That's because I was a guest, but now that I would be a resident, things are different."

"I don't want to give up this house, Kris," she said shortly. "You know how much work I've put into it."

On cue, the distant sound of a buzz saw interrupted our

terse discussion.

I frowned. "What's that? Is one of the neighbors remodeling?"

Destiny wouldn't make eye contact. "Er, no, I am, actually. Suzanne asked if I could do some touch-up on her bathroom."

"Why? It's gorgeous."

"There were a few flaws in the original work around the bathtub. Claudia's redoing it."

"That's insane! You spent a fortune fixing up her apartment last year. There's no way she could find another place as nice for the rent she pays."

"She didn't ask for anything," Destiny said, shifting in her seat. "I offered. Now could we please get back to what we were talking about?"

"Living together?"

She nodded impatiently.

"This could never be my home," I said, suddenly exhausted. "I love this mansion, but it's yours, and Claudia's and Suzanne's. You each have your own floor, your own energy. There's no room for me."

"I could make room."

"I don't think I could give up my apartment."

"Why not?"

"I don't like being on the ground floor. It scares me too much."

"You've never told me that before."

"Why do you think I live on the nineteenth floor, in a secured building, with security guards around the clock?"

"We could put in a burglar alarm."

"It wouldn't be the same."

"How about a dog?"

I shook my head.

Aggravated, Destiny took a deep breath. "You might have genuine safety concerns, but that's not what this is about. Even if I agree to move, and I let you choose the place, you won't live with me, will you?"

I formed a loud protest, then aborted it and mumbled, "Maybe not."

"What's really going on?"

I took in a deep breath and lowered my head. "I don't know."

"Do you love me?"

I sprang up and joined her on the couch. "God, yes!"

"Do you know that I love you?" she asked softly.

"Yes, but it's more complicated than that," I said uneasily. "It's about my family and me and how I need to be alone so much of the time. I have to have somewhere to go, where no one else is."

"If we stayed here, we could create a separate space for you," she offered.

"Where?"

"I don't know. Maybe we could convert the dining room into an office or a reading room."

"That wouldn't work," I ventured lamely.

"Sure it would! If we need to, we could knock out a wall or add one."

"You'd do that for me?"

"Kris, I'll do whatever it takes," she said firmly. "I want to be with you."

"Maybe we could—" I stopped short because my stomach had tightened, and the words caught in my throat. "It's more than just physical space. I can't stand to be this close. I can't do this," I said, disheartened. "Not now, maybe never."

Afraid of Destiny's reaction, I returned to the love seat and covered my head with my hands, curling into myself.

A long silence followed before I felt her move to the seat beside me. She put her arms around me and tried to quiet the sobs.

"I'll wait," she whispered, "for as long as it takes."

That night, Destiny and I slept with our backs to each other.

Over the next few days, although we both swore it wasn't by design, we managed not to see each other.

Just as well, because I had a lot on my mind.

Wednesday morning pulled around, and I stopped by the office only long enough to pick up supplies.

I drove to Children First and, through a back door, I hauled in three boxes of colored paper, sticky tabs, pens, and clip art.

When Jean McNaulty entered the classroom, she greeted me with a glancing hug. "You're an angel."

I shrugged. "We had extra stuff sitting around the office, and I thought the kids might like it."

She gestured to several goodies, still in their original packing material, and shook her finger at me. "You shouldn't have, but they'll love it."

I smiled shyly.

"They won your heart, didn't they?"

I nodded and began to unpack the boxes. "I can't stop thinking about them, especially Ashley."

Jean joined me at the art supply shelves. "You made quite an impression on her last week."

"A good one, I hope."

"Quite. Patrice and I have been talking about how we can persuade you to visit every week."

I laughed nervously. "I think I'll take it one field trip at a time. Which grocery store are we visiting today?"

"King Soopers. Tyler's mom wants us to work with him on behavior modification in public places. We'll try, but with him . . ."

Her voice faded when Patrice and the three kids, Ashley, Erin, and Tyler, entered the room.

"Ready to go?" Patrice said, perky. Ashley clung to the back of her leg, but peeked at me. I gave her a tiny wave, but she averted her gaze.

Thirty minutes later, we had everyone packed into the Children First van. Patrice and Ashley in the back, Erin and Tyler on the middle bench, and Jean and I up front.

As Jean drove, without prompting, she quietly predicted Ashley's future. At best, she would achieve a mental age of eight to twelve years. With proper support, she could adjust to marriage but not child rearing. She could be guided to social conformity.

Not a happy outlook. By the time we arrived at the store, I didn't know how much more I could stand to hear.

Fortunately, a scuffle in the back of the van diverted Jean's attention. As they had unloaded, Erin had smacked Ashley.

While Patrice comforted Ashley and Jean scolded Erin, I helped Tyler shed his heavy sweater.

"She always does that," Patrice said scornfully as she and I walked toward the store. "Ashley lets other kids hit her, and she doesn't react."

"Surely you don't want her fighting," I protested.

"No," she admitted, "but I don't want her giving up or giving in all the time either. She goes limp. I can see the hurt in her eyes, but she won't react physically."

"Is she okay?"

"I suppose. Erin never hits her hard, more pokes really."

"How about if I pair off with her while we shop?"

Patrice brightened. "Would you?"

"I'd love to."

"She likes to push the cart, but she's a little slow and awkward."

"I'm in no hurry," I said easily.

Patrice squeezed my arm. "I don't know what I'd do without you," she said.

Once inside the store, we split up. Erin and Patrice headed left to fill Patrice's list for her family. Tyler and Jean headed right to knock off Jean's shopping for school snacks. Ashley and I cut down the middle of the store.

"I have no list," I confessed to the five-year-old as she pushed our empty buggy. "I never go to the grocery store. Ever since I met my girlfriend Destiny, she shops for us. She puts food in my house and hers. Maybe someday, she'll only have to fill one refrigerator," I mused.

Ashley rammed the cart into a stack of potato chips. I backed it up and straightened it out. "How about if we each choose two things? Anything in the store, okay?"

She nodded intently. To start off, I chose the closest item I could reach. Ashley's eyes bulged as I hefted a bag of popcorn the size of a feed sack into the cart.

"Pretty big, huh? I like popcorn. This should last me a day or two."

Three aisles and four collisions later, Ashley chose her first item: a mop.

"How did you know I need a mop?" I fibbed, recalling the wall-to-wall carpeting in my apartment. "I used to have a friend who had hair like this," I said, fluffing the mop ends. "Okay, it was me," I confessed, as Ashley giggled. "Maybe I should have combed it more often."

I helped her steer around an elderly man who had a basket on one arm and a cane on the other.

Eventually, we passed the rapidly filling carts of Jean and Patrice, and after I nixed her live lobster selection, Ashley settled on her second choice. Following my super-size lead, she pointed to a giant can of pork and beans. I slid it onto the bottom shelf of the buggy, figuring I'd donate it to a shelter on my way home. Once they served the food, they could use the container as a wastebasket.

When we reached the loose candy bin, I prodded Ashley to choose one piece. After careful scrutiny, she picked a peppermint, and we dutifully inserted it into a plastic bag, along with my butterscotch.

Our rounds completed, we steered toward the check-out counter. There, I let her go first, and she tried to buy the sweets with a quarter I'd given her. The clerk glanced at Ashley with a measure of pity and disgust, then waved her through.

"She'd like to pay," I said breezily, as Ashley stood at the end of the counter confused, arm outstretched, coin in her palm.

"No need," the man replied, brushing us off.

"For the last thirty minutes, I've been telling her she could pay for the candy. Would you like to take her money," I remarked politely, "or should I call the manager."

"No need to get snippy," he said gruffly. He grabbed the quarter, knocking it to the floor in his haste. If I hadn't been on the verge of screaming, I might have enjoyed watching him scramble on his hands and knees to retrieve it.

The service deteriorated from there.

He set Ashley's change on the counter, unwilling to risk touching her. I handed it to her gently. He then proceeded to sling my beans onto the popcorn and almost stabbed me in the eye with the mop.

He filled my request for extra change for the soda machine by nearly throwing silver at me.

I took Ashley by the hand, led her to the bank of cold drinks, and lifted her to reach the coin slot. She inserted the money painstakingly, and cried out gleefully at the violent sound of cans crashing to the bottom.

Only when we sat on a bench near the sliding doors did I realize I was shaking with fury. I put the ice cold Dr. Pepper to my forehead and shook my head in dismay.

Ashley grabbed my arm. "Some people are stupid," I said.

To my surprise, she nodded vehemently, almost spilling her grape soda.

I laughed. "You're a pretty smart kid, you know." She stopped nodding but matched my wide smile.

"We're going to be great friends," I said, draping my arm around her shoulder.

She scooted closer to me and snuggled into the crook of my arm. "I could use a friend," I added softly.

The trip back to Children First passed uneventfully. No one fought, and Jean talked about an upcoming cruise with her mother instead of children's disabilities.

I helped unpack groceries in the classroom before saying goodbye to Patrice and the kids. When I hugged her, Ashley had trouble letting go, but Patrice distracted her with the promise of her peppermint.

Leaving, I couldn't exit the way I'd entered because a janitor, busily mopping the floor, had erected detour signs. The yellow placards directed me through a succession of hallways that eventually led to the parking lot.

I was in the car with my hand on the gear shift before it occurred to me. While cutting through the administrative offices of Children

First, I'd passed blithely by a door that said Wendy Henderson, PhD. Could she be Dr. W?

16

I shot out of the car and into the building. Out of breath, I knocked lightly on Dr. Wendy Henderson's door.

As the doctor worked on a computer, she never raised her eyes from its screen. "Be with you in a moment," she called out in a soft, preoccupied voice.

She finished her task with a solid, "There," moved her reading glasses to the top of her reddish-brown crown of hair, and finally met my gaze. "Yes?"

"Does anyone ever call you Dr. Wendy?"

"All the time." She smiled pleasantly. "May I help with something?"

"I hope so. Did Lauren Fairchild have thirteen appointments with you?"

The smile faded. "I'm sure I don't know the exact number of visits. May I ask why this concerns you?"

"My name is Kristin Ashe. Could I come in and talk for a few minutes about Lauren?"

She hesitated. "I suppose."

I walked in and shook her limp hand, careful not to press tightly against her three diamond rings. She dusted her fingers after I released them and straightened the cuff of the white silk blouse that protruded from her navy blue business suit. "What can I do for you?"

"I assume you've met Patrice Elliott." I began as I sat in a high-back chair across from her desk.

"Lauren's sister, yes."

"I'm not sure how much you know, but Patrice asked me to find out why Lauren committed suicide."

Dr. Wendy's pencil-line eyebrows arched a millimeter higher. "I see. Might I ask where I fit into all of this?"

"I'm trying to reconstruct the last days of her life, to get a feel for what she was going through. Your name, or rather the abbreviation Dr. W showed up in her calendar quite a few times."

"Ah."

"I thought Lauren might have been sick, or—" I paused and grinned sheepishly. "Or having an affair."

"You can rest assured the latter was not the case," she said, bristling.

"No, no, I'm sure of that," I fumbled nervously. "I've spent some time with Jean and the kids, and she spoke highly of you, but she didn't say what you do here. What is your role at Children First?"

"That's a good question." Her features softened. "My official title is Director of Special Services. I coordinate care with the team of professionals: occupational, physical, and speech therapists, for example."

"Do you work with the families?"

"Certainly. Most parents fail to realize a disability exists until their children reach an age when they should be able to do certain things, like walk or crawl or talk, and they can't. The way the family deals with this discovery will affect them for years to come. One of my professional strengths is in teaching parents to bury their child."

I gulped, and she noticed.

"At first blush, it sounds cruel, I know. Nonetheless, they must bury the child they had hoped for, travel through the stages of grief and, over time, come to accept their child for who he or she is. If they don't go through this process, they will endure a lifetime of disappointment."

"Isn't this, er, burial thing a little hard to do."

"Assuredly. It can be as traumatic as a death, but most parents rebound and learn to accept a child who is different, one who will require more care but is still a wonderful human being. Our programs at Children First are quite extensive. We teach families to work as a team and instruct them to be grateful for small advances. We also encourage parents to learn sign language and physical therapy methods, when appropriate. We provide tips on how to keep the strain and fatigue from ruining a marriage. We offer home visits, sending therapists out to work with parents and children together, and we give the family assignments. Twice a year, we sponsor Siblings Day. We invite brothers and sisters to take part in disability awareness exercises. Our goal is to help them understand their brother's or sister's plight. The healthy children spend the day in blindfolds or with slats on their legs."

"Does it work?"

She peered at me, slightly irritated, as if I had interrupted a presentation she usually delivered as a monologue. "Excuse me?"

"Do the siblings resent the disabled children less?"

Dr. W looked at me carefully. "Sometimes, but not always. A disability can destroy a family, and we can't always prevent that."

"Things have changed a lot, haven't they? None of this was available when I was growing up."

"Do you have a disabled sibling?"

In a thin, splitting voice, I replied, "My younger brother had, has, epilepsy, learning disabilities, and mental illness."

She nodded sympathetically. "How is he getting along?"

"Not too well. He's been in a coma at Denver Health for almost two weeks. He didn't take his medicine, and he had nonstop seizures." I paused. "I'm not doing so well either. My sister thinks he's responsible for all his problems."

"That's a common response. How do you feel?"

"I'm beginning to realize I know almost nothing about epilepsy. I can't recall my parents ever sitting down and explaining what was wrong with David."

"Many illnesses and disabilities are shrouded in secrecy and shame, epilepsy in particular."

"Why?"

"Society, as a whole, is intolerant. There's little room for anything different. Along come people who are disabled, who don't look or act 'normal,' and the first reaction is fear, followed by pity. We do what we can to educate people, beginning with members of the family, but we have a tough row to hoe. Often, despite all our support and intervention, parents give up their disabled children for adoption or institutionalization."

"Where do these kids go after they leave your preschool program?"

"In most cases, they're mainstreamed into the public schools, although there's considerable debate about doing that."

"What happens after they finish high school?"

"Unfortunately, it's over. Society has yet to develop an effective lifetime care program. Some individuals are ready to live on their own at eighteen, others at thirty, many never will be, but there are few provisions for that. You'll find pockets of excellent programs for the disabled, but no widespread, systematic approach, and the problem is compounded if the individual has multiple disabilities. You mentioned your brother's mental illness."

I nodded.

"That often proves to be the most difficult, if for no other reason than the patient is high-functioning in other areas or for periods of time. Families develop unrealistic expectations, often waiting for the mentally ill person to 'snap' out of it. There is a misperception that mood swings or depression can be controlled by sheer willpower. On a small scale, perhaps. In full-blown, clinical cases, absolutely not."

"Don't you get discouraged?"

"Frequently, but then a special child or adult comes along and raises my hopes. Lauren Fairchild was that kind of person."

"What did the two of you talk about?"

"Primarily, we planned an Ideal Care Program for Ashley."

"What's that?"

"A program that assumes there's no limit to the amount of money and resources available."

"But Lauren didn't have any money."

"I'm well aware of that, but she had plans for fundraisers, she had faith, and she adored her niece. That's all the criteria I needed to spend time with her."

"What did you tell her?"

"The same thing I tell all our clients: Disabled children today have the advantage of living in an age of technology and increasing mobility. I introduced Lauren to some of the state-of-the-art equipment that's been developed and encouraged her to read the latest literature. I also advised her to write to companies for more information and possible donations for Ashley."

"Did she follow through?"

"I assume so. She was a very determined woman. She seemed to understand, better than most, that disabilities last a lifetime, making it all the more imperative that each individual be given the tools to function at his or her highest potential. On one appointment, we discussed adult assisted-living programs."

"Wasn't it a little strange to talk about Ashley's care that far into the future?"

"Quite rare. Most family members can't see beyond next week but should be planning years in advance." She looked at me sternly. "I hope you'll be successful in your quest. It's a shame Lauren died. Her niece has lost a tireless advocate and a loving caregiver, an unusual combination."

After concluding her hollow memorial speech, Dr. Wendy made a point of studying the wall clock behind me.

I took the hint.

I rose, thanked her and, as an afterthought, asked, "Out of curiosity, how much would an Ideal Care Program cost for Ashley?"

Dr. W cracked a forced, mirthless smile. "More than you or I will earn in a lifetime."

17

From Children First, I headed to the hospital. On the eighth floor as I passed the nurse's station, I waved to Rose. She gestured back with a thumbs up sign.

I let out the breath I'd been holding but felt my stomach muscles tighten.

I shuffled toward David's area. Outside the glass cell, a teenage boy sat slumped in a wheelchair, shackled to the sides. I shot him darting glances and quickened my pace.

I burst into David's room and came close to bumping into Fran Green, who lounged at the end of his bed, her nose buried in a sports magazine.

I lightly tapped her shoulder. "Hey."

She started but beamed when she turned. "Kiddo, good to see you."

"What are you doing here?"

"Thought I'd stop by and see how your kid brother's faring. Love to visit hospitals. Reminds me of my professional days. The nurses ain't too hard on the eyes, either."

I looked at her with an air of quiet amusement. "Thanks, Fran. I—"

She cut me short. "Don't mention it. Gives me a chance to brush up on Fantasy Football."

"It's June," I exclaimed.

"No better time to start. Early prep work separates winners from whiners. We draft in fifty-two days. Truth be told, I'm a shade behind my normal pace. Any other summer, I'd already have the big guys, my top five picks. This year, time got away from me. No choice but to cram and hope for the best. Can't do worse than last fall."

"That bad?"

"The criminal with the gun destroyed my chance of winning. Plus, my number two guy blew his knee. Maybe just as well I didn't take it all, though. Got in a big stinkin' fight with Ruth. All the team owners chip in $50 to maybe win $500, but we have fun for sixteen weeks. Can't begrudge ladies a harmless distraction. You know, Ruth—she calls it gambling and doesn't approve. Wanted me to give my winnings to her chess club. To develop young players, she claimed. I wanted the dough to go to the breast cancer foundation. Argument ripped us to pieces, and I never won."

"The argument?" I teased.

"That, too. But, boy, I wanted that crystal football trophy and braggin' rights."

"Maybe this year," I said cheerfully.

She shrugged her shoulders in a relaxed fashion. "Enough about me. No work today?"

I took a deep breath, timed perfectly with David's respirator. "Not yet. I went on a field trip with Ashley's class. We spent the morning at the grocery store, practicing shopping."

"You could use some brushing up," Fran said, a gleam in her eye.

"Funny."

"Nothing pressing at Marketing Consultants?"

I pulled up next to her and sank into a chair. "Oh, there's plenty to do. I just don't feel like doing any of it."

"Can't blame you." She closed her magazine and leaned back until the sun coming through the window shined on her gray buzz.

I sighed. "I'm going to lose my business."

She didn't open her eyes. "Nonsense."

"I'm serious." I ran my fingers through sweat-drenched hair. "We missed a deadline on Monday."

"Happens all the time in business, Kris," she said easily.

"Not mine. I've done 3,000 projects and never missed one."

"You were due."

"Maybe." I blew the air out of my cheeks. "Yesterday, I yelled at a client."

"First time for that, too?"

"Of course," I said, offended.

"He deserve it?"

"She—and yes."

"Forget it then. Guilt is a useless emotion."

I stared at her blankly. "You, an ex-nun and lifetime Catholic, believe that?"

She peeped out of cracks in her eyelids. "Sure do."

I shook my head. "I wish I could let go."

"Comes with time." She leaned forward and patted my hand. "Looks like you've got quite a load there." She pointed to the full-size garbage bag I'd lugged into the room.

I opened it. "Fifteen stuffed animals."

She chuckled. "Never do anything halfway."

"David collects them. I thought he could use a few here to cheer him up. He has 150 at home."

"Sure enough?"

"He's into this big-time. He's given each one a date and place of birth. He keeps track of it all on an elaborate master list."

"No fooling?"

"Whoever is good gets to sleep with him at night."

"This fellow has quite the imagination. And now, he has," Fran halted to calculate. "165 total. Not too shabby."

I turned toward my brother. "Hey, Dave. On the news last night, they had a story about an Irish Wolfhound that ate ten stuffed animals and toys—even an Ernie doll."

No response.

I studied my brother's face, frozen in anger, and plowed forward. "A veterinarian did surgery and removed them all. I think the dog's going to be okay." I paused. "I hope you will be, too."

Fran draped her arm on my shoulder.

I leaned toward her and spoke so softly I wasn't sure I made a sound. "He had his first seizure when he was four. I was thinking about that when I woke up today. The day of my first communion. After church, we went to a pancake house for breakfast, and he slid off the booth. When he was seven, they thought he was well enough to take him off medications. On the way to the doctor's office, he had a grand mal, the big kind. The little ones are called petit mal. When he was a kid, every time David said, 'petit mal,' he slurred the words and they sounded like, 'pity me.' "

Fran remained silent, but I saw my misery reflected in her eyes.

"I should go to work sometime today," I said, without budging.

"So soon?"

I put my head between my knees and muttered, "Nah, who gives a shit about work?"

Fran rested her hand on the back of my neck. "That's the spirit. Now let's make ourselves useful—grab that pen and paper. Got to give these fifteen rascals names and birthdays.

I smiled at Fran. She had a knack for understanding life's priorities.

I worked the swing shift that night at Marketing Consultants and caught up on work in the quiet solitude of an empty office. For dinner, I ate from the giant popcorn sack.

The next morning, I called to apologize to the client whose deadline we'd missed and accepted an apology from the client I'd screamed at. I managed three productive hours in my five-hour stay.

At lunchtime, I made a beeline for Choices.

After inquiring at one of the front registers, I found Cecelia in the produce section, unloading a crate of bananas. She looked worn and haggard, and when she caught sight of me, she didn't pep up.

"There's more?" was her dispirited reply to my friendly, "Hello."

"Would you believe I'm here to shop?"

"No."

"Why? Is it that obvious I love chips and dip and Dr. Pepper?"

She eyed my body and smiled slightly. "No, you look healthy enough."

"Thanks."

"If you really eat all that junk," she added, amused, "you either exercise a lot or have an incredibly favorable metabolism."

"Exercise."

"I see." She resumed her banana stacking.

"Don't they ever fall?"

"What? These?" She pointed to the yellow pyramid. "Not usually, but the oranges are hell."

"I'll bet." I plucked one from the top to test her architecture, then delicately replaced it. "Listen, I stopped by to see if I could take you to lunch."

A deep frown etched her forehead. "I don't think so."

"If you've eaten already, we could go for coffee."

"It's not that," she replied, eyes downcast.

"You're too busy with the fruit?"

She tried to conceal a smile. "Not exactly."

I kept my tone intentionally light. "Too scared?"

She shot me a shrewd look but didn't reply.

"Have you talked to anyone about Lauren's death?"

"What's done is done. There's nothing I can do about it. What's there to say?" she asked, more resigned than angry.

"I'll make you a deal: Come with me to lunch, and we'll talk about whatever you want. If it's Lauren, fine. If not, that's okay, too. I'm a great conversationalist. Either way, you won't get bored."

"You'll buy lunch, and I don't have to say a word about Lauren?"

"Yep."

"Why?"

"Because I'm hungry, I hate eating alone, and you're the only one I can invite on short notice."

She smiled wryly. "At least you're honest. Give me five minutes to finish, and I'll meet you out front."

"Fair enough."

I walked a few paces before turning to give a hearty wave.

When I looked back, I caught her openly staring at me. A strange mixture of longing and sorrow flitted across her features before she returned a slight wave.

Over appetizers of vegetable dumplings at the Chinese restaurant next to Choices, Cecelia talked about running a health food store, and I rambled on about directing a marketing business and a detective agency.

Well into our main courses of lo mein and sesame chicken, Cecelia cleared the dishes from in front of her and leaned across the table. "Are you in a relationship?"

I pulled back and almost hit my head on the wall behind the booth. "Umm, yes. I have a lover. Destiny."

"Destiny Greaves?"

"You know her?"

"Only from television. I always wondered if she had a girlfriend."

"She's had lots," slipped out of my mouth. "Hopefully, I'm the last." That didn't sound right, either, so I stammered, "For now."

Bemused, Cecelia took a slow, careful sip of water. "Is Destiny the love of your life?"

"Maybe. No. Probably. I'm not sure. I can't imagine. I hope . . ." I sputtered, rested my cheek on my hand, and shook my head. "I have no idea."

I heard her laugh for the first time—a beautiful, infectious sound that began in her chest and resonated through her body. "You're unbelievable."

"Thanks," I said, hoping she'd meant it as a compliment. I quickly moved to safer ground. "Was Lauren the love of your life?"

Cecelia's joy vanished, and her brow furrowed. "I hope not. I'm too young to think the best is over. Forever."

An awkward silence covered the table.

I spoke up. "I miss her, too."

She raised one eyebrow. "Lauren?"

I nodded. "I know I never met her, but I've spent hours looking at her calendar, recreating the last days of her life. Plus, I've studied a photo of her and Ashley. You wouldn't believe the light in Lauren's eyes. And I've spent time with that amazing little girl. I can't fathom how Lauren could leave her."

I took a deep breath that hurt my chest. "I understand why she didn't go to Patrice or Nicole for help. All her life, she'd been Patrice's protector and probably couldn't reverse that role. Nicole, hell, Nicole was checked out. I can appreciate why she left without saying anything to them. She could have screamed it—whatever it was—and they wouldn't have heard her. What I can't grasp, though, and it's bugged me ever since we met, is why she didn't say something to you. She didn't, did she, Cecelia?"

Her answer was almost indistinguishable. "No."

"Because if she had, you would have stopped her, right?"

"I would have tried."

"But you never had the chance?"

"I should have seen it coming. I knew her better than anyone in this world. The last time I saw her, I was busy, and she breezed in and out. I gave her the Natalie Merchant tape, we chatted about nothing, and that was it. I can't believe I didn't see it coming. I should have intervened."

"You couldn't."

"How can you know these things?" Her voice softened with despair. "You come up with all these easy answers, and you know nothing about my grief."

I spoke in a near whisper and lowered my head to the level of hers, but she wouldn't meet my gaze. "My brother, who lives alone, has a slew of disabilities, including epilepsy. Two weeks ago, I called to invite him to the movies. No answer. The next day, I tried again. Still no answer. I decided to stop by his apartment, but got busy and skipped it. The next night, my sister called to tell me he was in a coma at Denver Health. Paramedics found him after he'd had a ton of seizures."

Her eyes, full of angst, finally met mine.

"Do you have any idea how many times I've replayed those days?" I asked, voice cracking.

"Probably a thousand, especially when you close your eyes."

"Not to mention every time I open them again. I can't stop thinking about it. If I weren't busy looking into Lauren's suicide, I'd have gone crazy by now. Then," I said, beginning to tremble, "I hear they found thirty bottles of medicine under his bed. He started seizing because he hadn't taken any of it in weeks, and suddenly, I felt enraged, because there was nothing I could do about that either."

"Except sit by helplessly and watch him die, right?" she interrupted. "How do you get it to stop hurting?"

I exhaled. "I have no idea."

"It hurts all over. I have this lump in my throat that won't go away. People come in and ask for Lauren—customers, suppliers—and it gets bigger and bigger. I relive the pain, as fresh as the moment I first knew she was gone, every time I hear her name. I can almost taste her.

"I wake up stiff from thrashing all night. My eyes are swollen from crying. I keep dreaming about her, the same dream. We're making love and I'm about to come when she disappears. Like that!" Cecelia snapped her fingers. "How could she do this to me? Can you answer that, Kris?"

I didn't try.

"There's so much I wanted to tell her. She might have been done with me, but I wasn't done with her. It was so sudden. How could she leave me?"

"You never stopped loving her, did you?"

"Never," she said fiercely, longing in her eyes.

I reached across the table to calm hands that had mutilated her napkin. "How did you two meet?"

"Years ago, we worked for the same catering company, Le Gourmet. When we were young," she added, smiling.

"What drew you to her?"

Cecelia's face lit up. "She had an energy I've never seen in anyone. If she smiled at you, you felt her happiness, as if it wrapped around you. Or if she cried, you felt the pain, as if it had sliced through you. She felt things deeply, and she made me feel them, too. Things I'd never felt before—good and bad. It's what brought us together and drove us apart."

"The intensity?"

She nodded. "Sometimes it came out in destructive ways."

"Was she violent?"

"A little."

"Against you?"

"Usually against herself, but I still couldn't handle it. It was the hardest thing I've ever done, but I left Lauren."

"How much did Lauren tell you about her childhood."

"Not a lot."

"Did she talk about her mother?"

"Never."

"How about her brother?"

"Not really. I know he died from SIDS, but that's about it," she said ruefully.

"Did you get that information from Lauren?"

Cecelia picked up on my astonishment. "It's not true? What did happen?"

"Lauren's mother hit him with an iron."

"Accidentally?"

"She hit him sixteen times."

She gasped. "Did Lauren know?"

"Yes. Read this." I fumbled in my backpack and retrieved a copy of the article Fran Green had found in the library.

Slowly, she pored over the words. As she read, the life drained from her ashen face, and her body tensed. By the time she came to the last line, her voice had changed.

Businesslike and abrupt, she said, "Lauren and I were lovers for four years and friends for twelve, and she never said anything." She tossed the pages across the table, narrowly missing the mustard sauce.

"She didn't tell anyone."

"Where did you get this? From Patrice?"

"No, she was too young to remember. My associate found it at the library, and I showed it to Patrice."

Cecelia retrieved the murder-suicide account and skimmed it again. "I can't believe this. The similarities are eerie. Lauren never had a chance—as if she were destined to follow in her mother's footsteps."

"By killing herself on her thirty-fifth birthday?"

"That, too," she said under her breath. She realized I had heard her, and her eyes fluttered with alarm.

"What else, Cecelia?"

"Nothing," she said brusquely. "I have to leave now."

I made three more gracious attempts to extricate information, but Cecelia wouldn't budge.

18

The next morning, after I picked up Fran Green, it didn't take long for the ex-nun to cuss.

"Hell's bells!" she said as she bent to extract a sticker from her white sweat pants. "A little gardening wouldn't kill these people, would it?" She shook her head with disdain at the sight of Noni Inlight's property.

The tattered siding, missing shingles, large-gapped picket fence, and unfinished paint job on the 1950s style ranch didn't escape her notice.

"Assuming I believe in spirits, which I don't, why would Lauren come to this dump? What would drive anyone to park on the front lawn?" She answered herself. "Maybe 'cause that carport's falling to the ground. For the life of me, I'll never understand why people leave trash cans on the porch."

"So they don't have to carry them as far to the curb?" I suggested, trying to be kind, a quality I'd perfected in response to Fran's incessant complaining during our thirty-minute commute to southeast Denver.

Fran shot me a sidelong glance.

"C'mon," I said, before she changed our minds. "The inside is bound to be better."

"Yeah, right! Who's ever heard of these voodoo notions: Doesn't charge for her gifts, doesn't want to turn it into a business, doesn't want to know who referred you." Fran's singsong voice trailed off when I gave her the bent eye. "Clearly she could use the cash," she added, unrepentant.

I rolled my eyes and rang the doorbell.

In seconds, Noni Inlight answered and invited us into a debris-laden foyer.

About the same age as her house, Noni didn't look anything like I expected. Her large black glasses and plump face without makeup reminded me more of a librarian than a psychic. Her attire did nothing to dispel the bookish image: light green dress, secured in the middle with a large white belt, tan nylons, clear nail polish, and a gold brooch in the shape of an aspen leaf. Her bun of bottle-black hair alluded to a bygone era—as if she'd chosen a hairstyle she liked in the '60s and never bothered to update. Her shoeless feet were her only visible concession to comfort.

I introduced everyone, and Noni shook Fran's hand, then mine, with her own clammy one.

As she and Fran exchanged preliminary pleasantries, I studied the dark surroundings. I judged the living room, decorated in reds and browns and stuffed with heavy, antique furniture, as the perfect place for a seance. Every window was covered with drawn, floor-length gold drapes, and the only illumination came from the flames of three chunky candles.

I started to walk into the room, but Noni caught my arm and led me and Fran down a hallway, through a kitchen reeking of garlic and suffocating from dishes. "The circle of energy is down here," she said, opening a door to the basement.

I followed her, careful not to trip on the dozen or so cats sprawled in the stairway. Fran walked a step behind and twice grabbed my back when a loud "Meow!" rang out.

At the bottom of the stairs, Noni instructed us to remove our shoes.

"Does that help with the transmissions?" I asked.

"No, I shampooed the carpet last week."

"Never know it," Fran said under her breath, noting massive stains on the off-white shag carpet, visible even in the limited light of a hundred candles. Intent on removing her sneakers, she missed my glare.

I tried to grasp why we were conducting a sacred ceremony in what appeared to be a rec room when Noni's booming voice startled me. "Here is where we will greet the one who has crossed over," she said, pointing to what I could swear was a ping-pong table, complete with net, covered in dingy white sheets.

Twelve folding chairs encircled it, and one stuffed arm chair rested at the head. An oak bar sat to the side of the table, above which hung an enormous pair of antlers, a dart board, and a neon Coors sign.

"Please, take a seat wherever you will be most comfortable," our hostess instructed.

She, of course, claimed the most plush chair, and Fran and I migrated to the opposite end. The seats we chose, despite their respective flowered and plaid pillows, were too low for the table. I sat on a crossed leg, and Fran improvised with ramrod posture.

On cue, the wandering felines settled in below the table. One stray chose Fran's lap over the ground, an unpopular idea. Fran picked up the cat as if it were a beaker of nitroglycerin and deposited it on the floor. The animal immediately returned to nap on her legs.

Fran let out an exasperated sigh.

"That is Shakra. She was sent here to heal people. Today, you are the chosen one."

Fran transferred the tabby to my lap. "Kris needs more healing than me."

No use. Shakra sprang back to the coveted spot.

"Let her stay," I said, to which Fran hissed, "I'll get you for this, Kris."

Oblivious to our bickering, Noni said, "I would like to welcome both of you to this blessed event. This afternoon, we will invite Lauren Fairchild to join us. However, before we begin, I would like to warm up my senses by starting with you two."

"Hey, that wasn't part of the bargain," Fran objected.

"Do not be afraid. The future is your friend—born of the past, nurtured in the present. You can either ask questions, or I can tell you things about yourself, whichever you prefer."

"I have a question," Fran began in a combative tone. "What are your credentials?"

I poked her in the side as Noni calmly replied, "It would take an afternoon to list them all."

"How about forking over the highlights?"

"I knew the stock market would decline at the beginning of the millennium."

Fran didn't look impressed.

"I also predicted the Broncos' four Super Bowl defeats."

Fran guffawed. "Big deal! Any pretty face who's watched two minutes of football would have known that. The trick was to predict their two wins."

"Very well. My divine perceptions aided others in solving the kidnapping of a six-year-old child. Perhaps you heard of the Bailey case?"

I chimed in. "The one last summer? Didn't the police figure out it was the father who stole the girl?"

"Who do you think pointed them in that direction, thereby ensuring the safe return of the child?" Noni asked smugly.

"You?" Fran said, doubtful.

Noni fixed on her, a glint in her eye. "I can see you will not be made a believer easily. Perhaps I can speed up your growth process by telling you Little F, whoever or whatever she is, is being neglected."

Fran began to blush. She turned to me and stammered, "What did you tell this broad about my sex toys?"

"Nothing! I swear," I whispered, barely able to conceal a smile. "What do I know? But I guess you better dust off Little F and plug her in."

"For your information, this particular one runs on batteries."

"If it'll make you happy," I said innocently, "on the way home, we can stop at 7-11 and buy some triple As."

"Try four double Ds."

"Whoa! That's more than my camping flashlight holds," I said, doing a mock double-take.

Noni put an abrupt end to our chit-chat with a startling prediction. "As for you, Kristin, you are contemplating a change. It will be a good one."

I frowned. "With Destiny?"

"You will be happy beyond your wildest dreams. The uncertainty you feel comes from external factors, not internal."

Before I could absorb all that, she added in a somber tone, "For now, you are going through a distressing period. I feel your helplessness and frustration."

"David," I said without thinking.

"These are old wounds. You must let go, but do not follow him."

"Visit him, you mean?" I asked, confused.

"No, follow him. He is a boy to you. You must let him become a man, in order to release him. Overcome the resistance. He must be free." Her prognostication gathered speed, and her features became animated. "He will be free. He is surrounded by energy beams, bathed in white light."

I couldn't follow her ramblings, but only one question mattered to me. "Will my brother live?"

"Yes, but not in the way you are used to."

"What's that supposed to mean?" I snapped. I hadn't even realized I was nervously tapping my foot until Fran nudged me.

"I am sorry, but that is it. I cannot interpret messages from the other side; I merely deliver them."

"Jesus Christ," I muttered.

Fran patted me on the thigh and buzzed in my ear, "Don't sweat. She's making this stuff up as she goes."

I turned to her and murmured, "Then how come it's so accurate?"

Noni clapped sharply. "We are ready to begin. We will commence by calling forth the natural psychic ability in each of us. I would ask you to join hands and assist me in welcoming Lauren Fairchild back to this realm."

We both glanced at her, unsure what to do.

She waved to us. "Come down here, and we will form a circle to focus the energy. I will invite Lauren Fairchild to return briefly."

With great trepidation, Fran and I switched to chairs on the other end. After considerable fidgeting on Fran's part, and a moment's pause for Shakra to bond with her again, the three of us held hands.

"Let us relax and let in the spirit," Noni said in a soothing voice. "Close your eyes, breathe deeply, and we will attempt to call Lauren Fairchild. We will begin by thinking about this woman who has passed over."

My eyes wouldn't stay shut, and when I caught Fran peeking out of half-closed lids, I almost burst out laughing.

Fran's crushing grip brought me back to my psychic senses, and I tried, not very successfully, to concentrate.

Noni's cry broke the unnerving silence. "I am getting a hit," she paused dramatically, then pointed a bony finger at Fran. "It is about you."

Fran's eyes bulged. "Me, why me? Skip my turn. Hate to hog all the psychic space."

"Soon, an old friend will come into your life. This is someone you cared about very deeply."

Temporarily interested, Fran perked up. "Man or woman?"

"Woman. Beware the consequences of a renewed liaison."

"What's that supposed to mean?" Fran asked, scornfully.

"No more messages are forthcoming," Noni replied, a touch contemptuously.

"This is bullshit," Fran muttered.

Luckily, Noni seemed more involved with the other world than what transpired inside the rec room, and she didn't respond.

"The energy particles are scattered. You must be still and focus. Soon, Lauren will join us."

We rested for at least five minutes. At one point, Fran's stillness led me to believe she was napping. A sudden twitch confirmed my suspicions.

Despite the cool temperature in the basement, my brow began to sweat. With the back of the hand that held Fran's, I wiped my forehead, which woke her up. She blinked a few times, looked at me for direction, then pointedly inspected her watch. I shrugged a reply and mouthed, "Five more minutes."

Noni, who had never opened her eyes but must have nonetheless seen our exchange, suddenly barked, "Focus! Focus! Focus! I can only bring into this room what is strongest in your minds. Visualize Lauren! Lauren! Lauren!"

In the ensuing silence, I tried to concentrate. I had almost formed a picture of the woman we were trying to revive when Noni began an eerie, low-decibel chant. "Lauren Fairchild. Lauren Fairchild."

The haunting summons must have done the trick, because without warning, Noni whipped her head in circles and cried out, "I have made contact. I am in touch with the spirit of Lauren Fairchild, and she is very agitated. I am afraid of the energy in the room. We must calm her down."

"Is she upset we broke into—" I began in a small voice before Fran kneed me. I rephrased the question. "Is Lauren angry about us getting into her doctor's files?"

Head bobbing out of control, Noni replied, "No. Something else is bothering her, something having to do with a message sent but never received. Do either of you have any idea what this means?"

Wide-eyed, Fran and I both shook our heads.

A hint of panic coated Noni's words. "We must shift the vibes to a more peaceful tempo. Immediately, bow your head and think of the best day of your life, and I will do the same."

I obeyed, remembering the day Destiny and I first made love.

I wondered what came to mind for Fran.

I almost leaned over and asked when Noni said, "That's better. Lauren pleasantly surprised me by joining in this exercise. She wants us to know that her special day was the child's birth."

"She's here?" Fran boomed, disbelieving, as I said, "Which child?"

"She wasn't specific. I simply felt her full heart welcoming another being to this planet."

"It must have been Ashley," I whispered to Fran.

"Could have been the brother, or a hoax," she muttered. Ever the skeptic, she squinted at Noni and demanded, "Have Lauren tell us something about herself no one knows so we can make sure she's the right spirit, that another one didn't get bored and pop in for the shindig."

"Fran!" I hissed.

Noni overlooked the obvious insult. "Very well. A child herself, she witnessed the murder of another child."

I lost my breath.

Fran didn't miss a beat. "Good enough! Let's get this sideshow on the road."

Noni rotated her head several times, lowering it to her left shoulder, then her right, and back again before she became still. "You may now reach out to Lauren with your inquiries."

"I'll do the talking," I said in a low voice to Fran before loudly addressing Noni. "Does Lauren have any regrets about killing herself?"

"Only one: That the message has not been received."

"What message?"

"Please," Noni cautioned, "don't ask questions about this. It will only upset her again."

"Okay, here's another one: Has she found peace?"

"Yes, eternal."

"Was she murdered?"

"No."

"Was her death an accident?"

"Most certainly not."

"Does dying hurt?" I asked, more for myself than to solve the case.

"Not as much as living."

"Hmm. Is she still in pain?"

"No. Her balance is restored."

"Can she tell us what caused her distress?"

"The signals are mixed on this. Please be more specific."

"Was it Nicole?"

"No."

"Cecelia?"

"I'm receiving a very strong reading." Noni paused. "These two women are strongly intertwined, but not in death. They are destined to meet in another life."

"Is it Dr. W? Is that why Lauren committed suicide?"

Noni's head bobbed uncontrollably. "No, but there is considerable energy there."

"Enough with the twenty questions," Fran said, exasperated. "Spit it out: Why did she bite the dust?"

Noni's body jerked, and her eyes flew open. "That's it. She is leaving. She will not remain in an environment that is clearly hostile."

Not sure whether I was talking to an aggravated Noni or Lauren, I nonetheless tried to smooth things over. "Wait, not so fast. Could I say something?"

After Noni responded with a sullen look and pout, I opted to forego the intermediary and attempt direct contact.

I pulled my hands away from the circle and folded them in my lap. As if praying, I said softly, "I'm not sure if you can hear me, Lauren, but if you can, I want you to know I wish we had met." I stopped, suddenly self-conscious, before I added, "I would have liked you as a friend."

Having said my peace, I stood to leave, but Noni yanked my arm and slammed me back into the chair. "You've done it!" she said, ecstatic. "I've never witnessed this before. You've brought her back, and she has something important to tell you."

Fran groaned, but I waited, riveted.

A full minute passed before Noni began to speak. It took several seconds for me to realize the words, delivered in a husky voice, must have been Lauren's own.

They made the hair on my arms stand on end.

"I put my hand to her chest and looked into eyes that were dead. Nothing I said or did could make her respond. She just laid there, silent, as I rubbed her head, begging her, willing her to make a sound."

"Holy fruits! What did you make of that?" Fran asked the instant we left the house. "That last bit sounded erotic. Ask me, Lauren was having an affair. Oldest reason in the book for suicide—unrequited love."

Squinting, I covered my eyes from the bright sunlight and almost ran into her as we both hurried down the uneven sidewalk. "I doubt it's that simple."

"What did you think of that Noni? Unknown would be a better name for her. Those kooks are dangerous. They should be state-regulated, have to get licensed, the whole nine yards. Some poor sucker out there might take 'em seriously. You didn't buy that home-spun hamming, did you, Kris?"

"Not all of it," I said hesitantly as I dove into the car. "But there was a ring of truth to some of it. And we might have found out more if you hadn't pissed Lauren off."

Fran slammed her car door shut. "You gotta be kidding. You're telling me you believed the garbage that came out of that Clairol's mouth?"

"Clairvoyant," I corrected, starting the engine.

"What a waste of good time and air. That's the last time you'll catch me at a sightseer's."

"Soothsayer."

"Whatever. I told you I don't take stock in psychotics."

"Psychics," I said bluntly, getting agitated.

"Yeah, sure! It was all a bunch of malarkey."

"You're mad because she was right on about your sex life," I said shortly.

"Not that it's any of your business, but my sex life is far from dormant. In fact, it'd be safe to say it's booming," she said affably.

"Really?" I grinned.

"Nah, Ruth's still a hothead about the shrink's office."

"What? Does she think we violated some ethical principle?"

"Heck, no! She's sore because she missed the beginning of the news."

She laughed, but I didn't join in. My mind was too occupied with other thoughts.

"Hey Fran, you don't think David's going to die, do you?"

"Heck no!"

"But what do you think she meant by all that stuff about being free. Could it mean he needs to be free of our expectations? Maybe that's it," I said hopefully.

"Don't have the slightest idea what she meant. Shoot, she didn't know herself, but whatever it was, wouldn't lose sleep over it."

"What about that part about Destiny?" I said pensively. "You think she was talking about our living together?"

"Got me. I ain't psychic. First I've heard of it. You two been discussing shacking up?"

"A little." I tried to gauge her reaction before revealing more.

She nodded approvingly. "You've got good taste in women, Kris. Destiny Greaves is a find. Never get two of her in this lifetime."

"What's that supposed to mean?" I said defensively. "Are you implying she's better than me?"

"Whoa, girl. Unsaddle that high horse and hop down. Doing nothing of the sort. What's the problem?"

"I don't know," I confessed. "I can't seem to make up my mind. When she first proposed the idea, it scared the hell out of me. Then it excited me. Then it distressed me. Then it cheered me up. Now, I have no idea how I feel."

The faster I talked, the faster I drove.

"I do know I love her, and I love to be with her. But what if something happens to her—she does travel a lot, and she certainly has a high-risk job. Or what if some woman comes along and steals her away—they proposition her all the time. Right now, as a matter of fact, this woman who lives on the top floor of her house, Suzanne, I think she's chasing her. What am I supposed to do about that?"

"Take a breath and slow down, girl. You got it bad."

"What?"

"Happiness."

"Pardon me?" I said irritably.

"You're happy, and you're waiting for it to end. Gads, you might even blow it up yourself."

"How would I do that?"

"Lots of things you can do to sabotage a relationship. Ruth and I have done 'em all."

"Like what?"

"Pick fights, be unavailable, get totally needy or totally self-suffi-cient, make demands, get attached to someone or something else. Sweetie, there are as many ways to destroy a relationship as there are to nurture it."

I could feel my face redden.

"Spit it out: How many have you done?"

"Most of them," I said, sheepish.

Fran looked at me intently. "When that crackpot told you to think about the best day of your life, what was it?"

I stopped the car in front of her house. "The day I met Destiny."

Fran hopped out onto the curb, but poked her head through the open window. "Enough said."

"What was yours?" I called out as she began a militant stride to-ward the building.

"I had two. The day I went into the convent," she bellowed with-out bothering to turn, "and the day I left."

All the way home, I pondered Lauren's message, the one "sent but never received." I had always known her meticulously planned death had meaning, but the session with the psychic confirmed my intuition.

The source of irritation for Lauren's spirit stumped me, though. What was the meaning, and why was it not being understood?

That last bit, about "eyes that were dead" and "begging her to make a sound" spooked me.

Maybe Fran was right. Maybe we shouldn't have tampered with the unknown.

Fortunately, the balance of the day brought me solidly back from the spirit world into the tangible one, as I visited Marketing Consultants and prepared a quarterly financial report for our accountant.

From work, I dropped by Destiny's and picked her up. She slid into the car and kissed me on the lips. "What's this surprise? Where are we going?"

I brushed stray strands of hair from her cheek. "You'll see."

When I parked in front of Ramano's, Destiny gave me a quizzical look. "Here?"

I nodded. "I want to try it again."

"Try what?"

"You'll see."

Inside, after we had ordered, I took her hand and clasped it between both of mine. "If it's not too late," I said, my voice a little shaky, "I'd like to change the answer I gave you the last time we came here."

Destiny's face fell. Dismayed, she said, "You don't want to live together?"

My smile vanished. "No, I do!"

"But that's what you told me the first time we came."

"I did?"

She nodded strenuously.

"I don't think I meant it then, but I do now."

"You're serious?" she said, her features registering hope and vulnerability.

"Of course I am. I want to live with you, and I want to do it as soon as possible."

"What about the other night, when you said no."

"I didn't mean that either."

"Let me get this straight," she said, confounded. "You didn't mean it the first time you said yes or the last time you said no, but this yes is for real."

I smiled broadly. "Exactly!"

Destiny dove around the table to hug me. After she returned to her seat, she said, "Now don't take this the wrong way, but what made you change your mind?"

"Would you believe a psychic?"

"No," she said grinning. "I know you too well for that. But I am curious, what did this wise woman tell you?"

"She predicted I'd be happy beyond my wildest dreams."

"Wow!" she said, impressed.

"That wasn't what really swayed me, though."

"Was it the thought of my naked body lying next to you in our bed, every night of your life?"

"No," I said, briefly returning her wicked smile. "It was you saying you'd wait for me, as long as it took."

"I would," she said, her green eyes sparkling.

"I know. After I thought about it, I realized I'd wait for you, too. You're a huge part of my life. I'm just afraid to admit it, because I keep thinking I'll lose you the second anyone knows you're important to me."

"You won't," she said calmly. "I wish you could believe that."

"I can. It's taken me awhile, but I finally get it."

"Just in time," she said lightly. "I was about to start an affair with Suzanne."

"Very funny," I said grimly.

"I'm kidding, Kris. Really, I am!"

In record time, we concluded our dinner and went back to Destiny's house.

For the next three hours, we made love.

I let Destiny in. I let myself out.

19

The weekend passed without drama. No work on the case, no visits with David. Quality time with Destiny and two nights of uninterrupted sleep buoyed me enough to stop by the hospital on my way to work Monday.

I had already deduced that the odds were good I wouldn't bump into my mother—she had a pattern of inactivity before noon—but I never considered the chances of happening upon my father.

I spotted his lightweight jacket and golf cap resting on the edge of David's bed before I saw him. He wore his customary leisure uniform: baggy dark blue shorts, red golf shirt, white socks, tennis shoes. I couldn't help but notice the effects of liquor and age: bulbous nose, pot belly, flaccid skin, wrinkles across his forehead and around his eyes, black hair with tufts of gray barely covering the front of his head.

Every instinct told me to flee, but when he spotted me, I came into the room. He offered me a hug, which I returned loosely.

"I thought you'd be at work," I said accusingly.

"I took the day off. How about you?" he asked, cordial.

"I'm going in late."

"How's business?"

"Fine," I replied gruffly, unwilling to elaborate. Awkwardly, I stood near David's feet, opposite my father who sat near his head.

"Have you and Ann been here many times?"

"I have. She hasn't come at all."

"Why not?"

"You'd have to ask her," I replied, knowing full well he wouldn't— he and Ann hadn't spoken in months—but I was tired of fronting for my sister.

He avoided my gaze, choosing instead to face my brother. "This really threw me for a loop. I thought he was getting better. He hadn't been sick in over a year."

"He went to St. Anthony's last fall for a broken collarbone—after he had a seizure on the street in front of his house."

"Was that when it happened? I thought it was longer ago than that."

As he spoke, the similarity between his slow, monotone speaking style and David's struck me. "No. It was the last week in October, right after my birthday."

"You're right! Well, at least he hasn't been in for depression. That's what he can't seem to shake. What do you suppose causes it?"

"I doubt you want to hear what I think."

"Try me."

I looked at him, incredulous. Did he really want the answers? I needed a list to keep track of them all. Let's see, potential causes of David's depression:

Epilepsy and/or the brain-deadening drugs he took to counter it.

Heredity. My mother had spent more time in bed than out of it.

Emotional neglect. Neither of my parents had bonded with him, or with me or my sisters, for that matter.

Diet. He had no cooking skills and lived off frozen, fast, or junk food.

Exercise. Or rather, absence of it. He never moved, indoors or outdoors.

Lack of focus. He had never held a job and had nowhere to go and nothing to do. Disability money from the government paid his bills, but it couldn't offer him a reason to get up every day.

Isolation and loneliness. He lived by himself and hadn't had a friend since elementary school.

Given the cumulative effect of his upbringing and lifestyle, frankly, it was a miracle something drastic hadn't happened sooner.

To my father, I said, "It would take too long to list all the reasons."

He looked at me peculiarly. "Maybe you girls were too hard on him. Maybe he couldn't live up to your accomplishments."

"Like that was our fault, that we did well in school and excelled at sports," I sputtered, touching my neck, trying to rub out the oncoming pain.

"I'm not placing blame," he said blandly. "Merely making a statement of fact."

If I'd had a sturdy instrument, I would have bashed him over the head.

I punished him with silence, but that didn't faze him. "You just missed Grandma. She came by earlier with her Bible study group," he said amiably.

"Too bad."

"She had a replica of Christ's cross, and she rubbed it over David."

My eyebrows shot up. "Think it worked?" I asked, fighting to keep my tone even.

He shrugged. "It couldn't hurt, and it makes her feel better."

"I hope David didn't get any splinters."

My father didn't smile. "She told me you found some medicine in David's apartment."

"Mom did, and how did Grandma know?"

"Ann told her. Is it true?"

I nodded. "Thirty bottles. I guess he stopped taking it."

"He never could keep track of his pills." My father rose and pulled his chair around. "Let's not shout over the poor bugger."

I felt trapped. He now sat between me and the door. "I think it's a little bigger than that," I said tersely.

"What are you saying?"

"Has it ever occurred to you he might not want to live?"

"You believe he did this intentionally?"

"I think he deliberately chose not to take his medicine. Whether he understood it would lead to this—or death—I don't know."

"He's had a tough go of it, but he's always been a fighter."

"As a kid he was, but he hasn't been for a long time."

"What makes you think that?"

"Remember seven years ago, his drive to McDonald's, when he totaled his car?"

"That was an accident," my father said firmly.

"He hit the side of a building at forty miles an hour. It was a suicide run."

"I can't accept that."

Of course not, I thought. You were the one who broke his heart.

After high school, David had lived with my father in a two-bedroom apartment in the suburbs. My parents had divorced, and my brother conveniently had become my dad's "buddy." Emotionally, they lived more like husband and wife than father and son.

David led a sheltered life, protected by my father who seemed determined to keep him dependent and immature, until the day my dad decided to remarry.

His new wife, Martha, wasn't about to have a twenty-five-year-old man live with them, regardless of his condition, so my father left him behind. Overnight, he abandoned him. He continued to pay for the apartment and David's bills, but he left him without any structure. David had no job, friends, life skills—or prospect of getting any in the future.

A week after my father moved out, my brother had the car accident. While he wasn't seriously injured, the episode was the first in a long run of decline, an extended, unheeded cry for my father to come back.

David spent three months of the next year in a psychiatric hospital, and his health—both mental and physical—had deteriorated every year since. And now this.

He lay between us, his most fervent wish granted. My father was there, but where was David? Suspended between life and death.

I looked at my brother's face, which on this day exhibited a deep sadness, and I said curtly, "What was he doing driving that day? He didn't know how, and he didn't have a license."

"He'd taken three driver's ed courses."

"And failed. The instructors told you he couldn't be taught."

"I didn't buy that, and neither did you. You took him out on a lesson."

"One! And he almost killed us. Just because he'd gone a year without seizures didn't mean he should have been driving. He didn't have the reflexes or the ability to process everything going on around him. He was a danger to himself and everyone on the road."

"Listen to what you're saying: It was an accident!" My father hollered, the jovial veneer dissolving.

"I saw him at the hospital after it," I said deliberately. "I'd never seen him like that. He didn't care, Dad. Not about anything, not about living."

"I was there, too, if you'll recall. I didn't notice anything unusual."

"You wouldn't," I mumbled.

"Pardon?" He glared at me.

"Nothing."

"I know my son better than you think," he retorted.

"How, if you haven't seen him in six months?"

"That was his choice, not mine," my father said coldly. "You may not like what I do, and your mother certainly doesn't, but I don't give a damn. What's between David and me is between us. It's no one else's business."

"Good, Dad," I said, sarcasm dripping from the words.

"David knows what kind of father I am!" he shouted as I left.

Funny he should chose those words, I mused, as I headed toward the elevator.

The week before David went into a coma, I had asked him what he thought of my father when we were growing up.

I had queried, "What kind of father was Dad?"

After careful consideration, David answered, "He sort of wasn't there. Like those kids who lose their fathers or their fathers die."

He paused for a long time before he asked, "Is that how you feel, too, Kris?"

"Yeah," I said, even though my father had spent every day of our lives with us until he and my mother divorced when I was eighteen and David was fifteen.

As I flopped into my car, I wondered if David was aware of my father's presence now, and if so, whether it soothed him or frightened him.

The day continued as it had started, overcast and tiring.

Right after I left the hospital, I tried to reach Nicole. Paige informed me she'd be out of the office all morning and would return my call at her convenience.

When I hadn't heard from her by the end of the day, I pressed again.

She came to the phone, exasperated. "What now?" was her unwelcome opening.

"I called to tell you Lauren wasn't having an affair with Dr. W."

"Oh, really—what a relief! One woman in Denver Lauren wasn't fucking," she said with evident satisfaction.

I continued calmly, "Dr. W was an abbreviation for Dr. Wendy Henderson. She's a PhD specialist at the school Ashley attends."

"I suppose you're going to tell me their relationship was innocent and platonic?"

"Trust me, if you met this woman, you'd know. I seriously doubt she's a lesbian. Plus, her explanation about their meetings is plausible. She told me she and Lauren were planning for Ashley's future."

"Isn't that sweet." she said tartly. "My lover seemed quite concerned with taking care of everyone except me."

"What do you mean?"

"Remember when I told you Lauren had no life insurance?"

"Actually, you told me she had a small policy through work."

"Yes, yes, but no extra coverage," Nicole said impatiently. "Did I mention how I paid for the cremation? I neglected to add I had to grovel to Patrice and Stephen for money and borrow from my parents. After all this, take a guess who's a goddamn millionaire!"

"What are you talking about?"

Her voice took on an ominous tone. "Money, you idiot. Cold hard cash. In the last three days, eight notices for insurance premiums have arrived in the mail, all addressed to Lauren, all for five hundred thousand dollar policies. God only knows how many more are on their way. I called every one of the companies, and guess, just guess, who gets it all."

I didn't dare. I remained silent while she continued her tirade.

"The first day, when two came, I thought it was a prank, but it wasn't. They're all legitimate. One final stab in the back from the woman I shared my life with for six years."

"These notices. You've never seen them before?"

"How could I?" she remarked airily. "Lauren brought in the mail every day. It was her favorite thing to do. She put hers in a drawer and mine on my desk. I never rifled through her stuff, and I certainly had better things to do than read her checkbook register in my spare time. I didn't realize there was a need to scrutinize every piece of paper that came into our house." She paused, and when she resumed talking, her voice had a downright cruel edge to it. "Humor me, Kris! Name a name, and I'll tell you if she's the lucky winner of the Lauren Fairchild suicide jackpot."

Knowing my guess, right or wrong, would raise her ire, I tried diplomacy. "Couldn't you just tell me?"

"What's the fun in that? That would be far too easy! How about if I give you clues? Clue number one: My precious life partner was fucking her. And in case you were wondering, their insignificant affair began long before mine."

"Nicole, really, I'm not comfortable—"

In words drenched in derision, she interrupted. "Clue number two: The recipient of this vast wealth has had a lifelong dream of opening a women's retreat in southern Colorado. The most peaceful, spiritual ground in the country. Down by Crestone, town of three hundred, in the heart of the San Luis Valley and the shadow of the Sangre de Cristo mountains. A convenient three and a half hours from Denver or Santa Fe and eight thousand feet above sea level. A haven for every mystic, healer, philosopher, and artisan. Our mystery woman and Lauren had big plans, very big plans. It made me sick to listen to them. They didn't have a hundred dollars between them, but they thought they could save the world."

"Is there any way—"

She hissed, "The two bitches probably caressed as they designed their pitiful village. High-desert land. Perfect climate. Good vibes. Glowing spiritual energy. Lesbians only. Build houses out of tires. New forms of agriculture. Solar-powered everything. No hierarchy or violence or meat or pesticides. Rituals and solstices. No men allowed, none whatsoever. No ageism, racism, or sexism. Hatred and homophobia not allowed. A place where all women could be safe. Blah, blah, blah."

"How about if—"

She sliced through my attempt to speak. "If it sounds like I have all this memorized, I do. If you're bored, join the club. I've heard the fantasy of their noble community until I could gag. It's all they talked about. I should have seen it coming. I complained to Lauren about how much time they spent together, but she wouldn't listen."

Her voice rose, forcing me to lower the telephone from my ear. "She said they were friends, as if friends kill themselves to leave other friends four million dollars."

"Maybe she—"

"I wonder how much money she wasted on those policies. This explains why she never had the money to travel or eat out. Last year, I had to go to Europe with a friend from college because Lauren claimed she couldn't afford it. She wouldn't join a health club. She bought these flimsy weights at Target and worked out on her own. She drove a beat-up car that was an embarrassment. I begged her to get a new one. I told her she was ruining our image, and she laughed and said she didn't want another car. I wanted a leather sofa for Christmas.

Guess what? She didn't have the money. She had one thing she allowed herself to spend money on, and it sure as hell wasn't me."

She snorted before continuing. "That wretched Ashley, that was it! Everything else in life was too expensive, except, evidently, loads of life insurance."

"How much did the insurance cost?"

"How should I know?" she said shrilly.

"Didn't you look to see how much she owed?"

"I couldn't be bothered. Reading things like that makes my eyes blur."

"I could take a look at the policies if you'd like," I said gingerly.

"Thank you, no. You've done enough. Poking around in my life, asking personal questions, all for nothing. I should call Patrice and tell her to give me credit, that I found out why her sister killed herself. The final sick act in a sick life. The ultimate co-dependent statement. But enough about Lauren, I'm robbing you of the opportunity to speculate on who benefits from her death. Have you come up with it, Kristin? You're supposed to be the super detective. Solve it!"

I was sick of being taunted and should have ended our call, but I couldn't. Silence was my only answer.

"Here's your last clue, and it's a biggie: They were lovers once."

Involuntarily, I said, "Cecelia."

After Nicole replied, "You're brighter than you seem," I slammed down the phone.

20

The day went from bad to worse.

Ann asked for the afternoon off but wouldn't say why. I barely avoided an argument there. Our two graphic artists missed another printing deadline, this time because the client wanted to see a tenth proof of the same line he'd changed nine times throughout the month. I didn't back down from that confrontation. I fired the client.

By the time five o'clock rolled around, I fled the office, eager to meet Destiny at my apartment.

Her late arrival did nothing to levitate my mood.

My scowl deepened when she offered the explanation for her tardiness: She'd had to stop by Suzanne's apartment to check on something, and it took longer than she thought.

I accepted her incomplete excuse at face value, only because I didn't have the energy to excavate more details.

The mystery of why Destiny seemed to want to spend more time in Suzanne's apartment than mine would have to wait.

The next morning, I had barely reached my desk when Ann accosted me. "Mom called last night. She wants us to divide up the responsibilities when David gets out of the hospital," she said heavily.

"Keep your voice down," I replied. "Come in and shut the door. We're trying to run a business here."

"Now you're concerned about that?"

"What's that supposed to mean?" I asked as she loudly closed the door to my office.

"You've been so busy with your suicide case, you've neglected clients and missed Angela's review."

I grimaced at the oversight. Angela had worked through the school year as an intern in our graphic arts department, and I'd promised a mid-June review of her full-time employment. "Why didn't you remind me?"

"Because you never forget anything," she said snidely. "Until now."

I sighed. "That's not fair. I've managed outside cases along with this business countless times. Has it occurred to you my work might be slipping because our only brother is lying in intensive care at Denver Health? Maybe dying."

"Maybe dead," she said dully. She shifted her weight from one foot to the other. "Take away all the medicine and the machines, and he's probably dead."

"Maybe."

"Better yet, he died a long time ago."

"Okay," I said, not willing to bicker, "what did you tell Mom?"

"That our family couldn't coordinate a bake sale, much less significant rehab. We could take turns, though, feeling guilty and managing crisis watches."

"If we did split the work, Mom would delegate all the jobs to us and think that satisfied her requirement," I countered.

Ann smiled lopsidedly and sat down. "I went to visit him yesterday."

I raised one eyebrow. "David? Why?"

"I wanted to do a meditation with him. I talked to him about choosing whether to live or die."

"Did he respond?"

"Not physically," she said rising, before adding curtly, "I'll give Angela her review."

"Thank you."

"By the way, I saw the stuffed animals you brought him," she said, and it sounded like an indictment.

"It was all I knew how to do," I said to the empty room.

After a few glum hours spent pretending to work on a dental newsletter, I pondered whether I should visit David or Cecelia.

I wanted to run to David's bedside and shout through his coma, "Don't listen to everything Ann says. You probably should make a decision soon, but you don't have to do it right now. If you want to stay and fight, I'll be with you. If you need to go, I'll miss you, but I'll understand."

Because chances were good he wouldn't hear me, I opted to visit Cecelia.

I had barely entered the health food store when I heard, "Hey, Kris!"

I turned to see Cecelia beaming at me. "You've changed your ways and started shopping here!"

"Not yet. Actually, I came to see you. Can we talk?"

"Right now?"

"If possible. It's important."

"C'mon, let's go to my office."

It resembled a large closet. Clutter everywhere. A Coleman beef poster adorned one wall, a year-at-a-glance calendar another. On a third wall hung a poster-sized photo of her and Lauren on top of Pike's Peak. I sat in front of their feet.

"I spend as little time as possible in here," she said apologetically as she cleared a seat. She balanced on the edge of her chair and added through a slight scowl, "You've got bad news, don't you?"

"Not hardly. What would you think if I said you're extremely rich."

"Very funny."

"I'm serious. Lauren left you a sizable chunk of money," I said earnestly.

A shadow crossed her face. "Kris, I wrote her paychecks. You can't save anything on what she made."

"It didn't come from savings. She had life insurance."

Cecelia became utterly still. "She followed through on it," she said softly as her lips quivered.

"What? The plans for a women's retreat in southern Colorado? Your Crestone dream?" Despite my best efforts, my tone had an accusatory edge to it.

Cecelia stiffened. "Who told you that?"

"Nicole. She's livid because she thinks you and Lauren were having an affair, and that's why she left you this money."

She systematically chose icy words. "Is she more upset about the alleged affair or the money?"

"Probably the money."

"That figures." She shot me an appraising glance. "And what do you think?"

"What am I supposed to think? There's a—"

She silenced me with a hateful glare. "I spent an entire lunch pouring out my guts to you. Do you honestly believe Lauren and I were sneaking around behind Nicole's back?"

"No," I said despairingly. "It's just that this insurance money—"

She interrupted. "Have you seen the policy?"

"There isn't one policy, Cecelia. There are eight, which total four million dollars."

She burst into wild, withering laughter. "Four million or four billion, what does it matter? None of it goes to me."

"But Nicole swore you were the beneficiary," I protested feebly.

"If that airhead had bothered to read the fine print, she would have seen I'm the administrator of a trust, not the beneficiary."

"You knew about this?" I asked, anger overriding incredulity. "And you never said anything to me?"

"I knew about one policy, but I never thought about it. A long time ago, Lauren asked me if I'd agree to be on her insurance, but nothing came of it. I had no idea she followed through and bought one, much less eight."

"What's the trust for?"

"Her niece, Ashley. You can't directly name minors as beneficiaries, at least that's what Lauren told me."

"When did she do all this?"

After a thoughtful silence, Cecelia replied, "I can't remember specifically. If I had to guess, I'd say it was a couple years ago, maybe a little more."

"Which means she and Nicole were lovers then?"

"Oh, yeah!" I could see the pain in her eyes.

"Why didn't she ask her to do it?"

"You'd have to delve into the intricacies of their strange, and estranged, relationship for that answer."

"It all goes to Ashley?"

"Every dime. Lauren made that very clear. I think that's why she chose me."

"Because she trusted you," I said, without adding the obvious implication she didn't trust her lover.

Cecelia nodded, and I let out a long breath. "I guess I have my answer. She killed herself for the money."

"It's not that simple, Kris." She fell silent, and I prodded her with raised eyebrows. "The money was her gift to Ashley, but I suspect the reason goes beyond that."

"To what?" I demanded warily.

"To honor. It all makes sense."

"Clearly you know something I don't. Would you mind filling me in?"

"I can't."

I pleaded with her. "Please, Cecelia, tell me the rest. Why was Lauren so attached to Ashley? You know, don't you?"

She nodded and met my eyes, hers full of regret.

"Why can't you tell me?"

"She's dead now. It's no one's business. They wouldn't understand anyway."

"Not even Patrice? She's the only one I'll talk to. If you're worried about Nicole, she doesn't have to hear any of this."

"How can you not tell her? She was her lover."

"But she's not my client. Patrice is, and she's in a tremendous amount of pain. She's the only one left in the Fairchild family, and she has no idea why. Why did her sister do it? Why did she give up her life for Ashley?"

Cecelia's cheeks flushed. "I can't say."

"Was she the real mother? Is that it? Ashley was her child, not Patrice's?"

"No," she said, with a wan smile. "You really are stubborn, aren't you?"

"I have to know. Please tell me."

"I can't."

"Did you promise Lauren you wouldn't tell?"

"No. She never knew I found out. One night when she was really drunk, she came over to my house and told me this horrible story. The next morning, she didn't remember she'd said anything. I never had the guts to bring it up again."

"What could possibly be that awful?"

No answer.

"It has something to do with Lauren's mother's suicide, doesn't it? That article I gave you triggered something, didn't it?"

"How do you do it?" she snapped, folding her arms across her chest and shifting her body until she had almost completely turned from me.

"Do what?"

"You are the most persistent person! The first time you asked me questions, I was determined not to tell you anything. It didn't seem right, having you know all these private things about Lauren."

"What made you change your mind?"

"That's just it," she said, anguished, "I never did, not consciously. Things kept slipping out, and you listened and accepted, and you never judged. You began to remind me of Lauren. I looked at you, and I saw her. The intensity. The isolation. You even look like her. Not physically, but your movements. The way you study me, your posture, your smile."

She hesitated, her body rigid with pain. "After our last lunch, I could hardly keep myself from calling you at home. I wanted you to be with me, to hold me, to tell me everything would be all right, like Lauren used to do."

I reached for her hand before she asked, "You know what's the most similar?"

Frozen with fear, I couldn't reply.

"The pain in both of you. You understand Lauren's, don't you?"

"More than you'll ever know." My voice sounded distorted.

"And you wouldn't think any less of her if she made a mistake, would you?"

"No," I answered honestly.

Cecelia examined me before she spoke. When her words finally flowed, I had to strain to catch them. "She loved Ashley so much, Kris. You have to believe that! It wasn't fair. She was trying to do something nice by babysitting. It was an accident. It could have happened to anyone."

My heart stopped. "Did she cause Ashley's injury?"

She nodded slightly.

"She dropped her when she was an infant?" I asked hopefully.

Cecelia ignored me and fell into silence. Before I could phrase my next question, she began to speak, in a lifeless tone, as if unaware of my presence. "She was trying to quiet her one night. She walked around for hours, but every time she tried to sit, Ashley would start crying again. Patrice and Stephen were out at dinner. Nicole was out with friends. Lauren didn't know what to do. She kept walking, until she was exhausted and almost delirious."

I gently interrupted. "Why didn't she put her to bed and let her cry herself to sleep?"

"She tried a bunch of times, but Ashley got so upset, she turned red all over and had trouble breathing. Lauren was afraid something would happen if she left her alone, so she kept pacing, but started to panic. She fed her, changed her, sang to her. Nothing worked. She tried everything. Absolutely everything." Cecelia broke off, unable to utter the conclusion.

"And then she did something to her?" I prodded, crestfallen.

She nodded numbly, and our eyes locked in agony. "She shook her, which quieted her."

"Forever," I whispered lamely before I could stop myself.

21

I couldn't let go of Cecelia's words for hours. I returned to Marketing Consultants, hunkered down in my office, and read back issues of *People* magazine—all the while pretending to work.

Activity buzzed around me. The phones rang, UPS dropped off packages, the printer picked up artwork, and my employees chatted merrily.

Yet, I couldn't focus on the same thought for more than thirty seconds without visions of Lauren and Cecelia interrupting.

It took two hours of inline skating around Washington Park to somewhat quiet my mind.

After the exercise, I went home and tried to nap but couldn't close my eyes. Destiny joined me at six, and we ate at a nearby Thai restaurant before returning to my apartment for the night.

As she unpacked her cosmetics in the bathroom, I stole up behind her and watched.

After a time, I spoke nonchalantly, "You know, if we're going to live together, maybe we could get a place big enough for David to live with us."

"Excuse me?" she said slowly.

"When he gets better, maybe he could stay with us awhile."

She met my eyes in the mirror. "Are you sure that's what you want?"

"No," I said tentatively. "But he can't live by himself again."

"What about your mom or dad?"

"They won't take him. They try to pawn him off on each other. No one cares about him, Destiny, except you and me."

"I've tried to be supportive of you, Kris . . ." She focused on the ground, unable to finish her sentence.

"But?" I prompted.

"This isn't one of your better ideas."

I stared at her gravely. "Why not?"

"He's not your responsibility."

"If my parents were dead, I'd step in."

"But they're not, and you might not be able to cope with all his problems."

I thrust my hands into my jeans pockets. "I could try."

She shook her head sadly. "It would change your life beyond belief."

"So?"

Destiny took a step toward me, but I retreated. "You're not being realistic, Kris. We dated for months before you even told me you had a brother. At the end of our outings, you're always frustrated with him, and that was before the coma. Who knows what he'll be like if he comes out of it."

"I could learn to be patient," I said, sullen.

"I couldn't, not that much anyway."

"Meaning what?" I stunned her with the sharpness of my tone.

Her eyes glistened. "I can't live with him, Kris."

I raised my voice. "How do you know if you haven't tried?"

"I know he'd ruin our relationship. I can't risk that."

"Then I can't live with you."

Aghast, she said, "You're not serious."

"I am."

"You're choosing him over me?" she asked, her face composed but pale.

"No," I said after a pause. "I'm choosing me over us. This is something that's important to me, and if you're not willing to at least consider it, I have no intention of living with you."

"But, Kris, you can't throw away your life like this. What about the plans we made?" she asked, devastated.

"Consider them canceled."

Furious, she snapped, "I'm not staying with you tonight, not when you're like this. Maybe tomorrow you'll come to your senses, and we can talk."

Destiny stormed into the bedroom and began to throw things into her bag.

"Don't bother calling me tomorrow. I won't have changed my mind," I screamed at her back as she stomped out the front door.

"Don't worry!" she cried, winning the last retort.

Five minutes later, I heard a soft tap on the door.

From my fetal position on the couch, I ignored it and barely flinched when I heard a key turn in the lock.

Seconds later, I was glowering at the tops of Destiny's shoes.

She gently touched my shoulder. "I can't leave like this, Kris. Could we talk?"

"I have nothing to say," I muttered, crushed.

"I do. Will you listen?"

I gave a noncommittal shrug, which she must have taken as a yes, because she lowered herself to the floor in front of me.

"I know you've been going through a lot lately, what with the case, and David, and seeing your family and all. I don't want to fight."

"Me neither," I mumbled between tears.

"Do you really want David to live with us?"

"No," I choked, burying my head deeper into the cushion. "I hate him."

"No, you don't," she said, stroking my hair.

"Yes, I do, because he takes and takes, and all I know how to do is give. Ann, she's the type who never gives anything unless she wants to, but I'm the opposite. I give until it hurts. I'll bet you she never spent one day of her life feeling guilty for how healthy we are and how sick

David is," I said scathingly.

"Probably not."

"I think about it all the time."

"I'm sure you do," she said tenderly.

I raised up from the pillow. "Remember when we took him to Bonanza last month?"

"How could I forget?" She nudged me playfully and put her arm across my back. "You wouldn't let him eat hot peppers in the car."

"He shouldn't have taken extra food from the salad bar," I said, a tad defensively before I smiled faintly. "Until he did that, he was the most normal one there. Everyone else in the place acted like pigs. Putting up with those paper-thin steaks so they could devour the salad bar."

"Remember the woman who sliced a piece of cheese off the slab and ate it standing there?" she asked, wincing.

"The worst," I chimed in, "the absolute worst was that man eating corn on the cob—"

"Oh, that beard drenched with butter," Destiny interrupted, nausea on her face. "Don't remind me."

"Why," I asked in a small, serious voice, "did everyone stare at David? A room full of the strangest people, and they had to judge him for a helmet his doctor ordered him to wear."

Destiny tightened her hold on me. After a long silence, I sniffled. "I don't hate him all the time."

"I know."

"Just some of the time."

"That's okay." She kissed my forehead. "He's not an easy person to love."

I sat up and peered at her. "Maybe it's not such a good idea for him to live with us."

"Maybe not," she said, unable to conceal her relief.

I lay back down and closed my eyes. "I know I can't heal him, but sometimes," I said, my voice barely audible, "I'm afraid I'll die trying to save him."

I slept fitfully that night, some of the time with Destiny in my bed, most of it awake on the living room couch. As the sun rose, I wondered how Destiny could sleep so deeply on her quarter of the bed, while I endlessly rotated in a space three times the size. I envied her the gift of an accurate clock and wondered when mine would right itself. When would I once again be alert during the day and tired at night?

I left Destiny a note thanking her for the night before and drove to the office, yawning all the way. I checked my jaw several times in the rearview mirror and ran my tongue over my bottom teeth. At the rate I was grinding and clenching, my fillings would be powder before the end of the case.

I stayed at the office only long enough to place a call to Fran Green.

After a few pleasantries, I zoomed to the point, "Hey, Fran, do you know anything about life insurance?"

"Just the basics. You planning on kicking the bucket?"

"Not any time soon, but something's come up with Lauren's case."

"What gives?"

"I think I know why she killed herself."

"For cash?"

"Exactly."

"Oldest reason in the book," she chuckled knowingly. "How much dough we talking about?"

"Four million dollars."

I heard a sharp intake of breath. "Whew, that's a lot of smackers. Who gets it all?"

"Her ex-lover Cecelia was— "

Fran interrupted with a sharp whistle. "Did have a thing going. Well, I'll be!"

"Not so fast. She won't get a cent. She's the administrator of a trust—"

"It all goes to some kooky charity, like research for frozen body parts."

"You should listen more and talk less, Fran," I chided. "If you'd let me finish my sentence, you would have heard the entire sum has been set aside for her five-year-old niece, Ashley."

"The one goes to the special school, right?"

"Yes, and you know why Lauren was so concerned about her future?"

"Sure, she loved the kid."

"She caused the brain damage, Fran."

"Get out!" she snorted. "You're putting me on, trying to one-up me for all the times I've strung you along with juicy information."

"I wish I were," I said earnestly, "but it's true. When Ashley was eight months old, Lauren shook her to quiet her."

"Deja voodoo." Fran coughed loudly. "Gimme a minute, Kris, I'm choking on coffee."

When she spoke again, her voice was raspy. "This is big! What's your source?"

"Cecelia told me. Lauren let it slip one night when she was drunk, too drunk to remember she told her."

"But if the brain damage was caused by shaking, how come she never got caught?"

"I don't know," I admitted. "That's some of what I want to ask Dr. Wendy, and I need to do it quickly before I break the news to Patrice."

"The sister doesn't know anything about the shaking business?"

"I don't think so." I looked at my watch. "Listen, I'm pressed for time. Can you help me by calling an insurance agent?"

"Case seems cut and dry. What's left to know?"

"I think this is why Lauren killed herself, but I'm not positive. For one thing, how do we know companies pay on suicides? Also, I'm curious to see if she really planned all this out and how she pulled it off. Four million is a lot of insurance for someone who made thirty thousand a year."

"Got yourself a point there. I'll call a gal I know, Mabel, runs her own agency. She's a straight arrow."

"Do it discreetly," I cautioned. "I don't want to do anything to jeopardize the claim. Do you think your friend can be trusted?"

"Heck yeah, she's an old flame. I'll stop by her shop and pick her brain."

"Ruth won't like that."

"Ruth won't find out," Fran said pointedly. "Tell me what you need."

As soon as Fran and I had concluded our business, I dashed off to Children First. There, I spent the morning with the kids. Erin and I worked on numbers, Ashley and I moved around colors and shapes, and Tyler and I rested on bean bag chairs.

At the end of the morning stint, I popped my head through Dr. Wendy's doorway. "Hi!"

Dr. Henderson looked up from a stack of paperwork. "Well, hello."

"I'm sorry to interrupt, but I was wondering if I could ask you a few questions?"

"Of course, come right in. I must say, I didn't expect to see you again."

"Me neither," I said vaguely, unsure how to begin. I stood behind the wooden chair across from her desk and took a deep breath. "I didn't know who else to come to," I paused.

She arched both eyebrows.

I blurted out, "Can shaking a baby cause permanent brain damage?"

Suspicion replaced friendliness. "Without question."

"Even if it's only done once?"

"Certainly. It's quite common."

"You've heard about this kind of child abuse?"

She smiled grimly. "I'm the resident so-called 'expert.' I keep up on all the literature. The condition you describe is prominent enough to have its own name, shaken baby syndrome."

"Could the brain damage be similar to damage caused by meningitis?"

She looked at me sharply. "Possibly. However, before I continue with a lengthy medical dissertation, might I ask why this interests you?"

I didn't answer.

"Does this concern Ashley Elliott?"

I changed the subject. "I also stopped by to tell you Ashley has enough money for her Ideal Care Program."

"How, may I ask, did she come by this sudden wealth?"

"Lauren left her four million dollars worth of life insurance money in a trust."

Dr. W pursed her lips. "I see."

"Do you think that'll be enough?"

"More than. That would ensure opportunities beyond the wildest dreams that Lauren and I discussed—" she stopped abruptly. "I have an uneasy feeling this revelation is related to your earlier questions. Is this true?"

I looked fixedly out the window behind her back.

"If you've implied what I think you have, you need to tell me."

"If I confide in you, will you promise not to tell anyone?"

Calm and detached, she answered, "Teachers and doctors are bound by law to report any incidents of suspected child abuse."

"You fall into that category?"

"If not by the strict letter of the law, most assuredly by my own code of ethics."

"You'd report what I told you, no matter what?"

"Absolutely."

"Even if the person who did it had died?"

She shuddered, then fell into a thoughtful silence. "That could make a difference, I suppose."

I dropped into the chair farthest from her desk. "Obviously, I need information, but not badly enough to betray a confidence. I need you to give me your word you won't say anything."

"My main concern is for the best interests of children, particularly if they're in our program. Will what you're about to reveal affect a child I know?"

"I can't see how it would at this point."

"All right," she said reluctantly. "Obviously, we're talking about Ashley Elliott and her aunt, Lauren Fairchild, am I correct?"

I hesitated before answering, "Yes."

"May I tape record our conversation?"

"I'd rather you didn't," I said crisply.

"I believe it's necessary."

"Why?"

"To avoid potential misunderstandings." She tapped her pencil on the arm of her chair. "I'm afraid I must insist on it."

I sighed. "Fine."

She pulled out a device the size of a credit card from a side drawer, turned it on, held it to her mouth and dictated the date and our names. She placed the recorder, like a barrier, between us.

"Very well. What have you discovered?"

"One night when Lauren was babysitting Ashley, I think she shook her."

"Ashley was what age?"

"Eight months."

"How unfortunate!" Her brow pinched. "Shortly thereafter, I presume, she was diagnosed with spinal meningitis?"

I nodded.

"That explains quite a lot," she said primly.

"Such as?"

"Her unusual attachment to the child. I took it at face-value as being driven by love, but I must say, it always baffled me. Now I would have to say guilt was most likely the motivating factor," she said, unveiling a tight-lipped smile.

"In other words," I shifted in my seat, "if Lauren hadn't caused the brain damage, you don't think she would have been as devoted to Ashley?"

"Correct."

"That's bullshit! You obviously didn't know her at all."

Haughtily, she replied, "You have a right to your opinion, and I to mine."

I felt slapped by her scorn. In a cool, level tone, I defended a friend

I had never met. "She was trying to calm her."

"No form of discipline, none whatsoever, is appropriate with an infant," she replied crossly. "Babies spend much of their awake time crying. One recent study found that normal six-week-old infants cried for approximately three hours a day. That said, no form of violence is acceptable as a means to solve a problem. None whatsoever!" Softening, she added. "Do you happen to know if Lauren was physically abused as a child?"

"Probably. Her mother beat her infant brother to death with an iron," I said sardonically.

Dr. Henderson's eyes widened. "Oh, my! That fits the profile."

"What profile?"

"Of an abuser. Abusive adults, such as Lauren, frequently have an unconscious desire for role reversal, wherein the adult expects the child to provide nurturing and protection. They may feel rejected by an infant whose social interaction consists of little more than distressing crying. Generally, injury is not the primary goal of abusive caregivers; rather, they simply want a submissive, subservient child. An infant who is temporarily dulled and drowsy as a result of shaking may seem desirable, and this outcome, regrettably, often reinforces the abusive behavior."

I gulped. "You're saying Lauren shook Ashley more than once?"

"Possibly."

"How come no one ever caught her?"

"With shaken baby syndrome, there are seldom external signs pointing to child abuse, which makes it difficult to diagnose."

"You mean it's possible to inflict permanent brain damage without leaving a trace?"

"Most assuredly. With this type of battering, often there are no cuts, bruises, or broken bones. While there is no direct trauma to the brain or any evidence of a fracture, the brain damage can be severe. I liken it to an extreme case of whiplash, in which all of the injury is internal. Young children are most vulnerable to this kind of abuse because they have relatively large heads, weak neck muscles, and soft brains."

"They can be hurt this badly?"

"The young ones, yes. This type of injury predominately is seen in children under the age of twelve months. Older children also may be affected, but their stronger neck muscles tend to modify the acceleration-deceleration forces that result in injury to the brain."

"When an infant is hurt, is it always for life, like with Ashley's disabilities?"

"Sadly, she may be one of the fortunate ones. The outcome could have been considerably worse. Of children who have been identified with shaken impact injury, approximately one-third die, one-third are disabled, and only one-third appear to develop normally. Among the children who die, most are admitted to hospitals in deep comas from which they never emerge."

"What would Ashley have been like after she was shaken?"

"Most likely she was vomiting and extremely sleepy. Possibly she also showed signs of pronounced irritability, rhythmic eye openings, involuntary motor movements. Bicycling movements of the legs and arms are common."

"These symptoms are similar to those of meningitis?"

She nodded once. "Nearly identical. Meningitis is a disease that affects the membranes covering the brain and spinal cord. As such, the most common results are fever, vomiting, loss of appetite, sleepiness, and sometimes seizures or uncontrollable jerking of the limbs."

"How depressing," I muttered, slouching in my chair.

"One aspect of this does strike me as peculiar. . . ." She paused, lost in thought. "There's one virtually fool-proof way to distinguish between shaken baby syndrome and meningitis."

I straightened with optimism. "Which is?"

"All across the country, they're alerting emergency room physicians to be on the lookout for retinal hemorrhages. It presents in almost every occurrence of shaken baby syndrome but rarely in cases of meningitis."

I slumped down again. Trying to keep the boredom out of my voice, I asked, "Meaning what?"

She shut off the tape recorder. "According to everything medical statistics demonstrate, if Ashley were a shaken baby, she would be blind."

"And she's not!" I gasped with joy.

22

My jubilation evaporated as I drove down the street, considering Dr. Henderson's last words.

As the walls closed in, the good doctor had blabbered on about a journal article she wrote comparing learning delays in toddlers with shaken baby syndrome to those with bacterial meningitis.

She lectured me specifically about the distinct, unmistakable differences between the two diagnoses.

I valiantly tried to follow her long-winded explanation, but it wasn't easy. Some of her sentences began in one minute but didn't end until the next.

As clearly as I could gather, however, she said something about cultures from spinal taps. In the next breath, she claimed seizures would have started immediately with shaken baby syndrome, not the next day as they did in Ashley's case. She maintained associated physical findings in shaken baby syndrome typically included broken ribs or chest bruises in the shape of the shaker's thumbs. She informed me small veins crossing the infant's brain would have burst and begun to ooze blood. She swore blood would have shown up in a culture, and there would have been an investigation.

None of it made much sense to me, but I had to trust the doctor's arrogance.

Her succinct conclusion: Lauren didn't cause Ashley's condition.

Too bad she never told her that in their countless "Ideal Care" planning pow-wows.

Really, though, none of this new information made a damn bit of difference.

Not a shred of it changed the fact that Lauren was dead. That she'd shaken the niece she adored. That this woman who could never escape the pain caused by a murderous mother had killed herself because of an outcome she hadn't caused. That Ashley would grow up with plenty of financial resources but without an aunt.

I left without further comment and drove back to the office as quickly as I could legally.

As I sat behind my desk, my mood improved only slightly when I realized I should call Nicole and tell her the money she coveted went to Ashley, not Cecelia.

Paige, the philandering assistant, put my call through without delay.

"Nicole, this is Kristin Ashe."

"You have some nerve calling. What, pray tell, do you want now? Some measly question you need to have answered?"

I didn't rise to the bait. Instead, I said as casually as possible, "I called to tell you the money doesn't go to Cecelia. It goes into a trust for Ashley. I thought that might make you feel better."

"How much does she get?"

"All of it," I said calmly.

"I see." There was a long pause before she added, "I guess we can't call the precious child financially disadvantaged, now can we?"

Her mean spirit had worn me slick. "Can't you give it a rest, Nicole?"

"I rather doubt you'd be pleased if you found out your lover left a fortune to her niece and none to you," she retorted.

I felt anger welling up. "Maybe Lauren thought Ashley needed to be provided for, and you didn't."

"Well, she was wrong, and she deprived me of what's rightfully mine."

"You think the money belonged to you?" I said, incredulous.

"Of course I do! It wasn't easy being Lauren's lover, and it definitely hasn't been a picnic telling everyone she killed herself. They look at me like I did it. I must have driven her to it, as if it were my fault. Please! Anyone who knew Lauren knew she was sick way before I met her. One day she drives into the mountains and swallows a bunch of pills. End of story . . . for her! But what about me? How am I supposed to explain all this to people? The least, the very least, she could have done was leave me some money. One of those policies would have been nice. It might have shown she cared."

"Even if you had the money, you wouldn't miss her less," I said, disgusted.

"That's what you think. What about my dreams? I'd feel a lot better right about now if I was living in Cherry Creek. I showed Lauren the house I wanted one time, on the corner of Fourth and Detroit. I toured it when it was for sale last year, even though it cost twice as much as we could afford. I went so far as to pick out furnishings for it. What about that dream?" she spat.

"Lauren probably—"

She cut me off. "I intend to find out what my legal rights are. I was prepared to take Cecelia to court. As it stands, I'll sue Ashley, if necessary."

"You can't be serious!" I said, astounded.

"I am."

"Maybe you should think it over for a few days, recover from the shock."

"I have no intention of wasting an hour, much less days."

My rancor rose to match hers. "I doubt you have any legal recourse, but even if there were a loophole, how could you possibly pursue it? These were Lauren's explicit wishes. She believed in them strongly enough to kill herself. She stopped living, for Christ's sake! Doesn't that mean anything to you?"

For the first time, Nicole didn't have a pithy reply.

"So you want a new house, who doesn't? You've got your health, something Ashley's never had. She's facing a lifetime of horror, and your biggest concern is what kind of couch you're sitting on. Lauren didn't die for a goddamn piece of furniture, Nicole!"

The dialtone did nothing to dampen my fury.

"Try looking different. Try talking so slow people interrupt you or finish your sentences. Try having a head three sizes too big for your body. Try living with your hands shaking all the time. Try having everyone ignore you because they can't stand to look at you. Try that, you fucking bitch." I slammed down the receiver.

Minutes later, I heard a knock, and Fran entered before I could muster a response. I smiled faintly at the sight of her shirt, which proclaimed, "Guns don't kill. Postal workers do." She'd tucked it into skin-tight workout shorts but hadn't bothered to smooth down the unsightly bulges. She tossed her mirrored sunglasses and Broncos cap onto the edge of my desk, flipped her fanny pack around to her belly, and sunk into the couch.

"You okay, kiddo? You look a bit peaked."

"I'm fine," I said, despite my pounding heart.

"Things okay with you and Destiny? You and Ann? You and David?"

I nodded after each guess. "Nicole just hung up on me. She wanted some of those millions, even though I doubt she'd take the disabilities that went with them. I can't wait for this case to be over," I said, exhausted. "How's Mabel?"

"Pretty as ever. Funny, too. Asked if I could pick her brain, and she said 'Pick away. What's left is yours.' Isn't she a card?"

"A real comedian," I replied, not quite as amused. "I take it the attraction's still there."

"Heck, no! I ain't sweet on her, but I'll bet she wouldn't mind getting me between the sheets again."

"Again?"

"Never mind that. She's sharp as a tack, too. The convent was a waste of her talents. She's built an empire over there. Carries a briefcase, calls it her 'traveling profit center.' Clever, huh?"

I looked at her sharply. "Are you sure nothing's going on between you two?"

"Nothing but business," she said briskly, cheeks red. "She told me so much about insurance, my head's about to bust! Quite the strain on the brain, but found out some fascinating things. Like eighty percent of car fires are started by owners. Don't go getting any ideas about torching that heap you own, Kris. They'll catch you in a heartbeat."

"You should talk. You don't own a car, and Ruth's looks like it's already been roasted."

"Easy, touchy. Good news is, if they catch you, they won't press charges. They just return your premiums and don't pay your claim."

"They don't prosecute?"

"Cripes, no, that'd cost money. Even if they won, it wouldn't generate any bucks for the company, and that's all they care about. If I didn't have such high scruples, I could get into this fraud business. Telling you, it's money waiting to be printed," she said confidentially.

"Fine," I said impatiently, "did you and Mabel get around to talking about life insurance?"

"Oh, sure! I know loads. Fire at me."

"Let's start with how did Lauren buy so much insurance on her salary?"

"Cheaper than you might think. Term insurance costs about fifty bucks a month for five hundred thou in coverage."

I did the math. "She had eight separate policies, so she paid four hundred a month."

"Give or take. Could she have covered that?"

"Probably. It would have been tight, but she was good with money. Still, wouldn't it have been cheaper to buy one big policy?"

"Sure, but no one would have sold it to her. Not enough net worth. Might have hawked that much to a high-powered exec who pulls down a couple hundred grand a year, but not to a deli manager. Ordinary gal like Lauren asking for that size of policy would have set off red flags."

"And a five hundred thousand one didn't?"

"Nope. That's the cut-off point, according to Mabel. Anything more and they do a financial investigation when you apply. Anything less, and they take your money and grin. Our pal Lauren knew what she was doing."

"Wouldn't it look odd if someone bought eight policies? Surely these insurance companies are linked into some kind of network that shares information."

"You hit it, but our friend Lauren got around it," she said gleefully. "That's why all the renewal notices came within days of each other."

I frowned, perplexed. "I'm not following you."

Fran spoke boisterously, "Bright bulb that Mabel. She figured if Lauren applied for all the policies on the same day, none of the companies could nose out that she had double and triple coverage. The information wouldn't have hit their main data bank yet. Also, the gal could truthfully state on the application she didn't have any other coverage."

"Technically a lie, but brilliant!" I sprang from my chair and paced behind the desk. "Do the companies pay on suicides?"

"Depends."

My heart sank, and I halted mid-pace. "On what?"

"Lots of things. Like there's this thorn called materiality. All the information on your application has to be accurate, or the company won't pay. Take for instance if a company normally covered suicides, but you lied from your crib at the mental hospital and said you were healthy, they'd toss out your claim."

"Could Lauren have been in therapy at the time and still received coverage?"

"Maybe yes, maybe no. You apply, they do a complete medical history, including a blood test. Mabel says she could have told the truth, and they would have written to her psychiatrist for info, maybe cleared her for coverage. Maybe not. Or, she could have lied. You with me so far?"

"Unfortunately, yes. Which means if she did lie about counseling, or if any of the eight companies finds out about Lauren's policies with the other companies, they can refuse to pay."

"Not so fast! That's where this hummer called incontestability comes in. Aren't these slick terms, Kris?" Fran asked, beside herself with delight.

"Wonderful," I said hurriedly. "What's it mean?"

"After you've paid into the policy for a certain period of time, the claim is incontestable."

"The insurance company has to pay, no questions asked?" My voice filled with excitement.

"You got smarts, kid. Exactly the scoop. Before the time expires, they dig like hounds, trying to find any technicality that'll keep 'em from emptying their pockets. After, they fork it over, no sleuthing allowed. Amount of time varies from state to state. Guess what Colorado's is?"

I high-fived Fran. "Two years."

She flashed me a shrewd look. "How'd you know?"

"Lucky guess," I said, grinning, thinking of Lauren's private party at Choices. The two-year anniversary celebration, complete with candles and a granola bar. The day her eight insurance policies had to pay out, no matter what.

I could barely conceal my delight. "As far as you can tell, there's nothing to prevent Cecelia from collecting the money for Ashley?"

"Not now. Once those two years are up, the men in suits have no grounds to hold up the cash."

"How soon will she get the money?"

"Should come within sixty days. Tell Cecelia she has to file a death claim with each of the companies. Needs to give them a death certificate or a copy of the obit, something like that. Better yet, have her ring up Mabel. My old friend said she'd help her through the red tape."

"And you're positive even if one of the companies discovers the other policies, or she lied about something else— "

"Tough luck. Too late. Lady paid her premiums and followed their rules. Insurance is a gamble. You take out coverage, you bet you'll die. Those suckers bet you won't. This time, they lost. Didn't figure someone would come along and plan two years ahead."

I paused, deep in thought. "There's no way all this is mere coincidence, that Lauren bought a bunch of insurance but killed herself for some other reason."

"No way. Too much work and too clever. Didn't leave one thing to chance. Case closed, girl. You're done!"

"Yeah," I sighed. "Now I have to find some way to tell Patrice."

"Don't envy you that," Fran said, leaning back luxuriously, hands folded behind her head.

It took me half the day to get Fran out of my office. I had to sit through a circuitous recounting of her complex relationship with Mabel. I would have bet Ruth hadn't heard a fraction of the details Fran revealed, and I too could have lived without the intimate ones.

Fran broke camp only after I told her I had to go see David. She offered to tag along, but I declined. I had a mission, and no one could accompany me.

I dropped Fran off at a nearby bus stop and sped to the hospital.

Outside his room, a nurse I'd never met kept me from entering until they finished cleaning him. She directed me to a lounge down the hall, and I nervously fiddled with magazines for the next thirty minutes. When a family entered, five members holding and supporting each other, my stomach dropped, and I left. I spent the next fifteen minutes sitting in a bathroom stall, breathing through my mouth.

By the time I returned to David's bedside, I was emotionally spent from rehearsing lines I knew I had to deliver. "Hey, David! How are you doing?"

I sat next to the bed and patted my brother's hand.

"I came to tell you I won't be stopping by for awhile."

I took a deep breath and forced myself to turn toward him. To my relief, he looked good, almost healthy: hair combed, mustache trimmed, skin clear.

I began, haltingly, "Every hour of every day, I've debated whether I should come visit. I want to be here, to show my support, but I just can't anymore.

"I get off the elevator, and I have no idea if you'll still be here. I brace myself to hear the news that you're dead, or that you're awake but can't function. It rips me apart to see you like this.

"I talk, but I have no idea if I'm getting through to you. It isn't even you. It's what's left of you, and it's not enough. For some reason, you're in this limbo. You're not here, but you're not gone either."

I cleared my dry throat. "I have to let go, little guy."

Nervously, I tapped my foot. "Every time I come to see you, this sick part of me hopes I'll run into Mom or Dad. I guess I keep wanting to form some kind of connection with them, but I never do. I never have.

"They were pretty lousy parents, weren't they? To both of us. I know they let you down. They gave the lowest level of care and demanded self-sufficiency. Maybe that's why you keep getting sick, to call them back, to give them one more chance to pull through. But they never do. They left you behind.

"Being around them these last few weeks has brought back all the pain we used to live in. I'm sure you heard me fighting with both of them, as if nothing had changed. I keep expecting it to, but it doesn't.

"I think that's why I need a break," I said, hoarse.

I squeezed his hand, placed it back on the bed, and covered it. I rose to leave, but abruptly stopped.

I shifted to fully face him. "Before I go, I need to know one thing. How come you didn't take your medicine?"

I searched for a sign on my brother's face. None surfaced.

I pressed both hands to my forehead, trying to ease the pounding headache behind my eyes.

"Mom thinks she saved your life by getting the paramedics to come to your apartment. I can't figure out if that's good or bad." I leaned toward him and lowered my strained voice. "Did you want to die?"

I watched for but didn't see the slightest movement.

I continued in a whisper, "It's okay if you did. You've suffered enough."

I patted his leg and walked away, eyes dry. Passing through the door, I cast one last glimpse. "See you later, Dave."

23

The next day, mid-morning, as I struggled to write creative copy for a pediatrician's brochure, Ann buzzed me. "Call for you on line one."

Harried, I picked up the phone.

"Kris, it's Cecelia. Did I catch you at a bad time?"

I brightened. "No, not at all. What's up?"

"I didn't know who else to call," she said, her voice breaking.

"What's wrong?"

"I got a letter today from Lauren."

"Oh my God! How? Is she alive?"

"No, but that's what I thought for a split second when I saw her handwriting on the envelope. It freaked me out until I noticed three postmarks. Lauren mailed it weeks ago, on her birthday, but somehow, the post office routed it from Denver to Kansas City and back to Denver again."

This had to be it: "The message sent but never received." A letter that should have traveled a dozen blocks had journeyed a thousand miles. Leave it to Noni, the psychic, to be exact in her predictions. This was what had agitated Lauren the day we contacted her. She'd paid her postage and, assuming death brought omniscience, had watched helplessly as her letter had veered off course.

That would have been enough to make anyone furious, dead or not.

"What's in the letter? Does she explain everything?" I asked, excited.

"Not really. There's a typewritten list of the names and addresses of the insurance companies. I guess she wanted me to know who to contact for the money."

"That's it?" I tried to mask my disappointment.

"No. There was one handwritten sentence at the bottom." Cecelia began to cry.

"Can you read it to me," I gently prodded.

"Just a minute, I'll get it." She set down the phone for a few minutes and returned, fumbling with papers. "Here it is," she said, after taking a deep breath. "'Cecelia, I did the best I could.'"

It wasn't easy after that, but I put in a full day at Marketing Consultants, all the while postponing my final meeting with Patrice. Sooner or later, I had to tell her why her sister had committed suicide. In fact, the sooner the better, but I couldn't seem to do it. My emotional reserve registered below empty.

Fran had volunteered, on numerous occasions, to take a more active role in the detective work. Maybe I could feign a sudden illness and pawn the task off on her. As soon as I had that cowardly thought, however, I nixed it. I knew I couldn't do that. Maybe to Patrice, but never to Ashley.

Right before I left the office, I called Patrice and made an appointment with her for the following afternoon. That salved my conscience a bit. I bought a little time, and also closure.

I drove home and was preparing to jot down thoughts for my meeting with Patrice when Destiny walked through my apartment door.

We shared a pleasant evening—pizza and sitcoms. After we'd both undressed and crept into bed, Destiny broke good news.

"I think Suzanne might be moving soon," she said coyly.

"Good," I responded bluntly. "She flirts with you too much."

"You think everyone likes me too much."

"Probably, but you two spend a lot of time together. She probably made up that literacy grant deal to lure you up to her apartment. I bet the whole thing was a fake."

Destiny smiled at my huffy attitude. "She got tentative approval yesterday for the first twenty-five hundred."

"I'll believe it when I see the cash."

Destiny traced my eyebrows with her forefinger. "You never did like her, did you?"

"You should never have told me you were attracted to her."

"I let that slip before I started dating you, when I thought you were my friend. More importantly, before I got to know Suzanne. Plus, it was superficial attraction. I used to think everyone was cute until I fell in love with you. You know why I like Suzanne now?"

"I have no idea," I said curtly.

"Because she's a good tenant. She pays the rent on time and keeps an eye on the house when I travel. Plus, she never uses the backyard. That's a big bonus."

"That's all you like about her?" I said dubiously.

"Please, Kris. She's too boring. Tedious and dreary."

"You two are sort of in the same line of work. You might be good together," I said seriously. "She's a helper, like you."

"Please, please, please, Kris, stop trying to set me up with other women."

"Mmm," I said, distracted by her meandering hands.

"You know what I'm attracted to in you?" Destiny asked in a husky voice.

"My brain?" I said lightly, trying to catch my breath between strokes of her hands.

"Your eyes . . . your shoulders . . . your breasts, especially this one . . . your legs . . ."

It took Destiny a long time to complete her list to our mutual satisfaction.

Afterward, the ringing phone couldn't awaken me from a deep sleep.

Destiny had to shake me several seconds before I became coherent enough for her to relay, "Kris, Rose at the hospital is on the phone. You need to go see David."

24

The next hours passed in a blur. Later Destiny recounted them for me.

It seemed I tried to leave the apartment wearing no clothes. She dressed me and drove me to my brother's hospital bed, where my worst fear was confirmed. We sat with his lifeless body until my father arrived. He tried to hug me, but I brushed past him into the hallway. I cried throughout the elevator descent but stiffened when I passed my mother, smoking a cigarette outside the hospital lobby. I ignored her.

We returned to my apartment, and Destiny called Ann to tell her David had died. My sister said, "Finally." Nothing more.

Destiny rang up Fran, who came by at dawn with bagels I couldn't eat.

As my lover and my friend made small talk, I kept repeating my need to go to Hanging Lake. To be alone with Lauren and David.

Ignoring their alarmed protests, I drove into the mountains in search of a peace I'd never found.

I don't remember pulling out of my zombie-like state until I'd hiked the mile straight up and had dipped my bare feet into the glacier-cold, blue-green lake.

If I'd paid attention on the three-hour drive, I would have noticed Ruth's unmistakable persimmon-colored car following. But I never saw the vehicle or Fran next to her, neck craned, binoculars raised.

At the top of the mountain, acutely conscious, I had an overwhelming feeling of relief.

Lauren was free.

Her freedom had begun the moment she planned her death. Those who loved her thought she left abruptly, but nothing could have been farther from the truth. She schemed and plotted and planned until every clever detail fell into place.

She made love to Nicole, somehow able to embrace her lover despite all her faults and infidelities.

She wrote to Cecelia and sent details of the insurance benefits. Nothing more needed to be said between the two women, briefly lovers, forever friends.

She spent her last lunch with her sister Patrice and made a final promise to care for Ashley.

Finally, she left four million dollars to the niece she adored. She killed herself to mitigate the irreversible injuries she thought she had caused.

As the only solution she could devise, Lauren Fairchild gave up her life. She died to atone for one mistake.

Maybe her final act was noble, perhaps foolish, but nothing about it was impulsive.

And David was free, too.

My brother's freedom began when he chose to reject the medicine that kept him alive but didn't give him a life.

Everyone believed David could carve out a decent existence in spite of his disabilities, but he never had.

He spent every waking moment on the verge of seizure, forever nursing injuries caused from crashes to the ground.

No wonder he slept so much.

When he was young, he was "harmless," and people accepted him. As he matured, however, his differences became more marked, and we all began to reject him.

The more he was hated, the more he hated himself, and the more pronounced his disabilities became. The more profound his disabilities, the more we discarded him.

He'd spent time in mental hospitals, boarding houses, nursing homes, and rehab centers, but he never could find that elusive place in which people who are different nonetheless belong.

My freedom would come the day I stopped apologizing for enjoying a life less wretched than my brother's.

Perhaps the end of his time would mark the beginning of mine. I thought about that all the way home.

I never did see Ruth and Fran tailing me back to Denver.

From Hanging Lake, I drove to my apartment, hurriedly changed clothes, listened to a message from Destiny reminding me to meet her at seven, and set out for Patrice's.

Lauren's sister answered the door in shorts that extended past her knees, an over-size Children First T-shirt, and an apron speckled with brown stains. She invited me into the house, where the smell of chocolate chip cookies greeted me.

Before I could muster the final explanation of the case, Patrice asked if I'd go outside and play with Ashley.

"But I'm done," I protested. "I've found out why Lauren killed herself."

"I know," she said. "I sensed that when you called yesterday. All night, I've tried to prepare myself for the news. Whatever it is, it can wait a few minutes. I'll finish baking off the last few batches of cookies, and you and Ashley can play in the yard. When she found out you were coming, I promised her you'd spend time with her before her nap."

"Okay," I sighed.

I cut through the living room, dining room, and kitchen, careful to avoid toys strewn everywhere. Outside, a blast of hot air hit me as I descended the wooden ramp. Ashley spotted me from the back of the yard and came running. Her awkward side-to-side gait sabotaged her forward motion, and she fell twice in the grass before she reached me. I knelt to hug her, and she kissed my hand. I carried her back to the pine tree cluster she'd left.

Once there, I exclaimed in delight at her secret hideout. Beneath three giant trees planted too close together, a sandbox had been constructed. Massive branches drooped to the ground and provided a shelter that felt almost as cool as the house.

At Ashley's beckoning, I studied her work in the sand and concluded—with a vivid imagination, for she'd assembled lots of piles that resembled nothing—that she'd built a town. Her vehement nodding confirmed my lucky guess.

I took off my polished black loafers and, unconcerned about my pressed white dress shorts and yellow silk blouse, I plopped in the dirt. I put my watch in my pocket, pushed up my sleeves, and began to construct serious piles of my own.

This delighted Ashley. We played for some time in silence before I spoke. When I did, she abandoned her projects, moved closer, and studied me intently. My hands kept moving.

"It's good to see you," I began. "We sure are having fun, aren't we?" She nodded. "I could sit here all day."

"I still have some popcorn left from our trip to the grocery store." Her eyes brightened. "I meant to bring you some, but I forgot. I'm not having a very good day. My little brother died this morning. He wasn't little anymore. He's big now. Was big. He used to be small, like this." I grabbed a twig from outside the box to demonstrate. "But then he grew, much taller than I am, but not quite as high as these trees. He didn't grow up on the inside too much, though, but he looked grown up on the outside. He was kind of a kid and an adult at the same time, which confused everybody. Not that it should matter, but people expect you to act a certain way, and he never could. He had a tough life."

I paused, suddenly keenly aware of my audience. "Do you understand any of this?" I asked.

The child nodded solemnly but immediately jumped up and ran into the house. A short time later, she reappeared and tapped me on the shoulder. I raised my head from my lap and took my fingers from my ears. I had been trying, unsuccessfully, to block out the incessant barking of a neighbor's dog.

Ashley handed me a warm cookie and a room-temperature bottle of water. I thanked her profusely, and we sat contentedly side by side until Patrice called her in for a nap. I hugged her good-bye and told her I'd see her next Wednesday morning, and I'd bring enough pop-corn for her and Erin and Tyler. She became agitated until I added, "Some for Mommy and Jean, too." She left beaming.

I ate my cookie and needed every bit of the water to get the food to pass through my swollen throat. I chewed numbly and sat in the box for a few minutes before I stood, brushed the sand away, and walked slowly, stricken, toward the kitchen.

As I entered through the back door, Patrice turned from the oven, where she'd placed her last batch of cookies on the top rack. "Your brother died?"

"How did you know?" I asked, astonished. I hoped she hadn't seen me slumped over in the sandbox.

"Ashley told me."

"She spoke?" I said, thrilled.

"Not yet." Patrice smiled sadly. "No, she showed me one of her books. One of the baby birds in it dies because he's too weak and falls from the nest. She pointed to the picture and went to the window and pointed to you."

"He died early this morning," I said quietly. "He never did regain consciousness."

"Is it for the best, like people say when they have no idea what to say?"

"I think it is," I replied and further surprised myself by adding, "Lauren's death might have been, too. She left your daughter four mil-lion dollars in insurance proceeds."

Patrice's hand flew to her mouth, and her gaunt, angular face lost all color. She staggered to the table and fell into a chair without bend-ing her knees.

I took a seat next to her and spoke slowly. "Please don't stop me, or I'll never finish. This is what I know . . ."

I told Patrice about Nicole and her girlfriend—how Lauren had known about but not objected to the affair. I outlined her sister's methodical process of buying eight separate insurance policies and naming Ashley beneficiary and Cecelia administrator. I recapped the information Dr. W had shared with Lauren, that this kind of money could make a profound difference in Ashley's life.

The entire time I spoke, Patrice whimpered, "How? Why?" as if chanting in a trance. She rocked back and forth and pulled on idle strands of hair.

Unable to reach her with mere words, I interrupted her dreamlike state by reaching for her jittery hands and quieting them in mine.

It took every ounce of courage I possessed, and some I borrowed from who knows where, for me to look into her troubled eyes and continue. "Because she hurt Ashley. One night when she was babysitting, she shook her to quiet her. Ashley's disabilities turned up immediately after, and Lauren thought she caused them. Without that shaking, Ashley would be healthy—at least that's what Lauren—"

Patrice interrupted, her voice calm but earnest, "You're wrong, Kris. Lauren was wrong."

"I know," I began. "Dr. W explained everything. The retinal hemorrhaging, but Ashley's not blind," I could hear myself blathering.

She cut in again, no emotion in her voice. "One morning, Ashley woke up fussy and feverish. I took her to our family physician, and he thought she had the flu. Stephen and I didn't want to cancel our plans, so Lauren babysat her that night. The next morning Ashley had a seizure. We rushed her to the hospital, and she stayed there two weeks. Bacterial meningitis. That's what caused Ashley's hearing loss and brain damage."

Patrice wrestled her hands from mine and gestured helplessly, palms upward. She continued, her voice lowering with every sentence until her words were almost indistinguishable. "If she shook her, it had to be that night. When we came home from dinner, Lauren told me she had trouble with Ashley. She vomited nonstop and screamed when she was diapered. The more Lauren held her, the more she cried.

The next day, the doctors at the hospital told us these were all classic signs of spinal meningitis, but until she had a seizure, we were still treating it like the flu. How were we supposed to know it was serious?"

"You couldn't have known," I said, uneasy.

"But Lauren never said a word about hurting her," she said despairingly.

"She was too ashamed. She didn't tell anyone except Cecelia, by accident one night. She only did that years later because she was drunk. The next morning, she didn't remember telling her. Lauren never even told her therapist," I added, hoping she wouldn't want to know how I'd obtained that tidbit.

"And now my sister's dead. All because of the shame." Patrice lowered her head and began to shake with weeping.

I put my arm around her shoulder and in utter silence watched tears puddle on the oak table, the first I'd shed since my brother died.

I prayed Patrice wouldn't ask, "Could the shaking have aggravated the meningitis?" Fortunately, she never did.

For I had posed that exact question to Dr. W, and she had answered it in her precise, clinical manner. "If the brain tissues were inflamed from meningitis, certainly it would have taken less shaking to provoke damage."

That response would haunt me the rest of my life.

25

One more person to talk to about Lauren's four million dollar suicide.

I drove from Patrice's house to Choices and couldn't help but grin when I saw Colleen at one of the front registers. My eyes darted from her pierced lower lip to her blue hair, artfully arranged in braids and beads. I tried to mask my shock as I shook her hand warmly. "You've been promoted!"

"You call this a step up? No way, babe. Handling the cash is too stressful. Plus, I'm morally opposed to promotions. One more tentacle the big establishment has in the little worker. No thank you. I'm just covering for a chick who went to Brazil."

"Is Cecelia in?"

"Sure thing. I'll call her." She picked up a private line. "She'll be down in a minute. She says to meet her at the juice bar."

"You didn't use the loudspeaker. You're slipping," I chided.

She smiled impishly. "My voice is a little raw. I went to an Indigo Girls concert last night."

I headed toward the back of the store but paused to graze at the food sampling table in aisle one. This could get addicting, I thought, as I munched my way through a handful of Colorado trail mix—peanuts, carob chips, almonds, and raisins.

Cecelia beat me to our rendezvous spot. Perched on a bar stool, she greeted me warmly. "Hi, stranger. Can I buy you a drink?"

"Sure. What's good?"

"My personal favorite's the peach smoothie."

"Sold!"

Cecelia turned to the young man behind the counter. "Jack, could you please make two of the usual?"

"Coming right up."

I sat down next to Cecelia, and she rotated her steel stool to face me. "What's new? How's your brother?"

I blew air out of my cheeks. "He died last night."

"Oh, Kris. I'm so sorry." She touched my arm. "How are you doing?"

I shrugged. "I don't think it's sunk in yet."

"Is there anything I can do?"

"No, thanks. I'm okay."

"If you need a ride somewhere, or someone to talk to, or maybe a meal . . ." her voice shrunk helplessly.

"Mmm. Thanks."

"I mean it, call me. I know what you're going through or will go through. It's not easy. You can't do it alone, and few people understand. You don't seem like you're the type to ask for help, but you have to."

My eyes watered. "Thanks," I mumbled. I had to change the subject—and fast—before I broke down crying. I cleared my throat. "I came to tell you she didn't do it."

"Who? What?"

"Lauren—she didn't cause Ashley's brain damage."

I could barely hear over the whir of the blender. "But she told me she shook her. Isn't that true?"

"Probably, but it turns out she did it after Ashley had contracted bacterial meningitis."

Cecelia put her hand to her mouth and turned ashen. "How can you be sure?"

"I just came from Patrice's. Ashley had symptoms of meningitis on a Friday morning, but Patrice thought they were the flu. She and Stephen went out that night, and Lauren babysat. Ashley would have been a handful—fussy and impossible to quiet—and that's when Lauren cracked and shook her. The next morning, Ashley had a seizure, and Patrice and Stephen rushed her to the emergency room. From there, she spent almost two weeks in the hospital, on heavy-duty antibiotics."

"Lauren didn't hurt her?" Cecelia asked, puzzled.

"No. If the shaking had been enough to hurt her, she'd have had retinal damage. But her eyesight is perfect. Her hearing's impaired, though, which is a classic result of meningitis. A specialist at Ashley's school explained all this to me."

Jack served our drinks. I took a big gulp of mine, but Cecelia didn't touch hers.

"What now?" she said, misery in her voice. "Lauren's dead. She may not have hurt Ashley, but she's still gone."

"There's nothing we can do about that," I said feebly. "But she did trust you to care for Ashley."

"I almost forgot. That's what's left. The money," she said bitterly.

"I know it doesn't do you much good, but it's what Lauren wanted, the legacy she left behind."

"What was she thinking? How am I supposed to know what to do with millions of dollars? I can barely balance my checkbook."

I reached into my pocket and pulled out a slip of paper. "Here are two women who can help. Mabel Armini is an insurance agent. She'll steer you through the red tape and make it easier for you to collect the money."

I put the note on the granite counter in front of Cecelia. "The other woman is the one Lauren visited so many times right before she died. Her name is Wendy Henderson, Dr. W. She works at Ashley's school, as a consultant to families. She and Lauren spent hours brainstorming, developing this plan for Ashley's future—what they'd do if money were no object."

"Which it isn't." She picked up the names and examined them, a vacant look in her eyes. "She took care of everything, didn't she? It's all set, every last bit of it, except one thing. She couldn't tell me." Cecelia fell quiet, her eyes closed.

I leaned forward and covered her folded hands with mine. "She never stopped loving you, Cecelia."

She peered at me, suspicious. "How do you know?"

I couldn't tell her I had found out in a basement rec room that smelled of cat pee, from a psychic in a bun. Instead, I said, "I just do."

Eyes filled with sadness, she looked past me and said awkwardly, "I'd better get back to work."

"Same here."

Neither of us moved.

"I guess it's over," she said, casting a glance at me.

"Mmm." I shifted on my stool and studied the counter.

"I'm going to miss our visits."

I lifted my head and met her sad gaze. "I know."

"You could always start shopping here."

"That might be too shocking for my body."

She smiled. "Don't worry, we have junk food, too. On your first trip, I could escort you personally and put unhealthy items in your basket."

In spite of my aching heart, I grinned.

"Even chips and dip," she promised. "I know where the good stuff is."

I laughed. "I'll think about it."

In a more serious tone, she added, "If you ever need to talk, about your brother or anything else, please call me."

"Thanks. You too. About Lauren or life or whatever. Good luck with Ashley. She's a fantastic kid. I'm going to be seeing her every week at Children First."

"You're volunteering there?" she asked, excited.

I nodded.

"Great. Maybe we'll see each other."

Reluctantly, I stood up. She rose and hugged me tightly.

"Lauren never had a chance, did she, Kris?" Cecelia whispered as I held her.

I sighed. "Not much of one."

She pulled back and said fiercely. "I miss her."

"I do, too," I said, fighting back tears. "More than you could know."

Leaving Choices, I realized the longest day of my life had almost drawn to a close.

I could summon barely enough energy to drive to Destiny's.

As I pulled in front of her house, my lover rushed from the porch, blindfolded me, and led me through the sideyard.

"Where are we going?" I asked, too exhausted for surprise.

"Up to the third floor apartment."

"Isn't Suzanne home?"

"Not anymore. C'mon, I've got something to show you."

"Is it bad?"

"Not necessarily."

My exasperation took hold. "What?" I reached to pull down the blindfold, but Destiny caught my arm.

"Follow me."

"Oh, God, it's mice, isn't it? Please don't make me kill them."

"No."

"Termites?"

"In Denver, in a brick house? Please, Kris, you're so dramatic."

Wearily, I protested, "A suicide? Did Suzanne kill herself up there? I couldn't take another one, you know."

"Keep walking, we're almost there."

"This is worse than the Hanging Lake hike," I muttered.

At the top of the stairs, I heard the door creak. We walked into the apartment, hand in hand, and when at last Destiny allowed me to look around, I almost toppled over.

Destiny steadied me with a firm hand as I blinked hard and tried to absorb it all.

The vast expanse of the sunlit space nearly blinded me. Gleaming hardwood floors, fresh paint, brand-new wooden blinds.

All that shocked me. But the flowers everywhere—more than I'd ever seen outside a florist's—and the enormous banner that spelled out, "I love you, Kris" dazed me.

I leaned into the wall and slid to the floor. "What's going on? Where's Suzanne?"

Destiny knelt beside me and stroked my hair. "She left. She moved out the beginning of last week. I wanted to surprise you."

"With what?"

"Our new home. What do you think?"

"Us? Live here? Together?" I started to cry.

"Yes!" she exclaimed. "It's not on the ground floor, and it doesn't have history for either of us. It's a fresh start."

"I can't believe you did this. No wonder you came up here all the time."

She laughed. "I was hoping you hadn't noticed. I was really worried last week when you came over early. You almost bumped into the woman I hired to wax the hardwood floors. She cleans the Lesbian Community Center for us when she needs extra cash." Destiny shot me a sideways look. "You didn't think Suzanne and I were up to something, did you?"

"No," I lied, dismissing the thought with a wave of my hand. "Never."

"Do you like it?"

I scrunched up my face, deep in thought. "Could we install a bunch of air conditioners? You know how hot I get."

"I already ordered three. They'll be here next week."

"And we'd have to hire movers. We could never get all our junk up those stairs by ourselves," I sniffled.

"Not a problem."

"Plus, I'd probably need leg massages at the end of every day, from all the climbing."

She dazzled me with her smile. "I'll give you one now, if you'd like."

We began to kiss but I pulled away. "I don't deserve someone like you."

"Yes, Kris, you do." she said, her smile fading into seriousness. "It's okay to be happy."

I tackled her with a hug. "What about a commitment ceremony? I'll never survive all the wedding stuff."

Destiny silenced me with another kiss. "This is the beginning of our ceremony," she said, drawing me into her.

I had to admit it. My heart felt a little less broken.